Sole Agent

Sole Agent

Kenneth Benton

Walker and Company
New York

All the characters and events
portrayed in this story are fictitious.

First published in the United States of America
in 1974 by the Walker Publishing Company, Inc.

Published simultaneously in Canada
by Fitzhenry & Whiteside, Limited, Toronto.

P24   ISBN: 0-8027-5286-1

Library of Congress Catalog Card Number: 73-90462

Printed in the United States of America.

10   9   8   7   6   5   4   3   2   1

CONTENTS

CHAPTER ONE

The Ingredients

IT DOESN'T MATTER *where they come from—sulphur from
the hot springs below Vesuvius, saltpetre from Taltal on
the Chilean coast and carbon from a charcoal-burner's hut
in the Pyrenees; but mix them well, drop in a match and
you know for certain what you'll get. A big bang.*

*With people you don't know—not until you bring them
together—and that is what this story is about : three people,
unwitting ingredients of an explosive mixture.*

*And it was pure chance that mixed them together and
laid the fuse, and touched it off with a careless finger.*

In Oxford it was a chilly evening in early spring, but
fine, and the man who was known there as Miloslav
Janek wrapped his scholar's gown around him and walked
bare-headed from his lodgings towards the Bodleian. To his
own disgust he had decided to let his fair, wiry hair grow
rather long since his arrival in England, and it softened
the puritanical appearance of his low broad forehead and
pale, neat features. His eyes, too, over the wide Slavic
cheekbones, were the palest of pale blue, and there was
indeed very little colour in the smooth open face. And this
was surprising, since the match in which he had just
beaten the captain of his college squash team had been
hard and protracted.

He was due to dine at the High Table of St Luke's later
on, but first there was a small chore to be done, as on
every Tuesday and Friday evening. It had always been an
abortive exercise, but it was an order, and he had been
well trained.

He ran briskly up the steps of the Bodleian, working out
in his mind, from the day and month of the current date,
exactly what he had to do. He showed his reader's ticket

and entered the reference library, where he took a number
of books from the shelves and went over to a table. Only
one of them, the first volume of the *Dictionary of National
Biography*, was of any interest for this exercise and the page
would be—he calculated—a hundred and thirty-six. He
turned to it idly and then forced himself to study the page
carefully, line by line.

He had reached half-way down when his face stiffened
momentarily. There was a faint pencil dot under one of the
letters.

He checked back quickly to see if he had missed anything
—but no, this was the first mark on the page. It was a 'g',
which meant, in his individual code, that the message
that followed would consist of five letters. He found them
one by one and memorized them swiftly, and then went
on as if he were looking up other references in other parts
of the book. Then he closed it and sat back, de-cyphering
the message in his mind.

After the 'g' came 'p', which meant URGENT. (Not so
bad, he thought. If the priority symbol had been 'w' he
would have had to ditch his dinner appointment and go up
to London by the first train to report at his accommodation
address. But this was a lower grade of priority : action within
a week. Time for him to fabricate a cover story.)

The rest of the message was 's' for TRAVEL, 'f'—
REPORT IN PERSON TO . . ., 'y'—ILLEGAL RESI-
DENT and 'e' (Oh God, it couldn't be that again!) for
LISBON. He picked up another book and began to make
some notes in pencil on the life of a Turkish law-maker—
genuine notes written carefully in a hand which showed
no sign of the rising worry in his mind. When he had
finished he reached out for the *DNB* again, found page 136
and appeared to read, tapping with his pencil. When
he closed the book he had left a faint mark under the last
letter on the page—MESSAGE RECEIVED AND UN-
DERSTOOD.

It was a clever little code, he thought, as he left the
library and crossed the Broad towards the great gates of
St Luke's. Clever and safe. Custom-built for each agent,

only twenty-six meanings to memorize and so seldom used that there was never enough 'depth' to give even a computerized cryptographer the ghost of a chance. And in any case thé other man—he had no idea who it was—who came into the Bodleian later, to note the acknowledgement of the message, would rub out the pencil marks.

He passed through the gates into the Outer Quad. Oddly enough, as it might seem to those in his own Service who didn't know about the ambience of ceremony and tradition in which he had been brought up, he was a man with a strong sense of history and a veneration for things and customs matured by age, and his eye lingered lovingly on the lichened Cotswold stone of the roofs and mullioned windows of the Quad, and the hallowed green turf. The message he had received would return to nag at him afterwards; for the moment his mind was at peace.

The staircase that led to the Senior Common Room was under the Gothic archway at the corner of the Quad. When he reached the top the oak door was open. He opened the inner door and stood inside waiting, smiling with a proper humility as his glance took in the scene in the ancient oak-panelled room. How typical, he thought with affectionate contempt, of this out-of-date society to which he had been so unexpectedly directed, this creaking dialectic of old and new ideas, this witches' brew of brilliant intellects bubbling away haphazard, with no sense of dedication to the State!

In the group of men toasting their behinds before the blazing coal fire or lolling in the deep leather armchairs he recognized several dons of international repute—the radio astronomer, the young mathematician who had his hair waved before every television appearance, the shaggy old philosopher whose message to the young on his eightieth birthday had been a rousing call to anarchy, a lawyer, a surgeon—and in the centre, holding court with effortless charm and complete authority, the Warden, with an alphabet of letters after his name, seventy-one years old and as straight as a tall pine.

The group turned like one man, with the in-built curiosity

of dons, towards the shy figure at the door. Then the
Senior University Lecturer in Roman Law came loping
forward and took him by the hand.

'Warden,' he said as he brought him towards the tall old
man by the fire, 'may I introduce my guest? Mr Miloslav
Janek, of the University of Brno.' As the Warden held out
his hand he went on : 'Like many of his colleagues, Janek
had to leave his country in 1968, and St John's were
happy to find a place and award him a research scholarship. So he is completing his thesis here, to our great
pleasure and profit.'

They made the young man welcome and someone put
a glass of madeira in his hand. The shaggy old philosopher
put on his glasses and peered at him. Then he slapped his
hand on the leather arm of his chair. 'I bet you fellers
don't know who he is,' he cried in his gravelly voice.
'But I do.' He snorted triumphantly.

The stranger turned towards him slowly, the shy smile
gone, the pale eyes half closed but hard and implacable as
crystal.

'Yes,' went on the old man, 'of course *I* know him, but
you lot wouldn't. He's the feller who beat young Chetwynd
last week. I saw him.' He added solemnly, 'He's a dead
snip for his half-blue if he goes on playing squash like
that.' With his skinny arm he tried to demonstrate a
squash back-hand and dropped his glass of madeira.

Amanda Harcourt was lying in a wickerwork chaise-longue
on the terrace of her parents' flat in Lisbon, listening to
a telephone voice pleading in eloquent Portuguese. It was
a pleasant spot, in the slanting evening sunlight, the
waxed dark red tiles of the floor contrasting with the blue
and yellow glazed *azulejos* on the walls and the green
awning overhead. The house had been built on the Estrela
hill—Lisbon is all hills and valleys—in the eighteenth
century for a rich merchant with many children and slaves,
and the terrace had been made ample and solid so that
people could take their ease and entertain their friends in
the cool of summer evenings. Through the brass railings

there was a view, over the red roofs, of the broad bosom of the Tagus, and the girl's eyes wandered idly from the ships and ferry-boats to the pile of books on the table at her side and then lingered with a certain satisfaction on the long brown legs stretched out in front of her. Then she looked at the student's notebook on her lap and gave the telephone an impatient little shake.

It had to be stopped, she thought. If it went on it could even be dangerous, and she was amused to find that the thought of danger gave her a perceptible sensual thrill. She spoke firmly and fluently, in the same language.

'Now listen, darling. I told you last week that we can't go on like this. Yes, I know. We had fun. Yes, you idiot, *fun*. I'm very fond of you, Joaozinho, and you made love with all the stops pulled out and I loved that and it was fun. But I don't want to marry you and you'll just have to accept it. Believe me, it's much better for both of us —I really mean this—if we don't see each other again. I mean alone. As it is, nobody knows, and I shan't ever tell anyone. And you mustn't either. Will you swear that, please, Joaozinho *querido*?' The other voice was raised angrily and at length. Suddenly she sat up.

'*No*! You must *not* call on my father. He doesn't know and by God he's not going to know. I won't have it, and anyway it wouldn't be the slightest use . . . Oh, don't be silly, darling. I know your blood is the bluest in Portugal—it isn't *that*. Oh, it's too complicated to explain on the telephone.' The other voice rose triumphantly. 'Oh well, all right, if you swear you'll stop telephoning me. It can't be this week because I'm going to stay with the Da Silvas tomorrow. Next Monday, then, after the Tissiers' party. I'll walk along the road towards the river just after half past twelve, and you can pick me up. OK, then. You can take me home—no, to *my* home, you goon—and we can talk in the car. But listen, *querido*. It really must be the last time. No . . . no, Joaozinho. Darling, I'm going to hang up now and if you ring me again I won't meet you.' She rang off and lay back in the chair thinking.

It was tough on Joao, because she *had* been rather in

love with him, and perhaps she'd led him on a bit. Quite a lot, come to think of it. But it had got to stop. He could be very persuasive when he got her to himself and she knew how easy and—oh hell!—what fun it would be to start all over again. And then all her plans would go for a Burton . . .

She walked slowly towards the door and then stopped, with a sudden thrill of amusement and fear. If only, she thought, she could tell him the truth. *That* would turn him off like a tap. But for Pete's sake, that was the one thing she couldn't do . . . Or could she? She turned to look at the river, and her face was brooding and very serious. As a last resort? If he went on refusing to be sensible? It was after all one way of shutting him up. And tight.

MV *Claudia*, Italian Line, was four days out of Rio and the equatorial heat was tempered a little by the Trade. But not much. Everybody was in or around the three swimming-pools and Peter Craig, lying by the topmost pool, was reluctant to leave it. It was a very comfortable ship, he thought, although there had been more vibration the previous night than he had noticed before. Until then there had scarcely been a tremor from the twenty-four enormous diesel cylinders which the Chief had shown off so proudly. Built for an aircraft-carrier, he had explained, and sweet as mother's love.

Craig got to his feet. Time for a shower and a drink before lunch, he thought, and then a long siesta. As he came out of the lift near his cabin someone called to him from the message centre and held out a radio envelope. He took it and went to his cabin, opening it as he walked.

It was signed 'Ferreira *Policia Internacional*' and had been dispatched in Lisbon. The text was couched in the leisurely style of a man who never paid for his own communications: 'Delighted to hear from you and look forward to meeting my distinguished colleague again with the greatest pleasure stop. Hope you can take luncheon with me on Tuesday 6th stop. Car will be at your disposal when *Claudia* docks.'

Very civil of Ferreira, thought Craig as he stripped off his bathing trunks and went into the shower cubicle in his cabin. He let the cold fresh water cascade over his body and wash away the sweat and the salt from the pool. They had met three years previously, when Craig was still in the Overseas Civil Service as Commissioner of Police in Bangasa, in West Africa.

There had been a lot of trouble on the Angolan border, with Free Angola Movement units using bases in Bangasa for re-grouping. The Bangasi leaders, already half-way towards independence, had undoubtedly been giving help to the Angolan rebels, and the Portuguese, knowing that nothing could prevent the British troops from being withdrawn within a year or two, had taken an understandably truculent line, while still preserving the fiction that the FAM, as such, did not exist—only bandits and 'Bangasi spies and infiltration units'. Their own spies were crossing into Bangasa in increasing numbers and Craig's Special Branch was heavily engaged. In the end Ferreira, head of the PIDE in Luanda, had met Craig, with minimum publicity, on the frontier and in a series of hard-hitting discussions they had worked a *modus vivendi* which reduced the tension and preserved at least some of the decencies.

They had come to like and respect each other, and when a period of comparative peace followed they had exchanged visits. Craig could no more approve of the methods used by the Portuguese military and police forces in stamping out the Angolan freedom fighters than Ferreira could condone the British determination to leave Africa to the Africans, but each could admire the other's competence as an administrator.

That had been three years ago, and now Craig was an Overseas Police Adviser in the Diplomatic Service, and Ferreira head of a department of the PIDE—the much-feared *Policia Internacional para a Difesa do Estado*—in Lisbon. Craig grinned. Poor Ferreira would be up to the eyes now in another kind of independence struggle, but this time in the heart of his own country.

He put on a pair of white shorts and a sports shirt and

made his way to the first-class bar, a cheerful gallery with wide-open windows facing forward. He had a few chapters of the proofs of his book on the Bangasi diamond smugglers to correct, and the little bar was usually empty at this time of day. Everybody else was enjoying the pandemonium around the buffet-lunch tables by the pool.

He settled down with a plate of olives and a planter's punch, tinkling with chopped ice, and took out his pen, but the effort of reading his own prose and trying to spot the small typographical and other errors he was supposed to correct became wearisome after a time. It was exciting stuff, in its way, but he knew it all by heart—the smuggling gangs, the escape routes through the bush to the Sierra Leone frontier, the secret caches, the court cases. And of course Graben, the man he had met again in Rio only a few weeks ago, and now dead. And Alcidia, too, the girl for whom, in that fight by the gold-mine, he had strangled a man to death with a steel chain.

It still worried him, used to regarding himself as a kindly, rational person who hated bloodshed as all policemen should, to recall how his feelings for that girl had led him from acts of sentimental recklessness to others where—he had to admit—he'd shown a ruthless ferocity which he'd never even known about.

He heard quiet voices behind him, and turning round saw the Captain and the Chief Engineer standing at the bar. They were too far away for him to overhear their low-voiced conversation, until the Captain called for more whisky and slapped his colleague on the back. '*Insomma, Alfredo,*' he cried encouragingly, '*arriviamo a tempo a Lisbona?*'

'*Magari!*' said the Chief cautiously. He swallowed his drink quickly and swore. '*Quel porco di cuscinetto!*' He left the bar, and the Captain turned smiling to greet some passengers who had just come in.

Craig was relieved. If there was anything wrong with the engines at least it apparently wouldn't stop them from arriving in Lisbon on schedule, the night before his lunch with Ferreira. So he could send off his reply. He was looking forward to seeing him again.

There was no one else he wanted to see in Lisbon and there would still be time to have a look at the town before *Claudia* sailed. He wondered idly what the 'little cushion' was that the Chief Engineer had disapproved of so vehemently. It was perhaps well, for his peace of mind during those last few days of floating luxury, that he didn't know that the *cuscinetto* would all but bring his earthly career to an end.

There they are. Three people, three ingredients. It was a week later that chance brought them together, on Tuesday, the sixth of April.

CHAPTER TWO

Tuesday Morning

Claudia was late in arriving at the mouth of the Tagus. It was eight o'clock in the morning when Peter Craig felt the big ship heel slightly and sway as she passed over the bar. He went on deck.

Astern, off the starboard quarter, the long Atlantic breakers crashed in fountains of spume against the Caparica coast, but inside the bar the broad estuary was still. The southern bank looked rather uninteresting, a line of low cliffs ending at the bar, where a long spit of uncovered sand narrowed the entrance to a few hundred yards. He went over to the port side and looked at the northern coast, low-lying at water's edge, with a great fort built on a promontory which thrust out into the estuary, but with hills behind, rolling back to the grey-green slopes and crags of Sintra, which he could just see above the thin layers of mist. It was a landscape of little fishing ports and villages, old houses and new hotels, a playground for commuters and tourists alike.

By the time Craig had dressed and had a quick breakfast the sun was well up and shining on the red spider-work of the Salazar Bridge, swinging high above the broad river, not graceful but impressive by its sheer strength and complacent air of achievement. The white tower of Belém, from which Vasco da Gama sailed, slid by at river level, mirrored in the smooth surface; the red roofs of the old town were appearing now, and farther off the tall baroque churches and the castle of St George. But the ship, once she had glided under the great bridge, slowed down and edged in towards the Alcantara Dock on the north bank. Craig went back to his cabin.

He had just realized that he would have to make a call at the Embassy. He knew no one on the staff, but if he was to see a senior member of the secret police he would have to let Chancery know in advance, and give someone a chance to explain HMG's attitudes, if any. Not that he had any intention of allowing Vicente Ferreira to draw him into a political discussion; he knew him too well for that.

What a bore, he thought. There would be even less time to stroll around the city, which he had only previously visited as a transit passenger between flights. However, it was one of those formalities which just had to be observed. And in any case, there was no need to change his light-weight tweed suit and he had put on a silk shirt and a dark red tie in preparation for his date with Ferreira. So he was reasonably presentable for a call on Her Majesty's representatives. He changed a traveller's cheque into escudos at the exchange counter, decided that he would not need a hat or coat and went on deck again. The ship was already alongside and instructions for transit passengers wishing to go ashore were being broadcast on the loudspeakers. When he was handed his landing card he was told to be back on board by four o'clock.

'So there's unlikely to be any delay in sailing?' he asked, remembering the cryptic remark of the Chief Engineer about the *cuscinetto*.

The officer hesitated. 'We don't think so, sir. But if

you'd like to leave an address in Lisbon we'll send a message there if there should be any delay.'

'I'll be at the Embassy about midday.'

'Very good, sir. We'll ring if necessary.'

He passed through the controls, and at once the long arm of the PIDE began to move. An airport official touched him. '*Da PIDE, Senhor,*' he said in a low voice, and unobtrusively passed over an envelope. It was a note from Ferreira, confirming the appointment for lunch at one o'clock at the Armed Services Club. While he was reading it a dark-skinned, stocky little man in a blue uniform came up, clicked his heels, bowed, and whispered: '*Com licença, Senhor Craig. O carro esta fora.*' He led him to a sleek black Citroën, standing outside the main entrance in a space marked for official cars only. He opened the door with a polite gesture of welcome which enabled Craig to glimpse the holstered automatic under his arm. Craig got in and spoke to the driver in his slow Angolan Portuguese.

'I have to go to the British Embassy to collect mail before I meet the Senhor Sub-Director at the Armed Services Club at one. Let's see. It's ten o'clock now, so that gives me two hours at least. I don't want to keep you from your duties . . .'

'The car is at the Senhor's disposal all morning. The Senhor Sub-Director's orders.'

'Yes, he did say that, very kindly, in his note. What's your name?'

'Agente Miguel Coelho, at the Senhor's orders.'

'What can you show me of your beautiful city in a couple of hours, Agente?'

The dark eyes gleamed with pride. 'Avenida Liberdade, *muito elegante*. Castelo Sao Jorge, *com boa vista*. Torre de Belém, *muito historico. Estadio de futebol*, biggest in the world . . .'

Craig stopped him with a laugh. 'We'll start with the Castle, and you can show me the *boa vista*. That's what I want to see most.'

The car rolled smoothly over the cobbled area around the docks, traversed the Estoril railway and the tramlines and turned east into the main road which led parallel to the river towards the centre of the city. To the right, beyond the speeding electric trains and the chunky little trams, a long line of warehouses hid the river from sight; to the left a jumble of graceful old houses and modern office blocks cloaked the steep hillside.

Traffic policemen, perched on their wooden drums beneath striped umbrellas, controlled the swirling traffic deftly. They evidently recognized the registration plate of the Citroën, because the driver swept through the impatient traffic without delay and on to a vast square, bordered on three sides by gracious eighteenth-century buildings. The fourth side had balustrades along the waterfront and a wide flight of steps leading down to the surging waters of the estuary. This was the Praça de Comercio, 'Rolling Motion Square', but Craig noticed sadly that the wavy black and white pavement had been coated with asphalt to form a huge car-park. But at least the triumphal arch still led to the grid of elegant streets built after the disastrous earthquake of 1755.

The car swung through the arch into a street of banking houses and expensive shops, and then turned right-handed into a maze of narrow streets which soon began to lead steeply upwards between tall houses faced with pale *azulejos*, with geraniums and jasmine tumbling here and there over the high garden walls.

They climbed through the outer defences of the castle and came at last to the gate into the open space within the battlements, where cars were parked in orderly rows beneath the ruined towers of the keep. Coelho ignored the car-park and drove along the battlements and drew up by a table with a panoramic view of Lisbon, done in painted tiles. Craig got out.

It was certainly a view worth seeing. The city stretched like a patchwork quilt across the steep hills and down into the valleys which radiated like outstretched fingers from the centre of the old town. The lovely outlines of the baroque churches crowning the hills were already being jostled by the stark cubes of modern blocks, but in the distance the castles on the heights of the Sintra range seemed to float dreamily above the hilly plain, monuments to the grandeur and whimsy of dead kings.

He looked southward. Beneath his feet the ancient houses of the Alfama clung like a cluster of swallows' nests to the hillside. Beyond the wide estuary rose tall factory chimneys, and far away on the horizon lay the long range of the Arrabida mountains. They looked mild and rather uninteresting. Craig didn't know that later that day he would be fighting for his life in those same hills.

By the time he had agreed to visit the Cathedral, several other churches—for Agente Coelho, rather surprisingly, proved to be a walking dictionary of saints and their shrines —the football stadium and the Presidential Palace, it was getting late and he asked to be taken to the Embassy.

Turning west along the river they came in time to the steep cobbled Rua Sao Domingos a Lapa. Half-way up was a long low building of rose-red stucco, faced with stone. Outside, a number of cars with diplomatic number plates were parked half on the narrow pavement, to leave the tramlines clear. Massive wooden doors in the yard-thick walls led directly from the street. There were heavy grilles on the ground-floor windows, but those on the first floor had little balconies of wrought iron. Inside the pediment of the doorway, above the Union Jack on its staff and the Royal Arms, Craig saw carved in stone the escutcheon of the Portuguese aristocrat who built the palace in the eighteenth century, a unicorn and a stag supporting a coat of arms above—of all things—a bed of roses. He wondered whether the present inmates of the Embassy found this apt. From what he had heard of Sir Roland Mortimer, Her Majesty's Envoy Extraordinary and Minister Plenipotentiary, he thought it unlikely.

The car stopped in the exact middle of the street and the driver opened Craig's door, stopped an oncoming tram and led him to the door. He went back to lean nonchalantly against the gleaming bonnet, watching with interest while the traffic struggled to pass on both sides. The PIDE observed its own traffic regulations.

After the brilliant sunshine the square hall seemed dark at first, but Craig could see a vaulted ceiling and a marble staircase, garnished with brass banisters, dividing at a half-landing to lead to the floor above, and at his feet an incongruously gay harlequin pattern of black, pink and white marble tiles. At the rear a stone-flagged passage led out to a garden, and he caught an inviting glimpse of a smooth lawn with tall old trees shading it from the sun.

A man in blue uniform with the Royal Arms on his brass buttons led him to a desk. Craig handed in his card and asked to speak to the Head of Chancery on an official matter. The messenger picked up his telephone and a moment later Craig was taken upstairs and along a passage to a pair of impressive walnut doors, one of which was opened to usher him in. It was a large room, with walls and ceiling painted with sporting nymphs and swans by a lake. All very gay, thought Craig—the bed of roses touch.

A tall, athletic man of about thirty-five—Craig's age—rose from behind a modern desk and came forward. In spite of the foot-thick stack of files in his in-tray he took his time over sitting his visitor down and offering a cigarette. He introduced himself.

'Simon Dickens,' he said. 'I'm First Secretary and H. of C., so I'm supposed to run the show and co-ordinate everything. I don't think we've met, but I see from the List that you were in West Africa. I was in Lagos a few years ago, in the High Commission, before all the trouble started, thank God.'

'I was in Sierra Leone and Bangasa, but I visited Lagos a few times.'

'Oh, well, there must be a lot of people we both know,' said Dickens, concluding the diplomatic opening gambit. 'How long are you here for and what can we do for you? Have you seen the Consul-General?'

'Good Lord no. I don't want to register. I'm only here for a few hours; I came in with the *Claudia* and we sail again this afternoon. I wouldn't have bothered you, but I thought I'd better let you know I'm lunching with one of the PIDE people. A chap I've known for years.'

Dickens got up and perched on the edge of his desk, looking thoughtfully at the broad-shouldered man in the armchair. Interesting face, he thought, a bit rugged-looking, with that broken nose, but the voice was easy and quiet, with a touch of Scottish in it, perhaps. The List had shown him as having been the top cop in Bangasa, but he looked pretty young still. Anyway, he decided, being discreet would be part of his job.

'May I ask,' he said, 'who it is you're lunching with?'

'Ferreira. Vicente Ferreira. He was stationed in Luanda for a time and that's where I got to know him.'

Dickens slid off the desk and stood frowning. 'Ferreira? Good Lord! You're not seeing him officially, are you?'

'Heavens, no!' exclaimed Craig, with a touch of impatience. 'Purely social. I told you, he's an old friend.'

'Well, well! Do you know what his job is now?'

'No idea.'

'He's head of the internal political branch of the PIDE. He's the terror of the call-up. If any poor little student objects to being patriotic and going to die in Africa—or at least, if he *says* so—it gets to Ferreira's ears within hours, and he acts very tough indeed.'

'I'm afraid there's no way of enforcing the Portuguese policy in Angola without being fairly tough, both there and at home. But Ferreira, when I knew him in Africa, was a good man and no sadist. And it isn't he,' added Craig, 'who makes the policy.'

'You're right, of course. And I don't know him—only his reputation. You like him?'

'Yes. He's not a bad chap, as I said. And a damned good police officer.'

'Oh, well, it's all right, of course, from our point of view. I hope you enjoy your lunch. There's nothing on the Embassy's conscience as far as the PIDE's concerned. But as you know, our relations with the Government here have been a bit tricky for some time, what with Rhodesia and our

African policy in general, and voting against—quote—our oldest ally—unquote—at the UN Assembly, and so on. So you may be given a lecture over your lobster Ericeira à la Cardinale.'

Craig grinned. 'It wouldn't be the first time. We used to argue like mad about politics. But as I told you, he's a friend and a good policeman, so we always found other things to talk about.'

Dickens suddenly slapped the desk with the palm of his hand. 'My God, that's an idea. Is he the sort of friend who'd do a small favour for you? And keep quiet about it?'

Craig's Scottish caution asserted itself. 'I'll not say,' he said warily, 'until I know what it is.'

Dickens laughed. 'It's all right, old boy, I'm not putting over a fast one. The thing is that we want some enquiries made, and if we do it through our usual channel, by way of the Consul-General and the Urban Police, we can't be sure there won't be a leak to the press. And then all hell would break loose.'

Craig was intrigued. 'What on earth is all this about?'

'The Defence Attaché's daughter's disappeared. She went to a party at the French Ambassador's house last night, was seen to leave at about half past twelve—and hasn't turned up since. But I think we'd better let Harcourt tell you himself. Then you can make up your mind whether Ferreira can help. OK?' He picked up the receiver.

'Oh, all right,' said Craig reluctantly. He had the feeling that he was being manœuvred into a position where he could hardly refuse. 'But how long have you known about this?'

'The MA only told me half an hour ago.'

'The Military Attaché?'

'Oh, Harcourt's both—Defence and Military. He's a soldier. His Number 2 is a Fleet Air Arm chap and he does Navy and Air. He wears a different hat according to what he's doing. But listen. The reason why Harcourt's in a bit of a tizz is that he's afraid now that she won't turn up in time for the official luncheon H.E.'s giving for a lot of the Portuguese top brass. At first he was sure she'd spent the night with a girl-friend and that she'd appear in time, so he wouldn't hear of my informing the police. But he'll have to agree now.'

'Does Miss Harcourt make a practice,' asked Craig drily, 'of staying away from home for the night?'

Dickens hesitated. 'This is exceptional. She wouldn't let them down like this without a reason, I'm sure of that. Between ourselves,' he added, cocking an ear at the door, 'she's a bit of a handful for her parents. They don't really understand her at all. But she'd know better than to ditch H.E. without warning; there's a lot of brain in that oh-so-pretty head. Here he is.' He stood up, and when Harcourt came in introduced him.

Brigadier Roderick Harcourt was a slim man of about fifty, of medium height, with a tanned smooth face, a carefully trimmed brown moustache and deep-set blue eyes. Craig noted on his left breast both the cerise and blue ribbon of the DSO and the purple and white of the MC.

He was wearing the Number One Dress of a former officer of the Royal Horse Artillery. The dark blue barathea jacket, close fitting at the waist, was buttoned up to the stand collar, which had scarlet patches and was lined by a linen strip which showed exactly a quarter-inch of white around the neck. The blue 'overalls', with their two-inch scarlet stripes, clung to his legs and were firmly strapped down to the spurred, black leather wellington boots. The aiguillette—the thick gold and crimson cord which is the badge of a Service Attaché—was looped over his left shoulder, and across the beautifully fitting jacket ran the RHA cross-belt of gold lace on black leather. Two gold lace slings from under the jacket held his sword. It was a dress of splendour and consequence, but Harcourt wore it as though it were the most natural, proper and comfortable clothing imaginable.

'I haven't got much time, Simon,' he said, with a look of apology at Craig. 'I think I'd better go and beard H.E.'

'You mean she's still missing?'

The Brigadier turned to look at Craig.

'Look, Rory,' began Dickens apologetically, 'I've told Craig—'

'Have you indeed?' The DA's voice was freezing.

'Yes,' said Dickens firmly, 'because I think he can help.' He explained about Craig's lunch-date with Ferreira. 'So you see he might—if you and he agree—tell the Sub-Director and ask him to make discreet enquiries. I mean— well, the hospitals, traffic police and so on. I hate to suggest these possibilities but—'

Harcourt interrupted him. 'My clerk's been listening to every radio broadcast, and there's nothing.' He turned to Craig. 'It's very civil of you to offer—' he began.

'Wait a moment,' said Craig. 'I haven't offered anything so far, and frankly, would rather not approach Ferreira. Let's forget it.'

'No,' said Dickens sharply.

Harcourt's icy voice cut in. 'What d'you mean, Simon? This concerns me only.'

'You're quite wrong, Rory,' said Dickens with equal coldness. 'H.E. plans his lunch parties very carefully and as you know he depends on Amanda to butter up the odd Minister.' He ignored Harcourt's angry gesture. 'So he's going to be very annoyed with us both and if *I* haven't been able to start a search he'll want to know why the hell not.'

'I'll take the blame, of course.'

'You can't. Once you've told me—and you were a bit late about it, you know—it's my job to find her.' He added more mildly, 'You're just hoping against hope that she'll turn up in the next half hour, I know, but you see you *can't* rely on radio bulletins. They'd miss out half a dozen accidents to cram in another commercial.'

The DA thought for a moment. Then he said to Craig, 'Dickens is right. I'm afraid I've got him into a jam as well as myself. But—well, it's so unlike my daughter. I'm sorry if I appeared rude.'

'You must be very worried,' suggested Craig, but Harcourt ignored that opening and went on :

'You know this officer well enough to feel you can ask

him to have some routine enquiries made—no more than that—without letting anyone leak it to the press?'

'Yes, I think so. As you know, loyalty to colleagues is a good point with the Portuguese and I could pitch it fairly strong, I suppose.' His manner showed that he was hardly looking forward to the task.

Harcourt said, with a smile of great charm, 'I am extremely sorry that we have to impose on you in this way. But if you'll agree to cast a fly over Ferreira I'll be eternally grateful.'

Craig had no alternative. 'Of course.'

'I'll just telephone the flat again,' said Harcourt, 'if I may use your telephone, Simon.' He went eagerly to the telephone and asked for a number. As he listened to the voice at the other end his face fell. He murmured something comforting to his wife and replaced the receiver. 'If she turns up now,' he said slowly, 'she'll have to miss it.' He turned to Dickens. 'You're not going to this one, are you? I wonder if Joyce would be terribly kind and—er—step into the breach. May I suggest that to H.E.?'

'Of course. I warned her earlier,' said Dickens drily, 'without of course saying why. She'll play.'

'Bless you!' He straightened his shoulders and moved towards the door. 'I'll go and tell H.E. now and then go round and see if I can help Lady Mortimer with the *place-ment*. I'm afraid, as I said, that she'll want to alter things a bit, as Joyce is—well, so much senior to Amanda.'

'What you mean,' replied Dickens cheerfully, 'is that her Portuguese is still just kitchen and women's talk, while Amanda's is bloody fluent.'

Harcourt smiled and went out without a word.

'Poor devil!' said Craig. 'If that girl isn't dead or un-conscious she ought to be spanked.'

'I would do that,' said Dickens grinning, 'with the great-est pleasure, but I doubt whether Joyce would trust my motives. She doesn't exactly take to Amanda. I can't think why.'

'So she's a very attractive girl?'

'She's a smasher. A big, beautiful girl with wide innocent

eyes and a rather special figure. And no morals at all. Her parents can't understand her—how could they?— but the Ambassador adores her and she plays up to him scandalously. Which is why he is no doubt tearing a broad strip off Rory at this moment.'

'What's he like—H.E., I mean? I've heard people talk about him and he sounds rather—well, difficult.'

Dickens considered. 'I don't usually discuss my boss, but you may well have to meet him and you'd better be warned. To put you in the picture, his last two posts were as Number 2, first in Paris and then in Washington, under rather severe taskmasters. So now Lisbon—'

'I see,' said Craig. 'This is a very important post?'

'The most important in Europe. And if the Office doesn't realize it yet the whole staff of this Embassy has got to prove it. You've known Governors like that?'

'I have indeed,' said Craig, feelingly.

'Well, there it is. He likes things to be done just so, and no—repeat no—slip-ups. But at least he knows what he wants done, and he's bloody good at his job, even if he can be tiresome.' He looked at Craig. 'It's really very good of you to help us. I know you don't want to do it. Have you got a car?'

'Yes. A PIDE one, standing in the middle of the street.'

Dickens chuckled. 'How like them! Their wings may have been clipped by the new regime, but they're still something of a state within a state. Well, good luck in the corridors of power. And you'll give me a ring after lunch?'

'Yes. I may only have time for that. The boat is due to sail soon after four. By the way, I told them to leave a message for me here if there was any change.'

Dickens nodded, and Craig went out and down to the street. He had only half an hour before his lunch-date, and with the midday traffic at its peak that was barely enough.

CHAPTER THREE

Luncheon at the Club

AT THE ARMED SERVICES CLUB the food was excellent and
after oysters, a sole, a steak and a sticky pudding, which
Ferreira insisted he should try, Craig was glad to settle
down with a cup of strong black coffee and a cigar and
allow his digestion a chance to catch up. This was the
moment to get Ferreira interested in the missing girl. The
Portuguese had shown clearly his pleasure in seeing Craig
again and talking shop. Politics had been avoided by common consent, but Ferreira was much interested in Craig's
account of his experiences as a lecturer at the Police
Academy in Chile and they had swapped stories of develop-
ments in forensic science. Craig glanced at his watch and
saw that time was running on.

'Vicente,' he said, 'I have a rather odd request to make.
I dropped into the Embassy this morning—'

'Naturally. To hear the latest horror stories about the
sinister PIDE, no doubt?'

'No, it was just a matter of routine—and they hadn't got
any horror stories, anyway.' He finished his coffee. 'It was
something—not up your street at all—but when the Head
of Chancery heard I was to have the pleasure of lunching
with you he wondered whether you might be kind enough
to have some routine enquiries made without letting anyone
know.'

'Anyone? Oh, you mean the press?'

'Yes.'

'But why?'

'The daughter of one of the staff has disappeared.'

'Disappeared? But they should have informed—Oh yes,
I see. They don't want the press to get excited. But that's
all very well, Peter. If they're not told quickly—but of
course you know this as well as I do. Is there a special
reason for secrecy? Who is the girl?'

'Daughter of the Defence Attaché.'

Ferreira started. 'Do you mean Amanda Harcourt?'

'Yes.'

'When did she—as you called it—disappear?'

'Last night. From the moment she left a party at the French Ambassador's.'

'Is it so very unusual for this young lady to stay away from home for the night?' There was a curious edge to Ferreira's voice.

Craig looked at him in surprise. 'I suppose so. Her parents are very worried, and so far as I know she wasn't back in time for a luncheon at the Residence where she should have been—so to speak—on duty.'

'I see,' said Ferreira vaguely. He looked thoughtful. 'I'll see what I can do. Have some more coffee?'

'Thanks. How is it you know the girl, Vicente?'

'I don't, except from her record,' said Ferreira wryly.

There was a pause. Then Craig said quietly, 'I think you'd better tell me what you know, if you don't mind. Perhaps it would help.'

Ferreira leaned forward and spoke earnestly. 'Listen, Craig. You've only got an hour or two before your ship leaves. Just keep out of this. You can't do any more. You've done what the Embassy asked; now leave it to me. I'll put out a general enquiry at once and, believe me, there'll be no publicity. If she's found your Head of Chancery will be told immediately by Protocol Department. That's the proper channel, and he must know it perfectly well. Just tell them that, and go off to your boat.' He stood up.

Craig groaned. 'Sit down, Vicente. Of course that's what I should like to do, but you know I can't. You said the girl has a record. You can't mean—well, just loose-living.'

'We are stricter about that kind of thing in Portugal,' said Ferreira primly. But his eyes met Craig's too boldly.

'No, it isn't just that, is it? Come on now. Tell me as a friend.'

Ferreira considered, taking his time. Then he said: 'All

right. I'll tell you as a friend, for your own information only. Is that clear? You won't act on what I say except by agreement with me?'

'Agreed. What has the wretched girl done?'

Ferreira drew on his cigar, then laid it down and spoke in a quiet official voice.

'Brigadier Harcourt was posted here two years ago. At that time his daughter was still at the University of Oxford and only came to Lisbon during vacations. She is a gay, attractive girl and she quickly made friends in the diplomatic corps and among the families of our land-owning and aristocratic society. She has long fair hair, and we Portuguese are very susceptible to blondes.' He added caustically, 'You have only to visit our expensive and wholly illegal brothels to realize that.'

Craig stirred uncomfortably. 'But you're not suggesting —?'

Ferreira laughed. 'I wish it were only her morals we had to complain about. She's a highly intelligent young woman with dangerous ideas in her head. Dangerous to my country.'

'Oh Lord, so that's it. She's been talking revolutionary socialism or whatever is the latest cry at Oxford.'

'The dangerous thing is that she *doesn't* talk adolescent politics—at least, not in public. In diplomatic circles— where I have reliable informants—' he frowned at Craig's smile. 'It's not funny, Peter, whatever you may think. As I said, in those circles she has never attracted any attention to her political views. But in private—ah, that's a different matter.'

'What do you mean—in private?' asked Craig impatiently.

'I'm trying to give you the whole picture. Among the more irresponsible of our rich young men is Joao Gonçalves Costa, who comes from one of our oldest and most respected families. His father is the Navy Minister. Young Costa is a firebrand. He is the head of a group of young men, mostly of the aristocracy but including some university lecturers and a few officers in the Armed Services, who have been plotting revolution for the past few years. We know all about them.'

'Well, then?'

'It was just talk—an escape of steam. To take action against them, with all the important names involved, would have caused more scandal and upset than it would be worth. So we decided to wait.'

'And Miss Harcourt?'

'She began by being a close friend of Joao Gonçalves Costa. Then he began to take her to meetings and she suddenly became an active member of the movement.' He made a gesture of exasperation. 'And *transformed* it. She tightened up their security, so that we couldn't bug their meetings any more. She actually found one of the mikes herself,' he added in an aggrieved voice, 'and pulled it out of the wall and showed it to them.'

Craig was finding it difficult to keep his face straight. 'That must have been a riot,' he suggested, in a shaking voice.

'It was. And it was *she*, with young Costa to back her up, who prevented the whole movement from disintegrating on the spot.' He shook his head. 'How a bunch of well-born young Portuguese could take orders like that from a *woman*—it astounds me! It just shows how effete they've become.'

Craig pulled himself up just in time. 'I realize how serious this is. If the Embassy had had any idea, I assure you—But how do you know all this? You said she found the mike.'

'I have a good informant,' said Ferreira shortly.

'Some young officer,' jeered Craig, 'who agreed to play rather than be posted to Portuguese Africa?'

Ferreira ignored the remark. 'After that they only met in private houses or out in the country, and at infrequent intervals. And under strict security control. She used to read them extracts from books about the famous Soviet cases—Klaus Fuchs, Greville Wynne, the Lonsdale network and so on—they're all full of information for amateurs.

Miss Harcourt became a sort of female guru. They used
to make a joke about it—"*Manda Amanda*".'

'Oh my God! "Amanda gives the orders",' said Craig
thoughtfully. 'The fat *is* in the fire. What a bloody fool
the girl must be!'

'That's not the word I'd use,' said Ferreira viciously.
'And then?'

'She told them to drop all their silly ideas of blowing
up my Headquarters and so on. Their only effective
weapon, she said, was illicit propaganda, and that is precisely the programme they've followed since she left them.'

Craig felt a wave of relief. 'She left them? She came
to her senses, then? Thank God for that! She's got
nothing to do with the movement now?'

'I'm not sure. Something happened last Christmas.
Either, as you say, she realized that she was heading for
trouble, or she fell out with young Costa. Or perhaps she
was telling them the truth when she said she had no time
to spare. She left Oxford last summer and came to live
here with her parents and study Portuguese. She had
learned other languages at Oxford, I think, and she had
decided to add ours and sit for the interpreter examinations
of the United Nations Organisation. I gather they're very
exacting?' He looked at Craig.

'They certainly are,' said Craig thoughtfully. 'To get up
to that standard in a new language would mean a lot of
work. And at least the girl seems to have character. Did
she stop seeing young Costa?'

'My informant says he has never mentioned her name
during the past three months, and he seems very unhappy
about it. As far as I know they haven't met. But I can't
quite believe,' he added slowly, 'that she wouldn't want
to know how their project was going. *Cristo Rey*,' he
exploded, 'it was her creation, however ill-conceived and
wild and—and un-Portuguese. They're not just going to
criticize the regime; they are going to distribute, clandestinely and all over Lisbon at the same time, leaflets slan-
dering every member of the Government, including even
the old Admiral for good measure; their families, their

business associations, girl-friends—every bit of dirt they can lay their hands on. Or invent.'

'But how can they distribute it all simultaneously without being spotted? It would need thousands of sympathizers to make it effective.'

'Rat-traps,' said Ferreira tersely. 'With time-fuses.'

'Good Lord, the old SOE trick. You balance a stack of leaflets, held by a weak rubber band, on the trap—the back-breaking kind—with a time-fuse to set it off. And you put it on the outside sill of a high window—'

'Lavatories,' said Ferreira sombrely, 'so that you can't see it from the inside. One distributor could set a dozen without any difficulty.'

'But the fuses? They can't buy time-fuses in the shops.'

'There's a photographic delay trigger which has settings of up to an hour,' said Ferreira. 'They were going to buy several dozen of those. They don't lack money.'

'Was that her idea, too?'

'Yes. She thought that one up.'

'And timed for—?'

'Timed for nine o'clock in the morning, when the street-cleaners have finished and the traffic is thick. And there's usually a morning breeze.'

'It's clever,' said Craig.

'She's a clever *puta*,' said Ferreira bitterly, 'with a dangerous turn of mind. I'd give a lot to get her inside for a few hours.'

'When is the project planned for?'

'Easter Day, with all the tourists up early to see the processions, the crowds going to mass and the middle-class leaving for picnics in the country. Perfect!'

'But damn it! You can stop it.'

'I hope so. If we can learn from our agent when and where the printing will take place we'll move in and take the whole stock. And burn it on the spot—I'm not going to take any chances. And of course pick up the men who work the machines and put them inside. It's a pity we can't risk waiting to pick up the distributors with their stacks of leaflets. But they've been chosen very carefully and some of them even we—the PIDE—can't touch without special ministerial authority. I daren't let it get as far as that. Even one of those leaflets, if it got into the hands of the foreign press, would be a major disaster, and when we act we'll do it without any publicity, so as not to give the foreign news-hounds a trail to follow.'

He paused, and looked grimly at Craig. 'I've told you too much, but it's important that someone on your side should know. I couldn't tell your Embassy without blowing my informant. And remember that I have your word that you'll take no action whatever on this information without my agreement.'

'Yes,' said Craig, 'that's what I said. Now let me get this clear. Although you feel—and bitterly, I can understand that—that Miss Harcourt is largely responsible for this plot, you have no evidence that she has any connection *at present* with the whole operation.'

'No evidence. I *suspect* she's still in touch with young Costa, but that's all. They have some meeting-place I don't know about, because it wasn't used for their so-called political meetings. All I know is that last summer they both disappeared for week-ends at a time—they became very clever at shaking off the trailers we had put on Joao Costa. I assumed they had become lovers.'

'Oh, for God's sake! Do you mean to say that Costa is still under surveillance?'

'Of course. He's the head of the group.'

Craig exclaimed. 'But look, Vicente. The girl can't be found. She might be with him.'

'You must leave that to me.'

'Of course. But couldn't you find out, *now*, what young Costa has been doing since last night. Don't you see, it might give us the solution to the whole problem?'

'And what happens then, Peter? If I find the girl is still meeting this traitorous young hothead in secret, do you realize what that means? If this is so, will you give me your solemn word that she will leave Portugal within twenty-four hours and not come back?'

Craig was silent for a moment. 'I should of course have

to tell the Ambassador what you have said about her activities. I'm pretty sure he would send her back to England at once, even if she hasn't any connection with the plot any longer, provided I convince him that she was involved as deeply as you imply. But—'

'You could add, which is the truth, that if she *is* in contact with Costa—even purely private contact—and we bring a charge against him as the organizer of the operation we shall also bring one against her. And diplomatic privilege won't prevent the story from getting into the press. Knowing a little of Sir Roland's earnest wish to improve relations between our two countries,' he added, smiling grimly, 'I doubt whether he would like that.'

Craig drew a deep breath. 'That's blackmail, Vicente, but never mind. I agree. Find your evidence before I leave —and find the girl, for after all I may be barking up the wrong tree—and she'll be out of the country within the next few days.' He paused, and hesitated for a moment. 'I appreciate your position, Vicente. I've no doubt you'd far rather that she landed properly in the soup.'

'Oh no, she'd make too much of a splash. I prefer the simplest solutions. Get her out of the country and you cut out a cancer. I don't want headlines; I want things nice and quiet.' He rose. 'Wait here. I'll telephone the Surveillance Section.'

He came back within a minute, walking quickly across the hall, his face dark with anger. But he sat down and crossed his legs casually, for appearance' sake, before he spoke.

'They've lost him,' he said bitterly.

'Oh damn! When?'

'Last night. Costa's parents were away from home. He told the servants he would dine at home and go to bed early. He asked them to rouse him at six this morning and get his chauffeur round at seven to take him to a riding stable. By eleven-thirty last night all the house lights had been turned out and it looked as if everybody was asleep, so the surveillance car was sent back to garage by the officer on duty. At twelve-five Joao Costa opened the door of the house garage and came out quickly and quietly in his Country Squire estate-car, leaving the door open. There was one agent left outside—and fully awake, I assure you—but he has only a Vespa and couldn't keep up. Costa hasn't been seen anywhere since.'

'A Squire? That's the American Ford, isn't it? A big car, and I think they put anything up to a V8 seven litre into them. Well, it ought to be pretty conspicuous. They alerted the watchpoints on the main roads?'

'Of course,' said Ferreira impatiently, 'but we don't have them on duty permanently. They were set up and in contact by radio with Surveillance Section by one-thirty.'

'It looks very much like a planned meeting, don't you think? I mean, the girl leaves the French Residence at twelve-thirty, he leaves home at five past—just time to shake off followers and pick up the girl as she left. And what's more, it's clear she must have known he was coming for her.'

'Why? I don't see that.'

'Because,' explained Craig, 'if he was just hoping to waylay her as she left the party he'd have turned up much earlier. He couldn't have been *sure* that she wouldn't leave earlier. Oh no, he'd arranged it with her beforehand. We're one step forward, anyway, I think. Find Costa, and we find the girl.'

'He hasn't telephoned her recently, as far as we know.'

'How d'you know?'

'Not from his home. That's tapped. I had to get the Minister's approval to do it,' he added in disgust.

'And I suppose her flat—'

'Not tapped. We have to get special permission, of course, for diplomatic numbers, and it's only granted for short periods, if at all.' He paused. 'So he could have rung her from somewhere else. I'm afraid that's what's happened.'

Craig stood up. 'OK, Vicente. We both act as agreed. I'll ring you before I go to the boat.'

'The car's waiting for you.' Ferreira put out his hand, and Craig shook it warmly.

'It's very good to see an old friend again,' he said with

a smile, 'especially one who entertains as royally as you do.
I'm sorry your young man and our young woman have
combined to give you so much trouble, but as far as she is
concerned I think you won't have any more. When she
does turn up, she won't find His Excellency in a forgiving
mood—not after what I shall be telling him.'

CHAPTER FOUR

His Excellency

IT WAS three o'clock. Craig was shown up to the Head
of Chancery's room as soon as he arrived. Dickens met him
at the door. A glance at his face was enough to tell Craig
that there was no news of the girl. Dickens waved him to
a chair. 'What happened?' he asked. 'It seems to have been
a damned long lunch.'

'It's a long story, I'm afraid,' said Craig. 'That's why I'm
late. And a bloody awkward one.'

'Has she been found?'

'No. But there's certain information about her which
you'll have to know.'

Dickens put out his hand for the telephone. 'I'll get
Rory.'

'No,' said Craig urgently. 'Don't do that.'

'What d'you mean? Is she dead?'

'No. And be a good chap and shut up till I've finished.
I'll tell you the essentials as quickly as I can and then I
think we'll have to see H.E. before we can talk to Harcourt, poor devil.'

'All right,' said Dickens, intrigued, 'get on with it.'

'The Harcourt girl has been involved with a revolutionary movement here. The PIDE are going to move in on
it.' Dickens jumped to his feet. 'And,' continued Craig,
'they've given us a chance to get her out of the country
first. If not, you may swing her diplomatic immunity but
you won't stop the story from getting into the press.'

Dickens swore. Then he muttered, 'But it's impossible. The girl isn't a bloody fool.'

'She was mixed up—emotionally—with a young man who's the head of the group. And it seems she is, or at least was, very active indeed, and I mean in the movement.'

'Was?'

'There's a pretty big chance,' said Craig slowly, 'that she's with him now, possibly completing the arrangements for a coup they've planned to bring off shortly. But no one knows where he is, either.'

'Oh, this is the most fantastic nonsense,' exclaimed Dickens angrily. 'You can't expect—' but Craig's cold voice cut him short.

'What I do not expect,' he said quietly, 'is that you should doubt my word. I assure you, I could not be more serious.'

'I'm sorry. You're convinced that this extraordinary story is true?'

'Of course it's true, in so far as it's what the PIDE *thinks* is the truth, and they're the ones who are going to put the fat in the fire. Look, Dickens. I've got less than an hour before my boat leaves. I take full responsibility for this story. Hadn't we better see H.E. at once?'

'Yes, you're right. And I agree that we must keep Rory out of it for the time being. It was just that—I was imagining what H.E. would say. But there it is. He's got to hear your story, however much he dislikes it. And believe me, he will.' He rang the Ambassador's PA and picked up his minute-board.

The Ambassador's room was on the same floor, overlooking the garden. It was about thirty feet long and panelled in rosewood, dark and gleaming softly. The desk was enormous, but when the small, plump man who sat behind it, fiddling irritably with an ivory paper-knife, raised his hot little eyes you didn't notice the desk. There was no doubt who was the boss in this rococo palace.

He rose politely to greet Craig, but his expression was hardly welcoming. 'I gather from Dickens that you kindly

agreed to ask a friend of yours in the PIDE—curious crowd
to find one's friends among, I would have thought—to help
us to trace Amanda Harcourt. Well?'

Dickens began, 'It's a long story, sir—'

'You know I don't have time for long stories, Simon. Has
the girl been found?'

'No, sir.'

'Dead?'

'Not as far as we know.'

'Has Mr Craig learned where she might be?'

'No, sir.'

'I see,' said the Ambassador in dangerously quiet tones.
'Well, Mr Craig, thank you for—er—*trying* to help us.
Simon, would you come back for a moment, please, after
showing Craig out. Goodbye, Mr Craig.'

Neither man moved. Then Craig said, 'If we left it at
that, sir, we shouldn't be doing our duty either to you or to
HMG. This is a very serious matter, of the utmost importance for your relations with the Portuguese Government.'

His Excellency smiled frigidly. 'Well, Craig, at least you
know how to obtain a hearing. But you'd better—dear me,
you *had* better justify what you've just said.' He put on
an exaggerated air of boredom, and even contrived a yawn.
'Go ahead. And sit down, for God's sake. Now, then. I
won't interrupt.'

And he didn't, except—during the early part of Craig's
recital—certain snorts of disbelief, which quite failed to
put Craig off his stroke. He talked fast for ten minutes,
without wasting a word. There was no need for repetition,
with those angry brown eyes boring into his, unblinking.
Towards the end Craig could sense a change in the Ambassador's attitude. He was listening intently, frowning
from time to time at the painted ceiling, and when Craig
stopped speaking there was a silence while he mopped his
face with a large silk handkerchief. It had become very red
indeed. But his voice was under complete control.

'You realize, Craig, that we only have the word of this
policeman Ferreira for these shocking allegations against
Amanda?'

'I know. But he could hardly have invented the story on the spur of the moment. After all, *I* brought her name up. I am quite sure that he believes it to be true, and short of some extraordinary muddle inside the PIDE that means it *is* true. Exaggerated, perhaps, but of course you will know, sir—I haven't met the girl—whether she fits the part. I mean, has she the strength of mind to influence a whole group of hotheaded young men *as a group*, which is what Ferreira says she did? And perhaps Harcourt can tell you whether she used to see a lot of young Costa.'

'What's his full name?'

'I'm sorry, sir, I forgot to tell you. It's Joao Gonçalves Costa, the son of the Minister of Marine.'

The Ambassador raised a startled face and swore loudly. 'That *does* ring a bell. They used to go about together when she first came out here. And it's quite true she dropped him. Oh, hell! And the business of being a good girl and concentrating on her work for the UN exams. Your PIDE friend has done his homework.'

'And her character, sir?'

'Oh, yes. She's got lots of guts, like her father, and as for brains, she can take on any of these young men-about-town and run rings round them.'

'So what do you think, sir?' asked Dickens.

'What I think of that filly's conduct, Simon, is not for your sensitive ears. I greatly fear that the story, however highly-coloured it may be, is true in the essentials. That "Manda Amanda" slogan sounded unpleasantly apt. I will admit that Craig's prefatory remark about the effect on our relations with the Portuguese was if anything an understatement. We are—or we could be, in a very serious position indeed. But if I can bring myself, as I always try, to be charitable, I will say two things. One is that, knowing the girl, I don't think she acted frivolously, or deliberately put the Embassy at risk. She is so damned sure of herself that she thought that as long as she was in effective charge the whole plot would work without a hitch. And secondly, it does look as if she realized that having planned the operation for them she had to leave this group before D-Day. And in fact, if we can prove that she has had no recent contact with them I think we can get away with it. Bluff it out, if necessary. No one is going to pay much attention in Lisbon, of all places, to what a girl is supposed to have *said*. But if she's still mixed up with Gonçalves Costa, even if it's only in bed, she goes home by the next plane. What a pity!' he added, with a cold smile. 'She was a useful girl to have around.'

'We could invoke diplomatic immunity,' protested Dickens.

'Oh, could we? You read up your Vienna Convention, my lad. In a matter of this kind, interference in the internal political affairs of a friendly country, the Office might well instruct me to waive diplomatic privilege. And I can't risk that. Dear God, no!'

'But sir—' began Dickens.

'You're not letting personal feelings influence you, Simon, I *hope*. I hope you know your job better than that. It may be tough on Amanda—and bloody tough it's going to be on Rory anyway. And Cynthia. But they should have more control over their daughter. You see,' he went on in a more friendly manner, 'the more I think of Craig's story, the more I believe it. She *was* a bit Bolshy when she first came out here, bursting with undergraduate ideas about Vietnam and the Sorbonne riots and the Establishment at home. I enjoyed arguing with her because she's got an unusually good mind and was as quick as they come. I thought I'd straightened her out. But it wasn't me. It was that damned group or movement, or whatever it is, ready-made for her to take over and organize. And that fits, too. She's a bloody good organizer. You remember, Simon, when Joyce was sick and my wife gave Amanda the Embassy stall to run.' He turned to Craig. 'It's an annual fair, for charity. Well, she ran it like a clock—best turn-out we've ever had. She told me at the time she liked organizing things.' He laughed, a dry cackle without much mirth. 'I tell you what I'll do, Simon. I'll give her a chance. If she can convince me that she's had no contact with young Costa since Christmas she can finish her course here and go home at the end of it. But she won't come back again while I'm at this post. Otherwise—the next plane, as I said.'

He slapped his hand on the desk and turned to Dickens. 'She has got to be found, Simon. At once. It's up to you, but no doubt Craig will be good enough to advise you. You're lucky to have a British copper available.'

'I'm afraid I'm not, sir,' said Craig stiffly. 'I ought to leave now to catch my boat.'

'Are you on an assignment?' asked the Ambassador softly.

'On leave. I'm on my way to Italy to stay with friends.'

'Come, come, Craig. This is a matter of great importance to our good relations with Portugal. Those were your own words. I'm sure you'll feel it your duty to help us out,' and he accompanied the words with a smile so threadbare and cynical that Craig let himself cool off for a moment before he could trust himself to reply. Then he said very firmly: 'I did not want to be involved in this matter. I have already done what I was asked to do. It is *not* my concern and with respect, sir, I am not on your staff.'

He could almost feel the Ambassador's hackles rising. His Excellency compressed his lips. 'That sounds to me a frivolous and irresponsible attitude on your part. But let's check the departure time of your boat. Which is it?'

'*Claudia*. Italian Line. At the Alcantara Dock.'

The Ambassador picked up his telephone. 'Miss Graham, would you please ring the Italian Line—' He stopped, frowning. 'You have a message for Mr. Craig. I see, you were waiting for him to come out. Here he is.' He handed the receiver to Craig, who received the message with a sinking heart, and then turned round.

'She has been delayed for repairs, sir. She won't leave until the same time tomorrow afternoon. Four o'clock.'

'Well, Craig, that's better,' said His Excellency with a triumphant smile. 'Surely it won't take an experienced officer like you more than twenty-four hours to solve our little problem. I was thinking,' he added blandly, 'that I should have to send a Most Immediate to the Senior Police Adviser and ask him to attach you to my staff for the time being. But now it's all settled and we needn't quarrel.'

Craig was caught, and he knew it, but at least, now that he was involved, it could be on his own terms. He thought for a moment, while the Ambassador looked at him with growing annoyance. 'All right, sir, provided—'

'What *provisos* have you in mind?'

'Just routine facilities, sir. So that I can make at least an attempt to sort this matter out.' He took his time, thinking it over, while Dickens, ignoring the look on his chief's face, took out his pen and picked up his minute-board.

'I must be fully in charge,' said Craig quietly, 'and I want orders given to all your diplomatic staff to co-operate with me, if required. Some of them will have to take turns on duty through the evening and night, if the girl is still missing.' Dickens was scribbling rapidly. 'The Embassy exchange to be kept served all night. A place booked on a plane leaving for London tomorrow afternoon, if there is one. If not, any time tomorrow. A cypher officer on duty or readily available. About—let me see—fifty pounds in escudos in my pocket, for possible bribes. And a further sum of at least a hundred pounds held here. A car and driver, of course—someone who knows Lisbon and the surrounding country really well.' He paused to let Dickens catch up. 'And—yes, I shall want a self-drive car hired for twenty-four hours by someone unconnected with the Embassy. It had better be available within two hours.' He stopped. It was a curious feeling to be in command of an operation again. He didn't realize that it gave him an air of complete authority.

The Ambassador looked at him thoughtfully. 'Why all the secrecy about the self-drive car?'

'I've got to tell Ferreira that you agree to his request. This is important for you, sir, because I shall say that you insist that Miss Harcourt, if found, shall be brought to the

Embassy at once. Meaning, of course, without interrogation.'

'I agree,' said Sir Roland impatiently, 'but again—why the secrecy?'

'Because it's no good my pretending to Ferreira that I'm leaving today. He'll probably hear the boat's been delayed anyway. So he will know that I have another day here and he will certainly suspect that I've agreed to help in the search for Miss Harcourt. He also knows that your staff will be doing their utmost to find her. So he'll keep tabs on all of us, hoping to follow any lead we may discover. I'm trying to put myself in his place. It is of the utmost importance to him, if he suspects that Miss Harcourt and Costa are together in some place where the propaganda material is held—and it does seem rather likely —to get there first. The last thing he wants is for us to stumble on the hide-out and scare everybody away before his boys can arrest them. That's obvious. So we, if only to prevent the girl from being the subject of over-enthusiasm by the PIDE agents, must get in ahead of them.'

'This *is* your friend Ferreira we're talking about?' asked the Ambassador with an exaggerated expression of disgust.

'Yes, sir. If I do find any leads I don't want his boys in my hair.'

'Dog eat dog, eh?'

'No, sir. Ferreira's a very competent police officer, with the best interests of his country at heart.' He paused. 'Like all of us.'

The Ambassador looked at him sharply. Then he smiled suddenly. 'You seem to know your job,' he said mildly. 'All right, you can have all the help you want. See to it, Simon. But first ask Rory to come and see me. I'll tell him.'

Dickens stopped on his way to the door and turned. 'With Rory, sir, you won't—'

His Excellency showed his teeth. 'I'll be kind and *very* understanding. That's what you mean?'

'Yes, sir.'

'I'm a naturally kind man, Simon, you know that. Now

get on with your job. And you, too, Craig. And good luck.' He added with a hint of a leer, 'I do hope I'm not doing you out of a pleasurable evening in the night-spots of Lisbon.'

CHAPTER FIVE

The Harcourts

'DO YOU OFTEN want to strangle him?' asked Craig, curiously.

'Oh yes. But he was at his sunny best this afternoon. However, as I told you, he's good at his job, and it makes up for a lot.'

They were walking back to Dickens's room. 'What about *our* job?' asked Craig.

'You can make your headquarters in my room. There are two telephones. I'll just run through with you the notes I made when you were laying down the law to H.E. —I enjoyed watching his face!—and then get on with them. What else?'

'I'd like to see Harcourt as soon as H.E.'s finished with him and then I'm afraid I'll have to ask him to take me to his house. I expect nobody's searched the girl's room?'

'No,' said Dickens shortly.

'Well, it's got to be done. What's Mrs Harcourt like?'

'She's a dear,' said Dickens unhappily. 'Never quite got used to mini-skirts and that sort of thing—she's really rather Edwardian. And awfully easily hurt.'

'Damn the girl,' said Craig furiously. 'I'd give a lot to be on that blasted boat. Why the hell did it have to go lame?'

This put Dickens back on his side. 'I do know that, Craig. But you're the only expert help we've got.' He opened the door of his room and cleared a desk for Craig to sit at. Then he read through his notes, adding details of what Craig needed.

The door opened and the Defence Attaché came in. His face was white and he looked at the two men without any expression. Then he said slowly, 'We'd better have a talk, Craig. Would you come to my room? We'll be alone there for your interrogation.'

'Look, Rory,' said Dickens urgently, 'Craig doesn't like this any more than you do.'

'That,' said Harcourt with a bitter smile, 'is hard to believe. But it's all right, Simon. H.E. told me he'd had to bully him into it.' He smiled stiffly at Craig. 'We'll give you all the help we can, of course. Come along.'

Harcourt led the way back to the top of the stairs and then into a narrow passage which ended in a blank wall, with a narrow stair ascending on the left. 'Sorry about this,' he said, 'but it's quicker.' At the top of the staircase they came into another passage with grilles built across it at both ends—all very security-minded, thought Craig—but Harcourt's room was large and well lit, with maps decorated with forests of brightly-coloured pins covering the green-washed walls.

He drew up a chair for Craig and produced cigarettes. Then he waited, sitting at his desk, very straight, and looking at a photograph in a silver frame.

'First, may I see what she looks like? I've got to be able to recognize her.'

Harcourt handed over the photograph without a word. Amanda was wearing a ball-dress and looking very elegant and self-assured. Her face was striking—pale hair swept up above her head, a broad bland forehead, delicately arched nose and wide, well-shaped mouth. Her bosom was small but firmly defined above a slender, but not too slender waist. A strong, healthy girl, well-gowned and confident. Her eyes—he remembered Dickens's words— 'wide innocent eyes and no morals at all'—it was a good description, probably. He returned the frame, handling it carefully, to the Brigadier.

'Thank you,' he said, without comment. 'Now let's see what we can work out as a plan of action. You've obviously discussed your daughter's disappearance with your wife

and racked your brains for any ideas. Have you anything
at all to suggest?'

'No.'

'Who gave you the time when she left the French party?'

'H.E.'s son. He was there.'

'How old is he?'

'Tony Mortimer? Nineteen, I think. He had—I mean
has—a bit of a crush on Amanda. He told my wife he'd
offered to give her a lift home, but she said she was fixed up
already. He didn't know with whom.'

'So she didn't take her own car, if she has one?'

'She has, but it's in the garage. She went there in my
car, and asked the chauffeur not to come back for her as
she would get a lift.'

'I see. Did Tony Mortimer say whether she was together
with some person in particular?'

'I asked him that, of course,' said the Brigadier impatiently, 'but he said no. She was enjoying herself and lots
of her friends were there and she danced with all of them,
he said, including him.'

'And there was nothing in what she said—?'

'No. He said she treated him as usual, like a big sister,
and I think he left her in a huff.'

'But he continued to keep an eye on her?'

'Obviously, since he says he knows she was there just
before half past twelve, because she was dancing with a
man he doesn't like, but a few minutes afterwards, when
he went to look for her, she'd gone.'

'Who was the man?'

'I thought of that, too. It was the French Ambassador's
son, young Tissier. He'd have had to stay the course in
any case. And young Mortimer, jealous, I suppose, made
sure that he was still there after Amanda had gone.'

'This was a party for young people, I suppose?'

'Yes. None of our staff was invited.'

'And other people who were there, whom you could
ask? And what about the chauffeurs and people at the
door?'

'I haven't advertised the fact that I don't know where my daughter's got to,' said Harcourt stiffly.

'I know. But we may have to, quite soon, if we can't get a lead. You realize that?'

'Yes, of course.'

Craig leaned back in his chair. 'Listen, Brigadier. The *only* lead we've got at the moment—and it's a pretty tenuous one—is the possibility that Amanda agreed to meet young Costa after the party—' he raised his hand to stifle Harcourt's protest, and went on—'agreed to meet him to tell him once and for all that she was no longer interested in his political ideas. Or, presumably, in him either.'

'She could have done that quite openly. They could have met anywhere.'

'According to Ferreira they had secrets—she knew a lot about Costa's political activities. If that's what he wanted to talk to her about he might well have arranged to meet her somewhere secret. H.E. told you—?'

'Yes, he did. But I still can't believe it.'

'Well, let's leave that for the moment. What's young Joao Gonçalves Costa like?'

Harcourt frowned. 'It's quite a time since I saw him to speak to. But he's not a bad young fellow. A bit wild-eyed and long-haired, as they all are these days. When he came to the flat he struck me as better than most—I mean, you know, he showed respect, flowers to my wife after a party, and so on. In fact, good manners. I admit I was a bit surprised when Amanda dropped him, but perhaps he had been showing rather embarrassing signs of infatuation. It was obvious, even to me.'

'And after she dropped him—that was last Christmas, wasn't it?—do you know for a fact if she has seen or spoken to him?'

'No, of course not. But she never mentioned him or suggested asking him to the house.'

'Never mentioned his name? It's a bit odd, isn't it? If she'd known him pretty well.'

'But for God's sake, Craig, you must know that they

don't *confide* in their parents these days. It's all so different.'

'I wonder,' said Craig. 'Did you confide in your people? I didn't.'

'Perhaps not. But we're men. Amanda *did*, at one time. We used to go long walks together—and she talked her head off.' He smiled as he remembered. 'She had no inhibitions at all, and no secrets either, in those days.' He added gruffly, 'Then she went up to Somerville, and became so remote—it was never the same relationship again.'

There was silence. Then Craig said, 'I must ask you this. Do you think she met Joao Costa last night?'

'That's poppycock! She's not a secretive sort of girl.'

'All right. Then we've got to find another lead. Have you searched her room?'

'I have not,' said Harcourt loudly. Then he added more quietly, 'But my wife did. And found nothing.'

'Still, there might be some indication—a note on a scrap of paper, for instance.'

Harcourt started to say something furious, and then stopped. 'All right,' he said curtly. 'We'll go there now.'

'Thank you. On the way I'd better check with Dickens to see how he's getting on and then—blast it!—I must ring Ferreira.'

'You can ring him from here. I'll go out.'

'Good Lord, no. He might have some good news. Please stay.'

He asked the exchange for the PIDE and got through to Ferreira without delay.

'Well, Peter, will you stick to our bargain?'

'His Excellency agrees, on the understanding, of course, that if your people find Miss Harcourt she will be escorted to the Embassy at once.'

'Once we find her she will be quite safe, I assure you.'

'I know. But that isn't what I said.'

'We'll bring her to the Embassy as soon as possible.'

'Listen, Vicente. The Ambassador is very seriously concerned in this case.'

'So he ought to be. But don't worry. I'll see she's all

right. I gather your ship hasn't left. They're replacing a big-end and it's had to be flown over from Genoa.'

'So that's what it was.' (He took a poor view of the *cuscinetto* which had landed him with a job he didn't want.) 'We're to leave tomorrow afternoon.'

'Yes, she should be able to leave by then. So you can have a quiet night, Peter. Or a pleasant night, anyway. Shall I let you have some telephone numbers?'

'No, you old devil. The Embassy's looking after me.'

'I have a feeling, Peter, that it's you who'll be doing the looking. But remember what I said. Don't get mixed up in this.'

'I'll remember what you say.'

'But it won't stop you, will it, Craig? Believe me, you must be careful. If you have a lead it may run you into more than you can cope with. Leave it to us.'

'Well, thanks for the advice. I shan't see you before I leave, so—'

He heard a chuckle at the other end. 'Oh yes, you will. I'll be at the boat to make sure you go. So long.'

Craig put down the receiver, frowning. He saw Harcourt's curious glance.

'It's as I thought. They want us to leave the search to them.'

'So that let's you off the hook.'

'Oh no, it doesn't. It only means we've got to be more careful.'

'I don't understand.'

'I think they'll do as they say, and if they find your daughter they'll send her here. But in spite of H.E.'s promise to send her home, if she's still in contact with young Costa they'll hope to catch her in a position of such compromise —I mean politically, of course—that they can make double sure that we'll do our part. Such as finding her with some of the other conspirators and a lot of clandestine material —'

'It's all such nonsense.'

'What matters, Harcourt, is what the PIDE *think*, and therefore what they're going to do. I've explained all this to H.E. but I'm most anxious that you should get the point. It is simply this; that *they* will want to get Amanda before we reach her, so *we* must try to get to her first. They will be watching us, therefore we must avoid surveillance, and if there are any people following us around, shake them.'

Harcourt thought it over. 'Yes,' he said, looking more cheerful at the idea of an opposing force to cope with. 'I do see your point. We've got to use any strategic advantage we have over the PIDE sleuths without letting them know. Right. Now, how can I help?'

'I'll let you know as soon as we can find something to go on. But first we must see Dickens. I wonder whether he's got that car yet.'

'What car?'

Craig explained as Harcourt led the way. He turned right in the passage and took Craig to the top of a main flight of stairs. 'You'd better see the proper way of getting up to this floor,' he said. 'It brings us down at the other end, beyond H.E.'s room.'

'What on earth are all the grilles for?' asked Craig. 'The security cage is on the first floor, surely, and I suppose anything top secret goes down there at night?'

'It does. But the grilles were put in during the war, when they thought they might have to stand a siege, I suppose, if the Germans overran Portugal. It's extraordinary to think of now, but after Norway nobody in Europe was safe. And there were a hell of a lot of real secrets here. This was the floor where the snoopers and the wreckers had their lairs. All madly suspicious of each other—this was before SIS and SOE were merged—but they did some remarkable work. They certainly had the old Abwehr guessing.'

There were the remains of more old grilles on the formal stairs, and half-way down, a large marble statue standing in an illumined niche. Craig glanced at it idly in passing, and then turned to stare. It was coy, but explicit.

'Is there any particular significance,' he asked cautiously, 'in preserving the statue of a hermaphrodite here?'

'None, whatever, so far as I know, although you can

imagine the rude speculations that blasted thing has occasioned. To me, it's typical of the FCO.'

'I don't like to think what you mean,' said Craig, laughing.

'Oh, I don't mean *that*. It's just that—well, in a regiment, for example, you respect traditions, and if a goat or an equally stinking Rock baboon illustrates some incident in your history you display it. It may seem silly, but there *is* a purpose. I find these Foreign Office types difficult to understand. They never talk about their traditions, but they never change anything unless they've got to. And yet they're as smart as paint, many of them, and tough. It beats me. That stupid sir-or-madam means precisely nothing in this Embassy except as something the junior archivist takes the new typist to giggle at.'

It was a good thing, thought Craig, that the man was letting his hair down a little. He glanced at him curiously. 'It must have been an extraordinary change,' he remarked invitingly, 'to come to a job like this after commanding a regiment.'

'It was,' said Harcourt laconically, and changed the subject.

In Dickens's office the Brigadier watched silently while they went again through the list. Rosters of duty had been made and the personnel concerned warned. The airline booking had been made in Amanda's name for the following day. 'Ferreira will learn about that,' said Craig 'and it's an earnest of our intentions.' The official car and driver were standing by. The money was handed over and Craig signed a receipt.

'What about the other car?' asked Harcourt. 'The one you hope won't be followed?'

'I haven't got round to that yet,' said Dickens. 'I thought Craig wouldn't want it for a bit, and frankly—' he hesitated, 'I'm not sure how—'

'I'll arrange that,' said Harcourt suddenly.

'Can you?'

'Yes, I think so. Jenkins will fix it. He'll be playing

bridge at the British Club. I'll go and see him at once.'

'I'm afraid they might have an informant there,' said Craig.

'He won't hear what I'm saying to Charles. I'll do it very casually.'

Craig wondered about that, but he said seriously: 'You'd better ask him to leave the Club, walk about for a bit, then take a taxi to a Hertz depot, hire a car for twenty-four hours, park it somewhere in the centre of the town and report to you with the ticket. Will he do all that and—discreetly?'

'Of course. He was a member of my regiment. Plenty of initiative. He hasn't got enough to do these days, since he sold his cork business.' He was speaking quickly and confidently, and his face had some colour in it.

Craig made up his mind. 'Good,' he said. 'Perhaps you could take me to your house as you go?'

Harcourt hesitated only a moment. 'Of course. It's only a few minutes away. We'll walk.'

They left the Embassy and turned into a street of fine old houses, most of which, Harcourt said, were taken by members of the Diplomatic Corps. The house they entered clung to the slope of the hill, and from the drawing-room of Harcourt's flat, lined with *azulejos* and comfortably furnished in traditional Portuguese style, they could see out through french windows across a broad terrace to a view of the river below.

Mrs Harcourt came into the room. She was wearing an old tweed suit of impeccable quality, and her face wore little make-up. It was a face of great charm, saddened with the lines of worry. The patrician nose and the broad clear brow were like her daughter's, Craig thought, but this was a gentle person, and sensitive. He did not look forward to bringing more unhappiness.

Her husband went up quickly and kissed her cheek. 'Darling, this is Mr Craig, a police officer whom Sir Roland has persuaded to help us look for Amanda.'

She gave him a distraught glance and then turned to

Craig. 'How d'you do?' she said, and looked round vaguely. 'Would you like some tea?'

'That would be very kind,' said Craig.

'He's going to ask you a lot of questions, Cynthia. I don't suppose you can help him but it's our duty to try. I won't stop for tea. I've got to go out on a job.'

She watched him go in some dismay. 'I hoped he'd stay for a bit,' she said. 'It's been such an awful day.' She made Craig sit down and rang a bell. A maid came in and was given her orders.

'Now, Mr Craig.'

'I know how you feel,' began Craig conventionally. 'Oh damn!'

'I beg your pardon!'

'There's nothing I can say which will do the least bit of good and I feel such a brute.'

'There's no need to exaggerate, Mr Craig. I'm taking this calmly enough, I hope, so I don't see why you shouldn't. Do you think Amanda's dead?'

'No,' he said loudly.

'There you go again,' she said with a gentle smile. 'Well, I don't either. Have you any idea where she is?'

'This is where I say "It is I who ask the questions, Madam!"'

She laughed quite gaily, and suddenly looked ten years younger. 'What do you want to know?'

'We're pretty sure that if she had been involved in an accident we'd have known about it by now. So it looks as if she went off somewhere last night, after the party, and for some reason hasn't been able—or willing—to come home. Someone else appears to be involved. Have you any idea at all who it might be?'

'No. I've thought and thought.'

'Was she—eh—involved with anyone in particular? I mean recently.'

'You mean Joao Gonçalves Costa? I wonder how you heard about him. But that's all over now.'

'How do you know it's all over?' asked Craig gently. 'Look. Let me explain. There is another reason—I'll tell you later—for thinking that she might have met him last night. You see, he's disappeared too.'

She raised a startled face. 'I'd no idea. I ought to telephone poor Dona Maria.'

'No. Please don't do that. In any case I think the Minister and his wife are away from Lisbon. But it's awfully important to know what her relations with young Costa are. It might help a lot.'

'She dropped him, I think, some months ago. It's very unlikely she'd have agreed to see him after midnight—like that, clandestinely.'

'I know. But something's happened. Please tell me. How well did she know him?'

She looked down at her hands in her lap. Then she raised her head and met his eyes. 'She had an affair with him last year. Rory doesn't know and I'd be grateful if you don't tell him yet.' Craig nodded. 'She never admitted it, but I *knew*. And in the same way I know that they're not lovers now. That she's not anybody's lover now. That would have been your next question, wouldn't it?'

'Yes, it would. And thank you. I suppose you've got no evidence? It's just what's called a woman's instinct?'

She smiled at him. 'A woman's instinct is mostly observation. When you love someone, even when they don't communicate with you very well, you can't help seeing how they look and—well, their state of mind. Even when it tells you what you don't want to know,' she added bitterly.

'But—I must ask this—have there been other men? I mean in that way?' As he said the words Craig knew he had struck the wrong note.

She looked past him, as if he were no longer in the room. 'No, Mr Craig. And if you've got the idea that Amanda strews her favours around Lisbon, you're quite wrong. I think that's all I have to say.'

The tea-trolley was wheeled in and they sat in silence while tea was served. When the maid had gone he said, 'I meant nothing of the kind, Mrs Harcourt. It was you who started talking about an affair, not me. I don't like asking these questions, you know, but I'm under orders from your Ambassador to find your daughter quickly. Before the PIDE find her.'

She looked up, horror-stricken. 'What on earth have they got to do with it?'

'They have reason to think that Amanda was—at least up until Christmas—fairly heavily involved not only with Joao Costa but with a group of his friends who are plotting against the regime.'

Her face went dead white, and for a moment he thought she was going to faint. But she recovered quickly. 'This is outrageous,' she said flatly.

'I'm afraid there is some pretty substantial evidence that she attended political meetings, and that would be enough for the PIDE. And if it does turn out that she was more heavily involved—which is what the PIDE is trying to prove—then she'll have to leave the country. That is the Ambassador's decision, not mine, of course.'

'Yes,' she said, in a low voice. 'Yes. She'd have to go at once. And the press would get on to it. And then we'd have to go, too.'

'Our whole object,' said Craig earnestly, 'is to get to Amanda before either the Portuguese police or the press. Then she can come straight to the Embassy and stay there until she leaves.'

'Then why are we just sitting here?' she cried. 'Can't you *do* something?'

'As I've told you, we've no lead to follow. I had hoped so much that you could help me.'

'I see.' She sat with her eyes closed, thinking. Then, without opening them, she said slowly, 'There was another man. Over a year ago. No, much more than that. When she first began to come out for the holidays. It's just conceivable that if she was in a fix she might go to him for help. But very unlikely. She's never mentioned him recently.'

'Who is he?' Craig tried to keep the excitement from his voice.

'A painter called Jack Davies, an Australian. I don't know where he lives, but it's in the Alfama, somewhere.

Amanda brought him to the flat once or twice, and he criticized our paintings—the family portraits in the dining-room. My husband didn't like him—he was a rather un-couth creature. But Amanda was fascinated by him for a time, and I think she visited his studio quite a lot.'

'May I look in your telephone directory?'

'Yes, of course. It's over there. But—it's no good, I'm afraid.'

'Why?'

'I'm sorry. I should have told you. I found his number this morning and spoke to him.' She stopped.

'What did he say?' asked Craig gently.

'I asked him if he had seen Amanda. He was very rude.' Her pale face flushed. 'But I gathered he hadn't. He—he made it clear that he thought I was prying into her private affairs and rang off before I could explain.' She added, 'He's a very impatient man, and quite graceless, I'm afraid.'

'I'll speak to him,' said Craig grimly. 'No. I'll go and see him. But first could we please have a look at Amanda's room? There might be an address-book, perhaps.'

She agreed, and took him into a room which led out on to the same terrace he had seen from the drawing-room. There were bookshelves, a desk with papers neatly stacked and a pile of notebooks, and a display of invitation-cards above the fireplace. A very orderly and pleasant room, Craig noted. The bed was still turned down, awaiting its owner.

He went across to the books, and saw at once a line of works whose names had made headlines—Krevitzky, Petrov, Fuchs, Greville Wynne on Penkovsky, Conolly on Burgess and Maclean, Philby on himself. That part of Ferreira's story, at least, was true, he thought. Then he turned to the desk. There was a leather address-book lying beside the Portuguese notebooks. He opened it, while Mrs Harcourt watched.

The addresses had been entered neatly in a rounded hand. Under 'Davies' nothing. He turned to 'J'. There was no 'Jack' but two 'J' entries, one at the top of the page and one lower down. The first ran: 'J. Sbda S. Jose. 25. 10. 25. 6432,' and the second 'J. QC. 349.'

He showed the book to Mrs Harcourt. 'Was that the number you rang, for Davies?'

'Yes. I think that's his address in the Alfama. It sounds like it.'

'And the other "J"?'

'I've no idea. I suppose it could be for "Joao Costa", but it's not a Lisbon number.'

'What could it be?'

'Somewhere in the country, with a small exchange.'

'Yes, of course,' said Craig admiringly. 'Come on, more ideas, please.' He had to get her interested in the search, get her imagination working. The rebuff she had received from Davies had left her with a distaste for the whole miserable business.

'Well,' she said, 'I can't think of any place called Q something, except Queluz, and there's no "C" to that. But it might not be the exchange at all. I mean, if it were a *quinta* somewhere, she might not have bothered to put the exchange, because she would know it.'

'What's a *quinta*?'

'A country house. There are hundreds of them near Lisbon. So it might be something like "Quinta Casal", and not the exchange at all.'

'Mrs Harcourt,' said Craig respectfully, 'you're doing fine. That is a possible line. If we can find out if the Gonçalves Costas have a *quinta* with those initials we're in business.'

'Yes. That's where they could be. In some secret place. They could be there now, while we talk, with the PIDE creeping up on them.' She shivered. Then she listened to sounds from the hall. 'There's Rory now. He'll know, of course.'

Harcourt came in quickly. 'Any news?'

'I'm afraid not,' said Craig. 'But we've got a possible lead, thanks to your wife.'

'Cynthia? Good Lord, you're looking better, darling. What's been happening?'

'Mr Craig's been practising a new police technique,' she said drily. 'You get the suspect to do the detection.'

'Suspect?'

'He suspected me of not wishing to collaborate. He's been very subtle, and kind.' She smiled at Craig.

'Would *one* of you,' said Harcourt, 'be kind enough to tell me what the hell this is about?'

'We think we know where Amanda may have gone,' said his wife, 'but not exactly. Rory, have you ever heard of a *quinta* called something beginning with C, belonging to the Gonçalves Costas?'

'No, I don't think so. Where is it?'

'That's just what we don't know,' said Craig, and explained about the entry in the address-book. 'Have you got large-scale maps covering, say, a radius of forty miles around Lisbon?'

'Of course. My clerk can bring them over from the office. But there are any number of *quintas*, you know.'

'That's what I said,' cut in Mrs Harcourt eagerly, 'but surely you know people you could ask?'

'Yes,' said Harcourt, and moved towards the telephone.

Craig stopped him. 'Please don't ring anyone about this. I'm afraid it's almost certain that your line has been tapped. If you ring someone and get the right answer the PIDE will get there before we can.'

'They can't do that to a diplomatic number.'

'Yes, they could, if they got special permission. And they could make quite a case, you know.'

'Blast their eyes!' said Harcourt furiously. 'What can we do? I could go round and find somebody at the Club. Or better—Charles will be here soon. He might know.'

'Charles Jenkins? Good Lord, I'd forgotten—'

'My set task?' said the Brigadier, smiling. 'Carried through without a hitch. I waited at the Club until he rang me to confirm. He was coming here with the car-park ticket as soon as he could find a taxi.'

'That's splendid,' said Craig. 'In the meantime, could we go on searching this room?' He went on quickly, 'Mrs Harcourt, would you go through all the clothes drawers and the wardrobe, and make sure there's nothing she's hidden—something she wouldn't want the maid to see —a letter, for instance, or indeed anything written. It might help.'

Harcourt saw his wife hesitate and said gently but firmly, 'It's got to be done, Cynthia.'

She turned without a word and opened the wardrobe door.

'Then there's the desk, and all the papers. If you'll do those, Brigadier, I'll do the bookshelves and search the rest of the room.' He began working systematically, taking down the books in batches, looking to see that there was nothing hidden behind and riffling through the books before returning them. He searched the other shelves, peered into some hand-made pieces of pottery and finished the other articles of furniture. Then he glanced at the desk, where Harcourt was going through the neat piles of translations, compositions, research papers and correspondence with the Faculty of Literature at Lisbon University. All very orderly, he thought. Remarkably so. The other two were working slowly and meticulously.

At the end of half an hour they had all finished, and the result was precisely nothing. There were no loose notes anywhere, no letters which could not be explained without difficulty.

'She's always been a tidy girl,' said her mother listlessly. 'Can we stop now?'

They returned to the sitting-room in silence, but as they entered the door-bell rang. A moment later a tall, heavily-built man in his sixties came limping in. His mottled red face glowed with an expression of imperturbable optimism.

'Just the ticket, what?' He laughed at his little joke and held out a scrap of paper. Craig took it.

'Oh, good man. Where is it parked?'

'Autoparque Elvira, half-way up that street that goes

off the Largo Moniz towards the Castle—Rua Elvira Chaves.' He turned to Craig. 'I don't think we've met, have we?'

Harcourt explained, and hurried on: 'Listen, Charles, we think we have a clue to where Amanda is. Do you happen to know the names of *quintas* belonging to the Gonçalves Costas?'

'Good Lord, man, they've got dozens. Up in the Minho and a hell of a lot of land south of the river.'

'The name begins with C, and it's probably near Lisbon.'

'Sorry, old boy. Doesn't ring a bell, I'm afraid.' He looked up curiously. 'But surely, Rory, all you've got to do is to ring Dona Maria, and ask her. I'll do it if you like. I used to go shooting with them a lot, when Henrique was a naval staff captain. Maria used to give very gay house parties.'

'I'm sorry,' said Harcourt, 'but that's just what we can't do. I'm afraid it's all a bit complicated. But look. The telephone numbers are all in one directory, so all we've got to do is to look up all the Gonçalves Costas. I hadn't thought of that. There are a hell of a lot of them but it won't take very long.' He went quickly to the telephone table and picked up the directory. There was silence while he ran through the list of names. 'No good,' he said slowly, closing the book, 'several *quintas* near here but none with a C. If it has a telephone it's ex-directory.' There was a long silence.

'Is there any close friend of the family,' asked Craig, turning to Jenkins, 'whom you could ask without attracting his curiosity? As Harcourt said, you couldn't do it on the telephone, I'm afraid, but—perhaps someone near, whom you could go and see?'

'There's old Monte Valmor, who lives in town—he's a walking Portuguese Debrett.' He thought for a moment. 'I know. I could say I was writing my memoirs. Can't remember all the aristocratic *quintas* I used to visit in me golden youth. He'd swallow that fly quick as you please. It surely can't hurt—I suppose you think this line's tapped? —if I ring him now and ask if I can come and consult him. That gives nothing away if we've got to be so hush-hush.'

'Yes, that's fine,' said Craig.

Harcourt was already looking up the number. He dialled and gave Jenkins the receiver. He asked for the Conde de Monte Valmor and listened for a moment. 'Not at home. Won't be back till six.'

Craig looked at his watch. 'Half past four. We don't want to kick our heels until then. There is just one possible line—'

'What's that?' asked Harcourt.

Craig caught Mrs Harcourt's eyes looking at him appealingly. 'I'd rather not discuss it; it's probably no good anyway. But I'll go off and try that and come back within an hour.' He rose to his feet.

'I've got a taxi down below,' said Jenkins. 'I can take you into town, if that's where you want to go.'

'Thanks,' said Craig. He knew that if he were seen getting into a taxi with Jenkins it would be followed, but he could sort out that one afterwards. 'There's just one thing,' he added, turning to the Defence Attaché, who was looking at him curiously. 'If by any chance I pick up a real lead I might make use of the car Jenkins has stashed away and try to follow it up. So I could be away for some time. But if so I'll ring you as soon as I can.'

'All right,' began Harcourt reluctantly, 'but—No, damn it, I *don't* agree. What you're saying is that if you find where this *quinta* is—from whoever it is you're going to see now —and I'm sorry but I can't see why you're being so darned secretive about it—then you'll go straight there?'

'Yes, of course. We can't waste time.'

'That's just the point. I don't want to be twiddling my thumbs here if there's any action. Your theory was that Amanda and young Costa met last night to sort out their personal relationship or her involvement in this damned group, or whatever it is. But it's clear that if it was only that she'd have been back last night. Don't you see, something's gone wrong? For all we know, she and Costa are being prevented from leaving by the rest of his group, or they've all fallen out among themselves. There may be serious trouble.'

'Yes, it's very possible. In fact, for all we know the police may be there now.'

'Well, there you are, Craig. If there *is* trouble it's *my* daughter and I want to be there. I've got diplomatic status, and if I go in and collect Amanda and take her away nobody's going to stop me. But you've got no official status here and what's more you'd be acting against the express wishes of your friend Ferreira. You'd be in enough trouble yourself—and no use to Amanda. I'm sorry to be blunt about this, but if you do get the address of that *quinta* you must let me get on with it. You'll have done your best and no one could expect you to do more. The same applies if you draw a blank and we have to wait to get the address out of Monte Valmor. So I'll go with—'

Craig broke in. 'I'm sorry, Brigadier, and I realize how you must feel. But I can't allow it.'

'*What* did you say?' asked Harcourt grimly.

'H.E. put me in charge of this operation. Oh yes, he did.' His quiet voice overrode Harcourt's furious protest. 'You can ring him or Dickens if you want to confirm that, but I insisted on it. Now please listen. It is all still pure supposition, even if we find out where the *quinta* is. But there may not even be a *quinta*—the "QC" may stand for something else. And while I'm off chasing hares Amanda may turn up at any moment and then you'll have a lot to do. And remember that if I did find your daughter in trouble with the PIDE I could still pull my influence with Ferreira, which would count more—whatever wrath he poured on my head—than your dip. card. In the short term, that is. And in the long term, if there is to be a show-down, I've no doubt that in H.E.'s eyes I'm expendable. You're not.'

'I don't like it,' said Harcourt.

'I dislike it intensely. But if she does turn up here somebody's got to find out at once whether she's been in contact with Costa, because—'

'Because,' finished Harcourt bitterly, 'if she has she

flies home tomorrow, without a chance to defend herself.'

'That's just it. And I think it'd be better for you to talk to her first, before she sees H.E.'

'He's right, Rory,' said Mrs Harcourt. 'At least we could make it a bit easier for her.'

Harcourt sat down slowly. 'I'm not sure I want to. But —oh well. I'll stay and do the staff work.'

Jenkins struggled to his feet. 'Half of what you've been saying is way over my head,' he said cheerfully. 'Can we go now?'

'We'll expect you both for dinner, if you can make it,' said his wife. She turned to Craig. 'You've been very understanding and kind. Thank you for that.'

CHAPTER SIX

The Alfama

As THEY WENT DOWN the stairs Craig said, 'Harcourt told you the reason for the car you procured so neatly. We're under surveillance, I think.'

'Yes. But there wasn't a car outside when I came here.'

'Well, we'll see. You go slightly ahead and open the door of the taxi and I'll come after you and ask for a lift. OK.'

'Right.' He strolled out of the doorway and limped over towards a taxi parked on the other side of the street, facing west. As he was getting in Craig ran out of the door and called out, 'Can you give me a lift into the town?'

'Yes, of course. Jump in.' The taxi made a U-turn and went off fast towards the Rua Sao Domingos. A man in a fawn suit and a dark, turned-down hat glanced at the cab as it went past and put his hand into his jacket pocket.

'Blast!' said Craig. 'That was a cop, and he's got a transmitter. We'll have a prowl car on our tail soon. You'd better drop me somewhere quickly and I'll get another.'

'Where do you want to go?'

'The Alfama.'

'That's easy. That's one place the prowl car can't follow you. I'll tell you what we can do, if you like. We'll drive to the Largo Santa Luzia, which is a place with a view, and there's a flight of steps there that leads down straight into the top of the Alfama. We can have a look at the view and the sunset and what-have-you and then you slip off by yourself.' He looked at Craig. 'I—er—know the Alfama pretty well, so if I can help—?'

Craig grinned. 'Thanks very much. Tell him where to go, would you please?' When Jenkins had given instructions, he added, 'It's the Subida Sao Jose.'

'I know it. There's a *fado* place there.' He hesitated. 'Why d'you tell me, when you wouldn't tell Rory? It's something to do with Cynthia, isn't it?' He laughed. 'I saw her give you a conspiratorial look behind Rory's back.'

'You don't miss much, do you?' said Craig. 'But you're right. It's something she doesn't want Harcourt to know about.'

'Amanda's got a boy-friend there, I suppose. Must be a poetic sort of bloke.'

'Artist. And an ex-boy-friend. His name's Jack Davies.'

'And Rory doesn't approve of him. All right, I'll keep mum.'

'Harcourt doesn't know that his wife rang Davies this morning and got a brush-off. It's a pretty slight chance but just worth trying. Even if he hasn't seen Amanda—that's what he told Mrs Harcourt—he might conceivably know where she could be.'

'Hm. Look, Craig. You don't know this girl and I want you to get something straight.'

'Go ahead. I'll be glad of anything you can tell me. I know very little so far.'

'Yes. Well, let me first tell you about Rory. I was a captain and he was a subaltern at Mersa Matruh, and he crawled up under fire and got me out of a hole made by the same mortar shell that took away a large part of my leg. It was one of the best-deserved MC's of the war.

He and Cynthia are—well, they're special people. I was at his wedding—and my God she was a peach of a girl —and I'd swear that from that day she's never looked at another man. Nor him either—at a girl, I mean. Now that's a—what would you call it?—a philosophy which I admire very much, in others. But I've never subscribed to it myself and I'm darned sure that Amanda doesn't either. The idea of one-girl-one-man simply wouldn't enter her pretty head. But this is what I'm trying to explain, it's not because she's a flirt or a popsy or something—I can only say it in Portuguese these days—it's simply because she's a girl who's still sort of exploring—like a tree, if you like, pushing its roots out to find the things it wants. She's just getting experience.'

'You can excuse almost anything,' said Craig drily, 'in that cause.'

'There you are. As I thought. You're prejudiced against the girl already.'

'Who wouldn't be, after seeing her mother today? I'm sorry. I'm really grateful you've told me this—'

'I know her better, you see. Better than her people do, ever since I used to stay with them in Germany when she was just growing up.'

'Everybody I meet understands her better than her parents do. And damn it, I'm on *their* side. It's time somebody who doesn't try to understand her shook some sense into the silly girl.'

Jenkins gave a great hoot of laughter. 'You do that, Craig, you do that. But I warn you, she's nobody's fool.' His laugh rumbled away quietly. 'Look, I'd like to be in on this. I've got nothing else to do and I might be able to help you. Say I get the old car from the car-park and wait for you somewhere down below, at the other entrances to the Alfama? Then if you've got any line to follow we don't have to depend on taxis. I know this town like the back of my hand.'

Craig hesitated. 'It's very good of you, but if they did spot me getting into the car it might be awkward for you afterwards.'

'What d'you mean? They wouldn't know who I was.'

'They'd find out, as soon as they got the number and checked where it came from.'

Jenkins gave another rumbling laugh. 'I gave a false name. I signed the form "Harold Wilson".'

'You old devil! Did you pay in cash then?'

'Of course. I always carry a few *contos* on me.'

'But what about taking it back?'

'Leave it at a garage and send the ticket back by post.'

Craig chuckled. 'It seems to me that you've done this sort of thing before.'

'Well, I was mixed up in a few ploys here during the war, when they'd patched up my leg and I was attached to the Embassy to look after the escaped POWs. There were a lot of them stuck for months waiting for transport, and I got a few bright lads together and we used to make life difficult for the German missions. You know, sugar in the petrol tank, tyre-busters at night outside their garages, ringing them up at all hours from call-boxes. There were some very tired men in the German Embassy. It didn't do much to win the war but it kept the boys' spirits up. And the Portuguese were very tolerant. They stuck their necks out quite a lot—all very unofficial, of course—to help the Allies, and I got to like them. That was when I decided to settle down here after it was all over.' He looked at Craig. 'Am I on?'

'Bless you, yes. When are you going to tell me how to get to Davies's place?'

'While we're looking at the view. We're coming into the Portas do Sol already. I'll tell the driver to wait while I do the Baedeker bit.'

He did it very neatly, leading Craig to the railing of a concrete platform built out from the edge of the Largo Santa Luzia above the huddled roofs of the ancient part of the town which forms the Alfama, cascading down the steep slope of the Castle hill to the waterfront buildings far below. Jenkins pointed out the sights with gestures of his big arms, all the time describing the route Craig would take through the labyrinth of alleys and steps. He finished, 'We'll turn now and walk back towards the taxi, but as we pass the top of the steps I'll point down there and you slip off. I'll pretend I can't go with you because of my leg, and I'll stand as if waiting for you to go and look at a fountain or something. Then after a bit I'll go off and try to get to the hire car without being followed. I'll be at the Beco do Mexias—the place I told you about—in half an hour.'

As they turned Craig saw the pale grey Anglia which had drawn up on the square. A man in a blue suit was standing near them on the platform, and when he saw them walking towards the taxi he turned briskly in the direction of the Anglia. Then Jenkins did his act, pointing down the steps and tapping his leg. Craig waved his hand and hurried to the top of the steps without looking back.

The flight of steps plunged down between a cliff of wall supporting a church, perched on the edge of the Largo, and a row of little houses with bird-cages hanging from the windows and flowers in rusty tins ranged along the walls. At the bottom he found himself in a street paved in black and white granite setts which curved away to the right, and there he saw the short flight of narrow steps of which Jenkins had told him. This led to an alley where fresh vines reached out to tangle with the green tendrils of their neighbours across the way. Swathes of brightly coloured washing, hung on wires precariously supported on spindly wooden brackets, looped and fluttered against the blue sky. Children, going home from school, chattered as they ran sure-footed over the uneven cobbles. It was an attractive, intimate little world of its own, thought Craig, utterly different from the cold busy streets only a stone's throw away.

He came into a square, with three streets leading downwards. His was the middle one, and he took it without looking back. There was an increasing smell of fish and cooking oil and the new alley became choked with women screaming and shouting as they bent over the baskets laid out on the slimy pavement and argued with the *varinas*, the sturdy fishwives who held up their iron balances and kicked away the cats skulking around the heaps of glistening fish. He pushed his way over the scaly stones between the solid hips and billowing skirts of the *varinas* and reached the end of the alley before he turned round. But as far as he could see over the bobbing pattern of women's heads, no blue suit was stalking him. He turned off towards a baroque church in a tiny square, with tall poplars and groups of medlar and oleander trees, and the vines strung across to give shade when summer came. There seemed to be children everywhere.

From one corner of the little *praça* a short alley under the vine trellis led up to a dead end, where there was a house with a flight of steps leading up to the first floor. It was Number 25. Below the steps was another entrance, to a grocer's shop, and as Craig climbed the steps he could smell garlic sausage and the tang of Portuguese oil. He rang the bell and waited, but the green door remained closed. He rang again, and this time there was a confused shout from within and a rush of footsteps. The door was flung open violently.

The man who stood glaring at him was well over six feet tall and his shoulders, made bigger by the loose smock he was wearing, looked enormous. What could be seen of his face, a rather craggy island entirely surrounded by a vigorous growth of hair and beard, was contorted with fury. But his brown eyes were surprisingly large and mild. He was shouting something in Portuguese as he opened the door, but stopped when he saw who it was.

'*Desculpe-me*!' he apologized gruffly, then looked at Craig's suit. 'Good Lord, you're a Britisher. Sorry, I thought it was those blasted children. What d'you want?'

'You're Mr Davies, I think. May I come in for a moment?'

'Sorry, but I'm very busy. Come on, sport, what is it?'

'Amanda Harcourt's disappeared. Can you help us to find where she is?'

'My oath! That's the second time today. Strewth! The sheila's of age, isn't she? She's a free agent. She hasn't got to ask her mum every time she goes out! She rang me up, she did, the sticky-beak, the prying old cow!'

'Shut up!' shouted Craig.

'Hold it, sport! Who the hell do you think you are?'

'I'm a police officer, if that helps.'

'Jeez-us, that's wonderful! That's the pay-off. They bring in a pommy rozzer to keep an eye on her, do they?'

'Oh don't be such a bloody fool. It's serious. Let me—'

'What's serious, cobber, is that you're wasting my bloody time. So just muck off.'

Craig put his foot in the door as Davies tried to close it. He said quietly, 'Look, Davies, I'm coming in.'

The big man opened the door quickly; as he lifted his foot to stamp on Craig's shoe he received a violent shove in the chest which caught him off balance. He staggered back, and by the time he had recovered Craig was inside and the door closed.

'All right, copper,' said Davies between his teeth, 'you've asked for it.'

There was some light in the narrow passage from an open door on the right and Craig could see the other man coming in with a rush. Davies had a powerful left, but he was too angry to be clever. His knuckles caught the skin of Craig's cheek in a glancing blow as he ducked, but the counter caught the Australian in the throat and stopped him. The sting in his cheek and a lot of built-up frustration put Craig in no mood to be kind. Everything he had went into the straight jab to Davies's jaw, and his grey eyes glinted as he saw the other man crumple and fall. Then he rubbed his knuckles and felt ashamed of himself.

He ran into the big studio on the right and found a bottle of brandy. He splashed some of it into a dirty glass and brought it back, got his arm under Davies's shoulders and called to him sharply by name. The bearded face moved and the brown eyes looked up at him, mildly astonished.

'Come on, boy, drink it up.' The Australian saw the glass and took a deep gulp, spluttered. Then he lay back and closed his eyes. 'That was a good wallop, friend,' he said sleepily. 'Dinkum, it was.'

Craig shook him. 'Listen. I'm not just prying. It's really serious. I must talk to you. It's for Amanda's sake.'

Davies sat up, and slowly got to his feet. Craig stepped away and watched him warily.

'It's all right, copper,' said the artist, grinning. 'Another time, perhaps, but not just now. For Christ's sake let's go and have a proper snort.' He lurched off towards the end of the passage and came back with two bottles of pale beer fresh from the refrigerator. He went into the studio, swept two chairs clear of the debris which lay around everywhere and sat down. 'Come in,' he said, 'be my guest.' He found two glasses, wiped them sketchily with a painting rag and poured the beer.

'My goodness,' said Craig thankfully, 'that's good beer.'

'Aussie friend of mine makes it. That's why it's in bottles. I can't stand that canned stuff. Blows you out.' He looked at Craig. 'Where did you pick up that pile-driver, friend? It was a beaut.' He rubbed his jaw.

'I used to box a lot at Cambridge. That's where I got this shape of nose. Sorry, chum. It wasn't a fair fight.'

'Oh yes it was. But out of my class. My word, yes! What's your name?'

'Peter Craig. I'm just passing through Lisbon.'

Davies chuckled and finished his glass. 'Pass, friend. Don't bother about the bloody counter-sign. Come on, Pete, what's cooking?'

'Amanda disappeared last night after a party. Didn't go home and didn't turn up this morning for an Embassy lunch which she knew she had to go to. So it *is* something serious. It seems possible that she went from the party with a Portuguese boy who at the moment is in bad with the PIDE. It turns out that he's disappeared too, and the cops are looking for him. Now if they're together, which seems likely, I'm trying to find where it is and get there before the PIDE turn up. D'you follow?'

'Jesus, that bunch! I'm with you. What can I do? Who is the boy-friend, Joao Costa?'

Craig's heart lifted. 'Yes.' He paused. 'Look, Jack. You obviously know something about Amanda and Costa. Have you any idea where they might meet—when they don't want people to know?'

Davies hesitated. 'Wait a sec,' he said, 'I'll get some more booze.'

When he came back with two more bottles he sat down, frowning at the stoppers as he removed them and poured out the beer. Then he looked at Craig. 'There's no other way you can find out?'

'We've tried every bloody thing we can think of.'

'This is a bit embarrassing, mate. If I tell you something will you swear—not as a copper; I know what coppers' words are like—but as a fellow human being, that you won't let Amanda know I've told you?'

'Yes. I agree to that.'

'Amanda's a super sheila and I love her, but we didn't always hit it off. Anyway, when she started going out with this Joao she told me about him and I got jealous as hell. And when it was obvious that she was going serious with him I did something—something I wouldn't have thought I was capable of. I followed them.'

'It was understandable.'

'The heck it was—not for me. My oath, no! And I don't suppose you would either, it's such a mucking sneaky thing to do. But we'd had a row, and she said Joao was waiting to pick her up and they were going to make a night of it—I tell you, she was as mad as hell or she wouldn't have said a thing like that. And I was nearly out of my tiny mind.' He stopped.

'Go on,' implored Craig.

'Well, she said she was meeting him at a café in the Rocio, so I got my car out and saw him pick her up. And I followed. I was going to wait till they got somewhere and then front up to him or something. I tell you, I was ropable. Over the bridge to Azeitao and then right. Farther on there's a turning to Sesimbra, which they took. I could follow all right because although he had a bloody great American car I had a Sprite, nicely tuned up. But on

the Sesimbra road I had to leave a bigger space, or he'd
have spotted me—and I was all for the element of surprise.
I saw him turn off to the left, towards the mountains. When
I got to the turning it was a little road—not much more
than a dust track—and I was charging up it, swallowing
his dust, when I suppose I came to my senses. I mean,
I was acting galah. So I went home, and got drunk of
course and finished up in some puff or other. I'm not
proud of it.' He hunched up, looking down at his long,
paint-smeared hands.

Craig drew a long breath. 'Thanks, chum. It was decent
of you to tell me. Have you got a map?'

'No, sorry. It's in the car and I've lent it to a pal.'

'How far was this turning from that first place—what
was it?'

'Azeitao. But you wouldn't reckon from there. You go
through Azeitao, quite a bit farther, and then the road
divides, left to Setubal, right to Sesimbra. About a couple of
miles along from the fork, I should think, but remember
this was over a year ago.'

'Could you find the turning again?'

'I might. But I told you, I haven't got my car.' He
was beginning to look apprehensive.

'I've got one, waiting down below the Alfama.'

'But, Pete, don't you see? If I took you there, and if
it is where she and that young bastard are hiding out, well,
she'd know I'd been snooping after them.'

'But for God's sake, the girl may be in danger.'

'Look, you promised—'

'Yes, I know. And I meant it.' Craig thought. 'There's
just a chance that what you've told me is enough. But
if it isn't I'll get another car and ring you—I know your
number—and you meet me where I say and lead us there.
And then push off. Right?'

'You're throwing your weight about a bit, aren't you?'

'You don't want Amanda collared by the PIDE, do
you?'

'She's got her little card. They can't touch her.'

'It's worse than I told you. They've reason to believe

she's been mixed up with Joao Costa in an independence movement, in quite a big way.'

'Good on her. That's my girl.'

'Oh, don't be silly. If they catch her with Costa and a bunch of his crazy friends she won't get off lightly, card or no card.'

'Oh hell! All right. You've made your point. I'll stay in for an hour or so in case you call.'

'Good man. Don't worry, I'll see she doesn't know you helped.'

'Thanks, Pete. If it wasn't for that I'd come with you like a shot, and be glad to, PIDE and all.'

'I know. I'll let you know what happens, if I can.'

Davies led the way to the door and opened it. 'I'm sorry now I spoke to the old—to her mum the way I did, but you know how it is.'

'You could always ring her and apologize.'

'Apologize? Jeez-us! But I suppose I could, at that. She must be going through a lot.'

'She is. So do it, Jack. But don't tell her I've been here. She'll guess it anyway and if anyone overheard you might have the PIDE on your doorstep. Thanks a lot, Jack.'

CHAPTER SEVEN

A Chase

CRAIG RAN down the steps and took the first street that led downhill. He had memorized Jenkins's instructions and knew that he had to work over to the right to strike the Beco do Mexias. The narrow streets and alleys branched away from each other like the veins in a leaf, each carrying its own small flow of life and activity. There were little dark shops with men hammering and tinkering in the gloom, and butchers, taverns, electricians, bakers—all on a Lilliputian scale but full of chattering, cheerful people. They seemed different from the sober crowds he had seen in other parts of the city; they lived as they had lived since the invasion of the Visigoths, happy and apart.

He found the Beco and made his way down to where it came out on to a busy square. And there was Jenkins. And the man in the blue suit.

It was no use pretending not to recognize Jenkins. The cop had seen them together and besides, Jenkins was already limping towards him, looking very pleased with himself.

'All in the bag, old boy.' He took Craig's arm and led him across the square.

'If we don't look out you'll be in it too,' said Craig quietly. 'Masquerading as Harold Wilson! Our little friend's just behind us. Either he waited for me here on spec or he followed you. It doesn't matter. He's there all right. And he may know the number of your car. We'd better get into it and think again.'

'Any luck?'

'Yes, I think so. Could you drive towards the bridge, and I'll explain?'

As they got into the Chevrolet he saw the blue suit walking quickly towards the grey Anglia. Same car, he thought; at least we'll be able to recognize it.

Jenkins turned into the Rua da Alfandega. 'The way I'd take is through the Praça do Comercio to the Liberdade, up to Pombal and then left to the autostrada. There's too much traffic along the river. But it'll take us some time to get to the bottom of the Avenida, at this time of day.'

'Do that. It'll give us time to talk. I may have to go back to the Alfama—it all depends on you. I've got a lead, but we'll have to work out the exact spot from a map. Have you got one?'

'I looked. Mr Hertz had left one in the glove pocket. Shows all the surroundings, if that's what you want.'

'It is,' said Craig, straightening out the map. 'There's a village called Azeitao—I've got it. And you turn right towards a place where there's a fork—oh, I see, it isn't on the main road at all. That's it, you turn right for Sesimbra.'

'Go on,' said Jenkins excitedly. 'Bells are beginning to ring loudly.'

'About a couple of miles from the fork?'

'Quinta dos Cisnes!' he shouted. 'It was at the back of my mind all the time, but it's all so long ago. Twenty years or more, when I first settled here. It's one of the Gonçalves Costa places, all right. I used to stay there. But they let the shooting go to blazes donkey's years ago. Henrique got arthritis in his trigger hand. I haven't heard it mentioned in recent years. It's probably derelict.'

'That's it. Good for you. Now can you tell me exactly how to find it? Then you can drop me and I'll take taxis and shake them off.'

'Not on your life, old boy. You'd never find the place by yourself. I'm taking you there. It'll save a lot of time anyway.'

'I know, but I told you I don't want to get you into a jam.'

'I'll do a bit of dodging and lose that Anglia.'

'It's no good, Jenkins. They've got your number and the one place there's certain to be a radio control is on that blasted bridge.'

'But they wouldn't stop us, for God's sake?'

'No, but they'd follow us to the *quinta* and then take over, and you'd be politely questioned and have to show your residence card, and then the whole story of the false name would come out.'

'Oh, that!' said Jenkins. 'That's easy. I'd tell them I'm being watched by a jealous husband and the snoopers are on my track. So I can't use my own car when I go to see the girl. Believe me, this has happened before.'

'With me in the car?' said Craig, laughing. 'It wouldn't wash, you know. Come on, let me get on with it.'

'No, Craig. Seriously. I'm more interested than you are in getting that girl out of trouble. Even when you get to the turning off the Sesimbra road there are half a dozen tracks turning off it. And none of them signposted until you get to the *quinta* itself. At least, that's how it used

to be and things don't change quickly in the country. Listen.
I can wriggle out of a jam. I've known half the Cabinet
for years, including Marcello Caetano. Let's risk it.'

'All right,' said Craig reluctantly. 'Of course we'll do
it in half the time in this car and with you navigating.
But we'll have to shake them, and no mistake, once we're
over the bridge.'

'I've got a thought about that, but I'll explain later.
For the moment, we go straight for the bridge?'

'Right.'

They drove up the broad Avenida da Liberdade,
thronged with people walking under the trees or drinking
at tables with a lazy foot outstretched, while a crouching
shoe-black smeared and slapped at the pointed shoe.

At the top of the Avenida the car swept round the dominating statue of the Marquis of Pombal and turned west-
wards into the Avenida de Aguiar and so on into the
beginning of the autostrada which runs west towards
Estoril and Sintra. Leaving the town, the road ran up to
the edge of a deep valley where, like the old Free Water
Aqueduct which Craig could see farther up the valley, it
launched itself across on tall pylons towards the higher
ground on the other side. But at this point Jenkins turned
off to the right on an approach road which curved under
the autostrada and led into the new highway which crossed
the Salazar Bridge. It was impressive in the evening sunlight—the surface satin smooth and rising gently on great
concrete pylons towards the towering supports of the suspension bridge itself.

They met road signs—radar control of traffic and speed
limits—and Jenkins slowed down. On Craig's side the
view was very beautiful, with the sun shining across the
mouth of the estuary and picking out the white walls of
the fort he had seen—it seemed ages ago—that morning,
and the yellow sand of the bar. Ahead of them was the
statue of Christ the King, high up on its concrete pedestal
on the far bank, not yearning like its counterpart over the
city of Rio de Janeiro but watching Lisbon across the water
with an air of detached benevolence. Beyond it he could

see the low line of the Arrábida range on the horizon. On its nearer slopes, he thought, hidden by the distance and the faint blue mist, must lie the Quinta dos Cisnes, and the end of his quest.

At the farther extremity of the bridge were toll-boxes on each of the four lanes, with men in uniform stretching out their hands for 20-escudo notes as the motorists passed. Beyond, the road widened to six lanes, with slender light standards arching overhead. The Chevrolet began to pick up speed.

'Is there anybody behind us?' asked Jenkins.

'I can't see the Anglia, but there's a black Fiat dodging in and out of the outside lane to have a peep at us. At least, that's what it looks like.'

'If we stay on this road we haven't much chance of shaking him, and in any case he can use his radio to warn the boys ahead. But we can get to the *quinta* another way, where we've got a better chance. Look at your map.'

'I've got it.'

'We'll take a turning to the right soon, marked for Sesimbra. It's a reasonable road, with lots of hills and bends. You'll see that at Santana it meets the Sesimbra-Setubal road in a T-junction. We go to the left, of course, but if we can draw ahead by then at least he won't know which way we've gone, unless he stops and asks, and that'll increase our lead.'

'Good idea. It won't take us much longer?'

'Only about a quarter of an hour, I should think.'

'Let's do it, then. Wait a moment. Is there any chance of slipping him when we make the turn? He can't turn round in this traffic.'

'Only if he gets right on my tail. The Sesimbra road leads off through open country.'

'Best not try, then. Use your indicator and slow down normally before the turn. Let's let him think we don't know he's there.' He turned round. 'Oh yes. No doubt about it. He could have overtaken that car easily, but he had a good look at us and dodged back. Still about two hundred yards behind. Is that the turning ahead, before the road narrows?'

'Yes. We adopt procedure as planned.' Jenkins chuckled. 'I haven't enjoyed myself so much for years. And the real fun is still to come.'

'I hope it's only fun,' said Craig. 'If it comes to speed you ought to be able to lose a Fiat without much difficulty.'

'She's a nice car, the Chevvy. She'd do ninety if I opened her up.'

'Let's hope you don't have to.'

They could see the road now, turning off to the right between fields and sparse pine woods. The road was tarmac, strewn with grit, and when they passed on to it the surface proved fairly smooth, although nothing like the satin feel of the highway. Within a few hundred yards they were into the trees and hidden from the main road, but Craig could see behind him the black Fiat taking up the chase. Jenkins accelerated, and the car surged forward.

The woods were still irregular and untidy, with stripped areas where the red soil showed through the scars of erosion. There were clumps of grey eucalyptus, and Craig caught the scent of the gum brought out by the day's hot sunshine. Wooden shacks were scattered here and there, with a few small houses standing forlornly by themselves. The car was moving fast, its light American suspension bouncing where the road was worn.

'There's a road to the right, to Alfarim, coming up soon,' explained Jenkins, 'another chance, if we can get ahead, to make him stop and scratch his head.'

They passed the Alfarim road and began to rise, winding through thicker woodland until they could look forward across a broad stretch of forest. They crossed a valley on a causeway and on the other side the trees began to close, the stone pines arching overhead. There were no more signs of habitation and nothing to see but the pines, the needles glistening on the ground and the cistus blossoms like scraps of white paper blown amongst the scrub. They came to a long straight stretch.

'He's still there, blast him,' said Craig, 'half a mile back and all out.'

Jenkins grunted and pressed his foot down. The Chevrolet began to sway alarmingly as the indicator went past the ninety kilometre mark. From higher ground they could now see the mountains of Arrabida, nearer and more impressive.

'They're higher than I thought,' said Craig.

'They're not so high, but precipitous. You see that castle, way over to the right ahead of us? That's Sesimbra Castle; it's at eight hundred feet but a sheer drop into the sea. And this part of the range is milder than over to the east, where you get near Setubal. The land goes straight up from the water to about sixteen hundred feet, with the road cut out of the rock. Wild country, and primeval forest on its landward slopes—very interesting for those botanical wallahs.'

When they came out of the *pinhal*—the pine forest—the landscape changed to one of plantations of fruit trees, olives and vines, and they passed men and women trudging home from their work in the fields, casting disapproving looks and imprecations at the speeding car. There were gaily-painted summer villas close to the road and here and there the mellow tiled roofs of a *quinta* behind its ancient stone walls.

'We're getting near Santana,' said Jenkins. 'Blast that chap! What's he got under that Fiat's bonnet? I thought I'd left him well behind.' He was looking in the rear mirror.

'You've got good eyes,' said Craig, turning round to see the glint of the setting sun on the black roof of the other car. 'But he's nearly a mile away now. That's the village ahead, I suppose?'

'Yes, we'll be at the corner in less than a minute. He won't see which way we've gone because of the houses, so I reckon he'll have to stop and ask.'

They roared into Santana, Jenkins braked fiercely, and they took the corner to the left and were accelerating fast along the dusty side road before the startled villagers could shout their protests.

'They'll remember which way we've gone,' remarked Craig drily.

'So they ought. It was a very anti-social bit of driving. Not like me at all.'

'What's the turning like—dirt road?'

'I expect it still is.'

'It's no good, Jenkins,' said Craig gently. 'Drop me when you get to the turning to the *quinta* and go on fast. With good luck he'll follow you.'

'Hell, no! I can hold him at this distance and when we get there we'll be up that little road in no time.'

'Leaving a cloud of dust for him to see? Look in the glass. We're making enough on this road, and it'll still be there when he comes along. And at the turning he'd see our dust stop suddenly on the road, with a fine thick cloud above the lane.'

'Blast it!' said Jenkins angrily. 'I wanted to be in on the act.'

'I know. And I'd far rather have you with me. But if you can make the other car think we've gone straight on you'll have given me a very useful start.'

'Why only that? I can go on foxing them.'

'Once you've gone through Azeitao someone will begin to wonder why you went the long way round, through Santana.'

'Oh nonsense! They're not as bright as all that. The average prowl-car driver—'

'It's not him we're up against. All the radio messages are being relayed back to that surveillance HQ in Lisbon, and someone there, with a map in front of him, is going to be quite bright enough to work it out. If I'm no longer with you at the next control they'll start working back and making enquiries. And I should think the Quinta dos Cisnes is a pretty obvious guess.'

'All right, then. I'm sorry we can't do it together. How'll you get back?'

'There may be transport at the *quinta*, but at the worst I can get a lift. And I've got money.'

'Wait a moment. There's one thing I can do. Instead of

going back to Lisbon through Azeitao I'll turn off before I get there and take the road towards Setubal. That'll hold them up a bit. And then there's a turning down the cliffs to Portinho. It's a little fishing village and I bet they won't have any sort of police post there out of the tourist season. I'll stay there a couple of hours and have dinner at the *estalagem*—it's called the Santa Maria, and you can find the number in the book. I know it's got one, because I've booked tables there before now. And if you get stuck, ring me there and I'll rally round.'

'Right. But look. As soon as you get there would you ring Harcourt—No. That's no good. It'd give away where you've got to, whereas we hope they'll think you've gone on to Setubal. We'll just have to leave him stewing, poor chap, until I can ring openly. I can probably do that from the *quinta*.'

'Is the other car in sight?'

'It's difficult to see for the dust. Wait till we get to the top of this rise . . . No, I can't see him. And I'm not surprised, at the speed we're going. I'll say this, you're a bloody good driver.' The car was swaying and twisting, but Jenkins's control appeared perfectly steady.

'Used to do a bit of rally-driving. That was good sport. But let me tell you how to get to the *quinta*.'

'Yes, that's been worrying me quite a bit. You said there were half a dozen unmarked turnings.'

'Well, I did—er—exaggerate a bit—to make it seem difficult, d'you see? So that you'd have to take me with you.' Craig burst out laughing. 'Actually,' continued Jenkins, 'it's quite simple. It's a dirt road, as I said, through a *pinhal* like the one on the Sesimbra road. Not as big as that one, but quite a large area of pine forest, with a few clearings. You pass two branch tracks, which you ignore, and about a mile from the road we're on there's a turning to the left— unmarked, or so it used to be—and that leads straight to the *quinta*.'

'What's the place itself like?'

'It's an old fortified manor-house, built several hundred years ago before the plantations were made. Four-square,

built round a patio with towers at the corners, and a sheet
of water at the back for the swans. Hence the name of
the *quinta*, of course. It was a damned lonely place, with
no home farm and nobody living near, and the Costas only
used it for the shooting and for honeymoons—that sort of
thing.' He paused. 'It may well be completely deserted, you
know.'

'Amanda went there with Costa about a year ago.'

'Did she now?' remarked Jenkins non-committally. 'I
suppose you got that from the chap in the Alfama who
marked your face?' He turned to glance at Craig. 'Did you
have a rough-house?'

'Yes. I wish you'd forget about that chap, Jenkins. He
made me swear I wouldn't let Amanda know he'd told me.'

'OK, OK. The number of shameful secrets I've kept in
my time. You've no idea the things that go on in quiet,
respectable little Portugal.'

'How far from the turning?' The road was twisting
through a pine forest.

'Quite near. These curves are splendid cover. I'll have
to slow down gently so as not to leave skid-marks. Then
you jump out the moment she stops and get into the
trees. I'll be at the place in Portinho in half an hour, and
that chap behind won't know which way I've gone at the
junction. I think I've got his measure now.' He peered
ahead. 'At the bottom of the next hill. The trees should
be close in, if they haven't been cut. You've got a gun, I
suppose?'

'A gun? Good Lord, no.'

'Well, remember that if you meet any PIDE boys
they'll be bulging with them. So if you're in a jam—
don't run.'

'Noted.' He turned to look at the big man, the red face
concentrating on the road ahead, the large freckled hands
guiding the bucking wheel with quick, sure movements.
'You're a good scout, Jenkins. I'll hope to have a drink with
you tomorrow before I get on to that boat.'

'Let's do that. I'll show you the Club. All right. Get
set now.'

He was braking even before he reached the top of the little hill, and slowed down smoothly on the other side, to stop dead opposite a gap in the trees. Craig was out already, and heard the car accelerating before he reached the first trees. He pushed his way in and crouched behind some bushes.

He could still hear the Chevrolet, already far off, when the sound of the other car came on his ear. It came shooting down the hill and flicked past his line of vision, its souped-up engine roaring through a lifted exhaust. Then suddenly it was gone, and droning away into the distance. He seemed to be on his own at last. Which was how he liked it.

CHAPTER EIGHT

Quinta dos Cisnes

CRAIG looked at his watch. A quarter past six. About an hour of daylight, he judged. The wood was still, except for the rustle of birds in the brush and a twittering in the arch of pine-branches above his head. The lane was scarcely more than a track through the soft sandy soil of the forest. He walked forward fast, glad to be exercising his legs and to be able to breathe the cool, pine-scented air. He passed two turnings, as Jenkins had instructed, and after a quarter of an hour found the track which led to the left through a thick copse of eucalyptus. It ran slightly upward, and at the top of a gentle slope ended in a pair of gates swung from old stone pillars. One of them bore, carved in an old marble panel, 'Quinta dos Cisnes'. Above the gates there was an elaborate arch of iron-work supporting a coat-of-arms in faded colours.

Beyond the open gates was an avenue of ilex trees which joined their branches and formed a long tunnel through the unkempt plantation of stone pines and eucalyptus trees. The gravel was partly overgrown with grass and moss, and Craig could see dimly the tracks of a set of heavy-duty tyres. As he went forward he had the curious feeling that he was being drawn up the long tube of the avenue into a vacuum. Even the birds were silent, and he could hear the sound of his feet on the grassy verge.

The house stood solid and uncompromising in the slanting light. From the end of the avenue he looked across a wide spread of gravel at the low, one-storey façade with the square towers at each end. The weathered walls, half-covered with ivy and blotched by gold and orange lichens, were surmounted by a row of castellations which hid the low roof. The only entrance he could see was a gateway set in the middle of the façade, but a pair of heavy wrought-iron gates, backed by metal sheeting, barred the view of the courtyard within. The arch above the gateway was filled by a fan of twisted iron around an escutcheon. There were closed wooden shutters behind the six square windows along the front of the house, and they stared blankly out through the heavy grilles affixed to the walls.

The place was as solid as a fortress, but the sense of proportion of the sixteenth-century builders, the moulded pagoda lines of the tower roofs, the stone facings and delicate tracery of the iron-work gave it elegance. Tall old trees hedged in the neglected gravel forecourt, but the high crown of a palm, towering above the roofs, showed that there was a garden behind the house.

A slight movement caught his eye. The first-floor window of the left-hand tower was not barred—it was a good twenty feet above the ground, anyway—and one of its wooden louvre shutters had been swung outwards but not secured. It was swaying in the evening breeze as he watched. He looked at the other tower, but its windows were securely fastened. Adjoining it an archway linked the main building to a stable block, and gave access to a cobbled yard, closed at the far end by a high wall.

The sun was almost below the trees, and its slanting rays caught the small disturbances in the gravel where the wheels of a car had passed. As Craig walked slowly towards the gateway he noted one place where the gravel had been scuffed up over an area of a square yard. It was not like the marks a tyre could have made, and he went over to look.

Then he stopped short. There were brown stains among the scuffed-up gravel and when he bent down to examine them he saw the dull gleam of coagulated blood.

He stood up and glanced back at the open window of the tower, but there was no movement there, nor any sign of life in the rest of the house. He looked around, and between the disturbed area and the stable archway saw a drop of blood, and a few yards farther on another. He walked over to the archway and into the yard. Still no one about, and the small door which led from the house into the yard was shut. There were no other signs to follow.

'Nobody here,' Craig said aloud, 'but us chickens.' They were wandering around aimlessly, pecking at the grass which grew through the cobbles and at the scraps of blown straw. Across the yard he could see where they must be housed. At the far end of the stable building which formed the right-hand side of the yard were two half-open doors, loosely tied together with a piece of string. The nearer end was obviously used as a garage, and he went over to it. The first door was open, and inside he could see a shining Country Squire V-8 shooting-brake. He opened the door of the car, and saw that it was empty. There were no signs of blood.

He glanced at the fascia. The ignition key was still in its lock. He turned it one notch and watched the petrol indicator creep half-way across the scale. Good, he thought. At least he had transport. There was garage litter around the walls, covered with dust, but nothing of interest. He looked at the wooden partition which separated the garage from its neighbour, and saw that it did not reach the roof; there was ample space between the top and the oak rafters. He gripped the top rail of the partition and pulled himself up, so that he could peer over it.

The space on the other side was no longer in use as a garage. At one end bales of straw had been stacked, and on top of them lay a young man, his arms and legs spread out on the uneven surface. His eyes were closed, and in the feeble light from the dusty window the livid white face appeared serene. He might have been asleep except for the dark blood which had stained the front of his silk shirt and spread downwards to form a dull pool on the stone floor.

Craig hung from his hands for a moment. Then he swung himself up and jumped down on the other side. He needed more light, and went to the door which gave on to the yard, but it was firmly locked.

He went to the body and gripped the wrist of the outflung right arm. It was quite cold, and when he looked more closely he could see the small hole in the shirt, just above the heart. The stain began lower down, and Craig examined the faint marks around the hole in the shirt. Then he stood up and looked at the man who had died. He would be about twenty-five, he judged; good-looking and intelligent. There was something Byronic—or was it the picture of that other dead poet, Chatterton, which was in his mind?—in the abandon of the slim body in death, in the appeal of the sensitive forehead framed in long, almost blue-black hair, the high arrogant nose and the slightly receding chin. The shirt was open at the neck and he seemed to have no jacket—only the shirt and the dark trousers and, oddly, no shoes. His feet were bare.

Craig looked around. Two saddles hung on the walls, and pieces of harness, covered in dust, lay on a bench. There was a saw-horse, more recently used, pushed into a corner, and a pile of sawn logs. The trunk of a sturdy young fir, stripped of its branches, stood against the wall by the saw-horse. There was the roof-rack for the car, a bow-saw, a cask of paraffin, some shooting-bags and gun-cleaning gear. But no gun. Near the door was a pile of wood-wool with a torn label lying on it. He looked at it briefly, pursed his lips in a silent whistle and put it in his pocket. There was nothing else.

He listened, but the silence was absolute and he drew himself up and over the partition and jumped back into the main garage. Without any attempt at concealment he walked out of the door and over the gravel to the house entrance. There was an iron bell-pull beside the gates.

The bell clanged somewhere away to his right, and he had to wait for some time before a little inspection wicket in the iron sheeting of the gate opened and an old woman's face, wrinkled and sunburnt, peered out at him.

'*O Senhorito nao està*,' she called in a high, trembling voice.

He is, you know, thought Craig. He's in that barn of yours, quite dead. The whole thing was becoming very curious. Aloud he said, 'It's the young lady I want to speak to, the English lady.'

She put her hand to her ear.

'*A Senhorita Inglesa*,' he shouted. '*Quero falar com ela. E muito importante.*'

She muttered something, made a gesture with her open hand for him to wait, and closed the wicket. Funny, he thought. She hadn't asked for his name.

It was almost five minutes later before she returned and opened the heavy gate, with a great slamming of bolts and creaking of hinges, to let him in. Then she closed the gate and shot back the bolts.

As he had expected, the entrance led through to the patio, dividing the front of the house into two wings, each entered by a small door inside the gateway. The right-hand one was open. The main entrance was directly opposite, on the far side of the courtyard.

The patio, with a silent fountain in its centre, was paved in stone, and around it the house was arranged symmetrically, with towers at the two rear corners corresponding to those he had seen from the front. But all the windows he could see were closed and barred, and he assumed that the old woman lived somewhere in the right flank of the buildings.

She took him through the door on the left into a flagged passage. Here the shutters on the courtyard were open and enough light came through the heavy grilles to enable him to see the closed doors of the ground-floor rooms facing the forecourt, and a stone archway at the end. Beyond it steps curved upwards.

The old woman went ahead and began to climb the spiral staircase, breathing heavily and muttering to herself. Half-way up was a landing, lit by an œil-de-bœuf window giving on to the patio, and opposite the window was an open door through which Craig caught a glimpse of a tiled bathroom. A man's slipper lay near the door, but Craig doubted whether she saw it. Her eyes seemed as weak as her hearing.

She panted slowly up the second flight, and now Craig could hear the faint sound of pop music ahead. She knocked on a polished walnut door at the top of the stairs and opened it, pulling Craig inside with a claw-like hand.

'O Senhor,' she announced, rather unnecessarily, and closed the door behind him. The music stopped suddenly and he could hear her shuffling steps on the stone staircase.

For a moment his eyes were dazzled by the bright light of an incandescent paraffin lamp placed on a table near by. The room seemed to take up the whole area of the tower. He could see a window—no doubt the one he had seen from below—in the wall facing the forecourt. The heavy velvet curtains were drawn. In the opposite wall a french window, set ajar, looked over the tiled ridges roofing the left-hand flank of the house. In the middle of the wall facing him was an enormous brass bedstead, with a brocaded counterpane whose colours glowed in the light of the small lamps on the side-tables. To his left, between the door and a hearth with a flickering log fire, was a walnut table bearing a silver tray of drinks.

On the other side of the fire a girl was sitting in an arm-chair, her hand still outstretched as if frozen towards the transistor tape-recorder which she had just switched off. Her heavy honey-coloured hair, falling over her shoulders, gleamed in the lamp-light. She was wearing a man's dressing-gown over a short, shimmering dress.

'Don't let me disturb your pop-concert,' said Craig coldly.

'It helps me to think,' she said, still staring at him in bewilderment. Suddenly she was on her feet in one smooth swift movement. 'And who the hell are you? I thought—' She stopped. 'I thought it must be one of my friends. Will you please explain who you are and what you're doing here?'

She was very like the photograph, he thought, tall and well-made, with those wide grey eyes. Very patrician. She could look beautiful, rather than pretty, but not now. There were dark shadows under her eyes and her expression, with those compressed lips and lifted chin, was hardly inviting.

Craig was in no mood for diplomacy. 'You're Amanda Harcourt,' he stated flatly.

'No. Who are you?'

'Of course you are. I saw your photograph this afternoon in your parents' flat. What on earth's the good of pretending?'

'I asked you who you were,' she repeated.

'Peter Craig. I'm a police officer.' He saw her wince. 'I've been helping your father to find out what happened to you. But don't let's waste time. I must let him know at once that you're all right—at least, physically. But there isn't a telephone here, is there?'

'Yes, there is. Over there by the bed, on the floor. It's ex-directory.'

'Good.' He walked towards the bed.

'No, don't. I forgot. It isn't any good. It doesn't work.' He was still moving across the room and she ran and seized his arm. 'I tell you it doesn't work.'

'I'll soon see. I may be able to make it go.'

She gripped his arm tighter. 'You can't. I tell you it's been cut off.'

He twitched his arm loose. 'I think I'll look all the same,' he said coldly. He reached the telephone in a few quick strides and lifted it off the floor. The whole of the cable came with it, and he saw that it had been jerked out of the wall. Then something caught Craig's eye and he looked at the receiver closely before putting it down. He walked over to the girl.

'Don't play games, Miss Harcourt,' he said roughly. 'Who did that? You?'

'Oh don't bully me,' she cried. 'You've no right to come into my bedroom—and start asking questions. Please go now.'

'Don't be silly. When I go—and I shall as soon as I know what's been happening—you're coming with me. You've caused enough trouble already. And what d'you mean—*your* bedroom? I thought it was Joao Costa's.'

She flinched, but rallied quickly. 'Since you insist,' she said defiantly, 'it's *our* bedroom.'

'It may have been,' Craig countered icily, 'but it can't be that now, can it?'

Her face went chalky-white, and for a moment he thought she was going to faint. She gripped the back of her chair, and then sat down suddenly. 'What do you mean?' she said in a low voice.

Craig was merciless. 'Damn it, you know perfectly well what I mean. He's dead, isn't he? And you know it.'

'Yes,' she said in the same tone, 'he's dead.' She turned away from him and stared down into the dying flames of the fire. Then she whispered, as if to herself, so that he could only just catch the words: 'I'd almost forgotten.'

'Forgotten?' cried Craig disgustedly. 'When did he die?'

'Early this morning.'

'You've got a short memory.'

'It's worse than that,' she said, 'it's incomprehensible. We slept in that bed last night and—in spite of everything he was considerate and sweet to me, as he always was. And now—it's as if he'd never existed.'

Craig was silent for a moment, looking down at her bowed head. 'It often happens,' he said gruffly, 'this delayed reaction. You'll remember him tomorrow.'

She drew in her breath sharply and straightened up, facing him. 'Don't talk about tomorrow. Today's bad enough.'

Craig shook himself. 'I'm sorry, but I haven't time to

go on talking about your emotions. Now listen, please, and answer my questions. Did you kill Joao Costa?'

'Oh *no.*'

'Did you help to kill him in any way?'

'I—no. No, I didn't help.'

'Good,' said Craig, breathing a sigh of relief. 'That'll do for now. I shall want the rest of the story later. We must go at once. Now listen. We won't attempt to pretend you weren't here. You obviously know what happened and you'll have to make a statement for the police. What about the old woman?'

'Maria? She doesn't even know he's dead, and anyway —'

'I thought not,' interrupted Craig, 'but the point is that she does know that you were here. It's all got to come out, as I said, but at least I can get you out of the way before the police come. So we'll take the car—I came without one—and get out of here quick. Then you can hole up at home and we'll say you're ill and can't be interviewed. That'll give us time to get your story in detail and think what line to take. They won't be able to touch you there. All right, let's go. Hang up that dressing-gown where it belongs and get your coat on. The PIDE may be on us at any moment.'

'The PIDE?' she cried sharply. 'What on earth do they know about it?'

'They don't know about Costa's death or they'd be here already. But they do know that he was plotting trouble—' he was careful not to say too much, remembering his promise to Ferreira—'and when he gave the people following him the slip last night, so that he could pick you up,' he went on, ignoring the startled look on her face, 'the PIDE suspected he was up to no good and started looking for him. They knew I was trying to find you, so they followed me, and although I shook them off before coming here I'm afraid they'll work out where you must be. And come here, hoping to find Costa.'

'They don't know about this place.'

'How d'you know? It's an obvious place to go for.

And they're clever, and tough. So come on, get moving.'

'No.'

'What d'you mean?'

'I won't go yet, and you'd have a hell of a job trying to make me.' She looked up at him with sudden decision. Before he could protest her expression changed and she was imploring him, humbly. 'Do just listen, please. You've got to let me tell you what happened. I desperately need advice. Five minutes. Then you can judge for yourself. I can't face Mummy and Daddy until I've got the whole thing straight in my own mind. And perhaps you can help me to do it.'

He looked at her, frowning. She was appealing to him now, as a woman, with those candid, wide-set eyes fixed on his face. 'All right. Just five minutes, if you really must.'

'Please sit down, then, so that I can talk to you properly.'

He sat in the armchair on the other side of the fire, watching her warily.

'You must be clever, to have found out all that about Joao and me so quickly. How did you know where I was?'

'Your address-book.'

She flared up. 'Who gave you—? Oh well. I suppose it's your job. But how did you guess? I mean, exactly—'

'We guessed. Now come on. You're supposed to be telling your story. You had an affair with him, is that it? Which went on after everybody had thought you'd stopped seeing each other?'

'We *weren't* seeing each other. I—I broke it off, I suppose you'd say, last Christmas.'

'Why?'

'Because I thought it'd gone far enough. You see, I didn't want to marry him.'

'Why?'

'For Christ's sake, have I got to spell it out?'

'Yes, please.'

'Well, then, if you *must* know, I took him as a lover but I didn't love him.'

'Then what are you doing here?'

'He kept pestering me to see him again, and said he wanted to call on Daddy—you know, this man to man stuff. And in the end I agreed to see him once more on condition he'd stop telephoning. He picked me up after the French party last night, as you know. We had agreed that we'd talk it over in the car, but he was in a really hairy mood and said he'd laid it on that we'd have supper here and he'd drive me back afterwards. There was something he wanted to show me, he said. I was afraid he'd make a scene or do something stupid, so I agreed. My God, how I wish I hadn't,' she added bitterly, turning her head away.

'So you had supper. And then?'

'Then he wouldn't drive me home. He said he'd keep me here by force, for days.'

'What for?' said Craig coldly. 'So that he could rape you at his leisure?'

She laughed scornfully. 'No, you idiot. So that I could be well and truly *compromised*. He tends to think in terms like that.' She stopped, and said more quietly, 'I mean he used to, poor little man. He *was* a man, you must realize that, and a very attractive one. But he had these archaic ideas about women.' She looked at the expression on Craig's face and half-smiled. 'You probably think the same.'

'Go on.'

'Well—in the end I stayed the night with him, as I told you. But in the morning I told him very firmly that he'd had it, and I walked out of the door and had got half-way down the stairs when he came chasing after me with a gun. And that made me livid, and we had another argument down below, and I told him I wouldn't marry him if he was the last man left on earth.' She looked at Craig appealingly. 'It's the sort of thing you say when you're very angry. I don't suppose I meant it.'

'And then?'

'I pushed him away and got out of the gate, and he

followed. And then—' She rose from her chair and turned away.

'Well?'

'He shot himself.'

'How?'

She turned to face him, exasperated. 'How? Well, he turned the gun against his chest and backed away, staring at me, and calling me a lot of names. So I ran at him. I was furious and I didn't think for a moment that he'd do it. But he jumped back and—and did it.'

'What with?'

'What do you think? With the gun, of course.'

'What did he pull the trigger with—his thumb? It's difficult to do it with your forefinger.'

'Is it? I suppose so.' She paused. 'You're a cold fish, aren't you?'

'I'm a policeman. What was he wearing on his feet?'

She looked at him, and hesitated. 'Oh yes. Slippers. They must be around somewhere. They fell off while I was carrying him to the garage.'

'I see. And why did you do that?'

She pushed up her hair in a childish gesture of bewilderment and peered at him between the soft thick strands. Then she leaned towards him, and he could almost feel the force of her will.

'I know this may sound silly,' she said earnestly, 'but it's true. When I saw him on the floor, bleeding—and quite dead, I had to think what to do, desperately. And I couldn't, with him staring at me. I had to get him away somewhere, so that I could think—I knew what a jam I was in. And then I thought of the garage—the part that isn't used. He wasn't very heavy. Maria is deaf and she was asleep, I suppose. She didn't come anyway, so she couldn't have heard the shot. So I went to the bathroom and got a towel, and put it folded on my shoulder to—well, to—'

'To catch the blood. And then?'

'I told you he wasn't heavy, and I'm strong. I got him across my shoulder and took him to the garage and left him there. And locked him in.' She stopped and looked at him sharply. 'How did you get in?'

'And what did you do with the key?'

'The key? I—I don't know. I think I threw it away. Yes, I threw it over the wall.' She sat down suddenly and covered her face with her hands. 'You must believe me. I was so shocked—but not until then, not until I had got him out of sight—that when I got back to the house I just collapsed. I lay on the bed—and I've never cried so much, and I couldn't think straight, and in the end I went to sleep and only woke up late this morning.'

'What did you do then?'

'I couldn't telephone, because Joao had pulled it out of the wall when I threatened to ring home. And I thought and thought. Nobody knew I was here except Maria, and at first I thought I could take him away somewhere and leave him. But she'd still know I'd been with him, and it would all come out.'

'It has to come out; I told you.'

'I didn't believe that, but I had to have more time to think. So when I rang and Maria came I told her Joao had gone out shooting and would be back later. And she gave me some food and then—I went to sleep again. I suppose it was shock,' she added in a lower voice, which trembled slightly, and looked at Craig, willing him to believe.

'Who closed his eyes?' asked Craig, and then her resistance crumbled.

'They weren't closed,' she said wildly. 'They were staring at me, as I told you. Why must you ask me all these questions?'

'Because I want the truth, not a pack of lies.'

'I've *told* you the truth.'

'I'm not going to waste any more time.' He reached forward quickly with both hands and twitched the dressing-gown off her shoulders, pulling it down so that she could not raise her arms. 'As I thought. No sign of a stain on your dress, or of washing it clean. The towel wouldn't have stopped it all, not with his weight on it. You never carried him anywhere. *Then who did?* And for that matter who killed him?'

'He killed himself.' She held her face high and stared at him defiantly.

'Oh no, he didn't. There were only slight marks around the bullet hole in his shirt. He was shot from at least a few feet away. And who closed his eyes? I don't think it was you. For once you were telling the truth. Then who did?'

'There was nobody else.'

'There *was* somebody else, someone you were expecting when I came in. Why did you tell Maria to let me in without asking who I was?'

'There wasn't anybody else.'

'There was somebody who not only broke the telephone cable but pushed a knife through the microphone diaphragm, so that I can't hook it up.'

'There wasn't.'

'All right. Have it your own way. Since I can prove Joao Costa didn't kill himself, you must have shot him yourself. Your diplomatic immunity won't get you off a murder charge, so I'll turn you in to the Portuguese.' He moved towards the door.

'Stop.'

He turned to look at her, as she stared down into the fire. 'I let you go on talking,' he explained quietly, 'although I knew it was mostly lies, because it was the only way of making you realize that you *can't* get away with that kind of deception. Not with professionals. *Any* police investigator would have torn up your story as soon as he began to check. And then you'd be much worse off than if you'd told the truth.'

'You believe in the truth, don't you? You think there's some sort of implicit virtue in *the truth*.'

'Yes, I do.'

'And if I don't tell you what really happened, you'll go roaring off and tell the police to come and get me?'

'Yes. That's what I said.'

She looked him estimatingly for a long moment. Then she said, 'If you'll sit down and listen quietly, without firing so many bloody questions at me, I'll tell you the truth. But you won't like it.'

'All right, but please do it fast. Can't you understand what your people are suffering at this moment?'

She sighed. 'I know, poor dears. I'd give anything to let them know I'm all right. But I can't—yet. Do sit down.'

He sat on the arm of the chair. 'Go ahead, let's have the truth. It was one of Costa's group, I suppose?'

She started. 'You seem to know an awful lot. What *do* you know about his group?'

Craig swore to himself. He said carefully, 'It's generally known that Joao Costa and some of his friends don't exactly approve of the Caetano regime.' He shrugged. 'If there is more to it than that you'd better tell me, especially if there's a connection with this murder.' He paused. 'And Amanda—'

'Well?'

'Cut out the feminine allure this time. It was an impressive performance but it made my head spin.'

She glared at him. 'It's nothing to do with the group, as you call them; they've never been here, as far as I know.' She laughed—a laugh with a tremble of hysteria in it, and no mirth at all. 'It was a Russian who shot Joao. A Soviet intelligence officer.' She paused, then looked him straight in the face, and added : 'My boss.'

CHAPTER NINE

Sole Agent

'OH FOR GOD'S SAKE !' exclaimed Craig angrily. 'Don't start another fairy-story.'

She glanced at her watch. 'If you stay here long enough you'll meet him. That ought to satisfy you.'

'All right, I'll buy it. Who is he?'

'Miloslav Janek. That's his name in England and it's

enough for you to know. He's a GRU officer—that's the Military Intelligence Service, you know—'

'I did know,' said Craig grimly. 'And how did you meet him?'

'When I was up at Oxford. He's got natural cover there, as a research student—a Czech research student. That's where I met him and where, later on, he recruited me. I'm the only agent he's got.'

'Very frank and open, these Russian spies!'

'Shut up!' she said coldly. 'There was a reason why he told me more about his work than he should have done.'

'Good Lord, pillow confidences! You *are* a Mata Hari. And why did you agree to work for him? I suppose they framed you first and then blackmailed you into it? It's the usual procedure.'

She hesitated. 'No, it wasn't like that, but I'm not going to explain. You wouldn't understand.'

'But what on earth's he doing here?'

'He came over specially to stop me getting mixed up more actively with Joao and his friends.'

'It fits, of course. It's extraordinary, but I'm beginning to believe you. Did he warn you off once before—last Christmas?'

'Yes. But Joao went on insisting, and in the end—'

'That bit was true, then, Joao persuading you to come here. And your case officer heard you were going to see him and turned up—when?'

'Early this morning. I had slept here, as I said.'

'But that was another thing I thought sounded wrong. How would you have explained—?'

'That's why I had to leave so early, to square one of my girl-friends. I couldn't telephone because Joao *had* pulled the telephone cable out of the wall. She'd have said I'd spent the night with her. She's done it before. And I had to get home—'

'I know. For the Ambassador's lunch. Do go on. You quarrelled with Joao?'

'Yes. All that part was true. I was an idiot to sleep with him but—oh hell, I was fond of him, and he swore it'd be the last time. But of course in the morning he made a scene just as I told you and came running behind me with the gun, and I was desperate. I knew I had to make the break with him complete. If Milo found out I had disobeyed him it would have spoiled my plan.'

'Your *what*?'

'Oh, never mind. But I did the only thing which would make him wish never to see me again. I told him I was a Russian spy.'

'God Almighty!'

'I told him I'd been reporting all along about his group and their plans. Which wasn't true,' she added thoughtfully. 'Milo simply wasn't interested, except to tell me not to touch it with a barge-pole. He said I had to keep myself free from any contact with political activities, let alone foreign ones, until I'd got myself nicely established as an interpreter. You see,' she explained with the hint of a smile, 'from the GRU point of view I am a long-term spec. Nothing more.'

Craig drew a long breath. 'You left Joao chasing you out through the gateway with a gun,' he said carefully.

'Yes, that's where I turned on him and shouted that I'd been spying on him, and who for. Then I ran towards the garage—he always left the key in the ignition—and there —there was Milo. I still don't know how he got there or what he was planning to do, but he was actually coming across the gravel towards the gate. I called to him, "Look out, he's got a gun!" and then Joao came storming up and shouted at me—in English, that was the trouble— "I'll kill you, you filthy Russian spy!" and I saw Milo's face.' She shuddered. This wasn't acting, thought Craig. This had actually happened to her.

'And then?' he prompted, as she paused, looking down at the floor.

'Joao saw Milo and waved the revolver at him vaguely. He was only interested in me. And Milo took an automatic from his pocket quite slowly and shot him dead.' She added fiercely, 'Joao had no chance. It was like putting down a mad dog. Milo said so afterwards.'

'It sounds more like deliberate murder.'

'What do the words matter?'

'But why did he do it?'

'Because I'd spilled the beans to Joao. If I told anybody else he'd kill them too, I think.'

'Like me, for example.'

'Yes. That's a thought. Like you. It's as I said, I'm his sole agent, so far. It means everything to him. If he knew I'd told you about it he'd kill you too.'

'Well, thanks,' said Craig wryly, 'it's just as well to know. And incidentally, what are we waiting for? What's he doing? How long has he been away?'

'Since early this morning, when it happened. About eight o'clock, I suppose. He was coldly furious at first. He asked me where the key of the barn was and I showed it hanging on a hook inside the garage, and then of course I began to bawl him out—and he just knocked me aside. But hard—I'd no idea he was so strong—and I lay in the corner of the garage while he picked up Joao's body and carried it into the barn and locked it in.' She stopped, and looked at Craig with fear in her eyes. 'Did you really mean that his eyes were closed when you saw him?'

'Yes.'

'Well, it must have been Milo who closed them. Because they were open, open and staring, as I told you.' She shivered. 'He's an odd person. Very odd and sensitive, sometimes.'

Craig laughed shortly. 'Have you the slightest idea of the kind of fire you've been playing with?'

'Oh yes,' she said, quite soberly, 'I understand them all right. I've read a lot, you see.'

Craig groaned. 'Book-learning! Yes, I've seen your books. But there's no time to argue with you. Why didn't you leave with him?'

'He wouldn't let me. He said he'd got a lot to organize, but he'd come back tonight with everything prepared, so that he could make Joao's death seem natural—I don't know what on earth he meant by that—and cook up a cover story for my disappearance. He wouldn't trust me to go back and appear at the Embassy lunch and meet him afterwards. I tried that on him, but he wouldn't wear it. And I think he guessed I was just trying to get away, because he said very coldly that I had to stay here and explain Joao's non-appearance to Maria, and then wait for him. And then he took his gun, which he'd wrapped in a handkerchief in his pocket, and forced me to hold it, and put it away again. And he told me that if I didn't do as he said he would pin Joao's murder on me. He had friends here who would witness against me.'

'But—'

She went on, disregarding his protest. 'He said he would only come back in the dark, because he needed darkness *and* moonlight, whatever that meant.' She looked at Craig questioningly, but he did not reply and she went on, 'But he'd need a hell of a lot of time to arrange everything, because—'

'Well?'

'This is pure guesswork, because he didn't say anything about it, but as you know there are no Iron Curtain Embassies or even trade missions in Lisbon.'

Craig started. 'My God, you're right.' He looked at her with unwilling respect. 'So no chance of a Legal Resident, only—'

'Yes, only an Illegal Residency, under cover. And the cover must be pretty tight, with the PIDE on their tails, so when a young colleague turns up from outside, wanting facilities in a hurry—' she looked at Craig.

He finished, 'He won't get them unless they get through to Moscow on their emergency W/T link and ask for authority, and even then it would need a lot of persuading before they'd stick their necks out. You're right; it would take up a lot of time.'

'Yes. You see how well we understand each other when you stop trying to trip me up at every word.'

'What are you trying to get out of me now?' said Craig cautiously.

'A free hand. I want to play it my way. Don't interrupt, please. Let me say my piece. I've had the whole day to work this out. If you took me away from here, what would happen? Milo would conclude I'd thrown him over and take his revenge as he threatened to do. He'd have to forget Oxford, and all his plans, and disappear, that's obvious, but my God he'd carry out his threat, if only to discredit my word.'

'But—' protested Craig.

She stamped her foot at him. 'Let me go on. What would you do? Could you arrange to dispose of Joao's body?'

'And play into the hands of the man who murdered him? Not bloody likely.'

'All right. Could you pin the murder on Milo, while putting me in the clear?'

'I don't know. My first duty is to get you out of this mess, if not for your sake, for the Embassy's. But after all you're the only witness against him. You'd have to give evidence.'

'Oh, fine! And the whole story would come out, me and Joao, me and Milo, me and—' She hesitated.

'You and the group?' suggested Craig.

She bit her lip, and continued quickly, 'Don't you realize that if you won't agree to get rid of poor Joao, whatever you try to do for me will be quite useless as far as suppressing my connection with him is concerned? Which, in my view at least, is the object of the exercise.'

'So what's your alternative?'

'You leave here, by yourself, now.'

'And let the Russian take charge? What d'you take me for?'

She looked away from him. 'I don't know you, do I?' she said mildly. 'I can't tell what you'd do, except that your law-abiding mind would prevent any plan from being effective. You'd try—I'm sure you'd try honestly to hush things up as far as you decently could, and Simon Dickens would go dashing round to the Chief of Protocol, and H.E. to the Foreign Secretary. And nothing would have the slightest effect as soon as Milo and his friends began to operate.' She paused, and added very quietly, 'And then —I know it sounds old-fashioned, but that's what he's like

—Daddy's heart would slowly break up into little pieces.'

'So you've thought of that, at last,' said Craig in disgust.

'Oh, be quiet!' she said furiously. 'I love him. I love them both, even if I can't talk to them. But it's no good expecting you to understand, any more than they can. What I *must* make you see is that Milo *can* do it. He's utterly uninhibited and he's trained to cope with a situation like this. I *trust* him. I trust him because he's got a paramount motive for getting me out of this frightful mess and restoring the *status quo*. He'll stop at *nothing* to put me back where I was, his sole agent, the proof that he's a real intelligence officer, and not just his father's son.'

'What *are* you talking about?'

'His father is—or rather was, a marshal in the Soviet Army.'

Craig jumped. 'If he told you that you can be quite certain it isn't true.'

'Well, he did. And you're wrong; it's quite true. I can't explain it all now, but that's part of it. I mean, why he's so desperate to prove himself.'

'Let's go back to the bit about your trusting him. You'll go along with him, help him to hide the evidence of what he's done? Cold, bloody murder?'

'I've got no choice. That's how he's fixed it.' She added, in a low voice, between clenched teeth : 'I'll settle my account with him later, the bastard.'

'I've told you you're playing with fire. Can't you understand that? You wouldn't have a chance of crossing him up, not on your own, you stupid girl. Can't I make you see sense? And anyway, I thought you said you worked for him. You're on his side, aren't you?'

'No, I'm not. The murder was bad enough—I do hate violence—but he shouldn't have threatened me with a murder rap.'

'But—good Lord, I forgot! I tried to tell you twice but you wouldn't listen. If we act now it's an empty threat. He was bluffing.'

'But for Christ's sake, he's got my fingerprints on that gun.'

'Oh, use your brain. How did he get hold of the gun? How does he show that they're your prints? And remember that as you said he'd have to disappear the moment you're free to make a statement. He must fix it that only patriotic Portuguese give evidence—people with nice clean records, patriotically snooping around this den of licentiousness and subversion, who actually saw you pull the trigger and were able to pick up the gun afterwards—that's the only way he could play it, and how long d'you think it would take to set up?' He laughed shortly. 'Weeks, at least. All the trouble finding the right chaps, and the briefing and planning. They may be very good, the Russkies, but they can't work miracles. And by tomorrow evening you'd be back in England. We've booked the passage.'

She stared at him. 'What a bloody fool I've been,' she muttered. 'And I thought I'd worked out all the options. But wait a minute—don't you see, it would still have to come out—the meetings with Joao and his boys, and Milo, and all the lies. I told you and I meant it. It would break their hearts.'

'I won't say the obvious thing,' said Craig, 'but listen to me carefully. You're right; you'd have to go through with it, but it needn't be as bad as you think. You could explain that you'd dropped Joao because you'd learned about his political shenanigans, and as for the GRU you never in fact did any spying for them—that is true, isn't it? Yes. Well then, you always intended to play him along a bit further and then contact the Security Service. And tell all.'

'You mean MI5? But that's what I always did intend to do.' She smiled at his evident bewilderment. 'When things had hotted up a bit further.'

'It didn't occur to you, I suppose, that you might have mentioned that little detail earlier,' he said sarcastically. 'But I don't believe it anyway. Whatever you are, you aren't just in it for the kicks. There's *some* strange purpose in your crazy, beautiful head.'

'Yes, there is. And it's no part of my purpose to please either your Establishment or the Russian one. They're both equally rotten.' She lit a cigarette and watched him speculatively through the smoke.

'It's my Establishment, as you call it, that's going to get you out of this mess now, if I have to haul you by the hair. So drop that cigarette and—' He stopped. Through the open window he could hear, all too clearly, the deep clang of the bell at the gate.

CHAPTER TEN

Janek

AMANDA started violently. 'He's much earlier than I thought. You'd better hide or something. He's armed. He's got Joao's gun, too.'

'I think I can cope. Will Maria open the gate?'

'No, she'll come and ask. When I told her to let you in—I thought it was Milo—I told her she wasn't to admit anyone else.'

'Is there nobody else in the house?'

'No.'

Craig opened the door and listened. 'She's not coming.'

'Oh God, I've just remembered! She goes out with a lantern after dark to make sure her precious chickens are safe. There's a fox.'

Craig swore. 'What door would she use? The side one into the yard, of course. How do we get to it?' He plucked her out of her chair.

'Through the kitchen on the other side of the gateway. Wait. Let me take this off.' She wriggled out of the dressing-gown, picked up a torch from the table and ran out of the door, down the spiral staircase and was in the passage when he caught her up, and stopped her. He whispered: 'If it is the Russian—and there was no police siren—he mustn't know there are two of us. So quietly across the entrance.'

She nodded and he opened the door softly and they stepped out into the cool air. On the stone pavement under the gateway their footsteps made little sound, and they heard nothing from the other side of the gate.

The door opposite led into another passage. There were rooms on the right, one of which, presumably Maria's, was open, with a light inside. At the end they turned left under the corner tower and found themselves in an enormous kitchen, which the girl illuminated in flashes as she ran forward. Craig caught fleeting glimpses of the long stone table in the middle of the floor, granite sinks along the walls and a huge open fireplace with a canopy which reached up to the roof.

In the opposite corner of the room he could see light coming from outside. There was an entrance set in the thickness of the wall, with its oak door swung inwards. He groped for Amanda's arm, took the torch and switched it off. His arm found her shoulders and he pulled her towards him and spoke in her ear. 'Run out of that door and hide in the yard—in the chicken barn if it's still open. If Maria's there keep her with you. I'll go round to the gate and deal with your friend Milo. He's going to get a surprise.' He picked up an iron meat-spit from the table and hefted it in his hand.

'No you don't,' she whispered furiously. 'I told you he's the best hope I've got, and I still mean it. And he's armed. You go and I'll keep mum. He won't hurt me, but you'll be for it if he finds you here. All I want to do is to see that Maria's all right, and then I'll go and let him in.'

'Wait,' whispered Craig urgently. He could see the reflection of a wavering light on the surface of the door. He pushed the girl behind him, and tightened his grip on her wrist as she struggled. He dragged her forward until they reached the open door.

They could see the old woman trying to run across the

yard, but she was coming not from the chicken barn, as he had expected, but from the part of the stable building nearer the archway. A hurricane-lantern in her hand was swaying wildly, and she was shouting in her weak, cracked voice, '*O Senhorito é morto! Bandidos! E morto o pobrinho! Chama a policia!*' Then there was the vicious, dry crack of an automatic, and she fell forward on her face.

Craig got his hand over Amanda's mouth before she could scream. She bit him, but he held her tight and got his mouth to her ear. 'Watch. Keep still and watch.' He pulled her away from the door.

The lantern lay on the ground, flickering but still alight. They saw a man come quickly out of the dark and bend over the still figure. He turned the old woman over and shone a pencil torch on the wrinkled face, while with the other hand he held her wrist and waited. Then he bent forward and gently closed Maria's eyes and arranged her dress, saying something in a low voice which they could not catch. Then he slowly straightened up and switched off the torch.

With a violent effort the girl broke away and ran to the door. Before Craig could reach her she had shouted into the dark 'You murderer! You filthy murderer!' and slammed the heavy door shut. The solid bang of the door closing almost drowned the shout they heard from the other side. Then the girl was sliding the heavy iron bolts into their sockets in the stone. They heard a voice calling outside and someone beating on the door. She snatched the torch from Craig's hand, shone it on the bolts and hinges and shouted, 'You won't kick or shoot your way through this, you swine.' Then she sobbed suddenly and dropped the torch, putting her hands over her face.

Craig's arm was around her shoulders, holding her tight, but after a moment she shook him off and began to walk back towards the other end of the kitchen. He picked up the torch, which had fortunately not been broken, and followed her.

'That's torn it,' he said. 'I could have fixed him nicely

when he came to the door, and after that you could have kicked the daylights out of him for all I'd have cared. But never mind. At least you've shown your colours.'

'I told you I hate violence, and he's acting like a mad dog. She was such a decent old thing, and kept her mouth shut about us. She adored Joao.'

'Well, let's see where we stand. One, he knows you're still here. Two, he doesn't know I am. Three, after your very pungent remarks he'll expect you to go straight to the police if you get out of here. Four, so he'll try to make sure you don't.'

'Where does all that fine logic get us?'

'Is there any other way in?'

'No. Only the main gate. And you saw how strong that is.'

'Yes. And it fills the arch, so you can't climb over.'

'What do you want to do, withstand a siege?' she asked, contemptuously. 'After all, we're two. He's only one.'

'How d'you know? There may be others with him. And there's no chance of catching him now with his guard down. What's more, I haven't got a gun, unless you can provide one.'

'No,' she said, more soberly, 'Joao's was the only one here. I'm sure of that. Not even a shotgun. Telling Maria that Joao had gone shooting was just bluff; she wouldn't know, poor old thing.'

'So what are you suggesting? Sallying forth, bare-handed?'

'No. I'm sorry—What did you say your name was?'

'Peter Craig.'

'I'm sorry, Peter. I don't know why you should stick out your neck for me anyway.'

'I'm always suspicious when you act friendly.'

'It's all right. I *am* friendly now.'

'And me with the blood dripping from my wounds.'

'Ooh,' she said, 'I forgot. Let me see.' She shone the torch on his hand. 'You fraud! It's even stopped bleeding. I thought so; my heart wasn't in it.'

'What d'you do when it is? Go for the jugular?' There was something in his voice which made her stop still. Her voice came to him through the darkness, quiet and serious. 'That is what you really think of me, isn't it? A sort of vampire.'

'Your word, not mine.'

'Oh Lord, I suppose I'll have to explain to you some time. I'm not at all like that, really I'm not. And if you're going to say that but for me two people would be alive, don't. I know it's true and it's very hard to bear. You see, some day I suppose I'll turn into a wonderful wife and mother, but not for a long time yet. I've got more important things to do.' She went towards the passage.

Craig was utterly baffled by her, but he said nothing. At the main gateway he shone the torch on the locked gate and tested the bolts. There was no sound from the outside and they went on, closing the passage door behind them, and up the stair.

When they were again inside the lighted room he looked at her appraisingly. She was standing by the fire, arranging her hair, quite composed now. There was no sign of weakness or shock in that assured, wide-eyed face, but her hands were still trembling. She frowned and put them behind her.

'We'll leave your odd motivations for the moment,' he said. 'There's something I want you to do.'

'What d'you want?'

'We'll see if he's done a bunk. If he hasn't I want you to talk to him.'

She flared up instantly. 'I won't. You saw what he did.'

'I saw him bend over Maria and do things which struck me, in the circumstances, as very odd, but perhaps he's a mixed-up kid. But neither you nor I saw him fire at her. I want you to get him to admit it. And I want to hear him say it.'

'I see,' she said scornfully, 'your plodding policeman's mind is rooting around for evidence.'

'Yes. And there's something your brilliant analytical mind hasn't grasped, I think. If he ever did try to frame you for the murder of Joao Costa, do you imagine he'd leave it at that? He'd frame you for this, too.'

'But you said—'

'I know. I don't think he could do it, but we can't be sure, can we? You seemed to have such a high idea of his competence.'

She hesitated, and before she could speak Craig went on: 'If the two of us could hear him admit to both murders we should have a very useful piece of evidence. And what's more, we could find out if he knows or even suspects that I'm here, which is very important, whatever plan we make.' Her expression was still doubtful, and Craig added casually, 'But of course if you don't feel you can face him—I mean, I realize how difficult it'd be to hide your revulsion. It would mean playing a part, and that's not everyone's cup of tea.'

'Of course I can do it. But how?'

Craig went quickly to the lamp and turned down the flame. 'Do the same with the others, while I ease the shutters open.' She obeyed, and when the lights were dim he opened the heavy curtains on the window facing the forecourt and peered through. One of the louvre shutters was already ajar and he pushed it back and opened the other very quietly. He could now see sideways and there was already a little light from the moon, rising behind the trees. It shone on the fair hair of a man who came walking slowly from the direction of the main gate; and on the long-barrelled revolver he held in his hand.

He stood back behind the curtain and motioned to Amanda. 'Tell him to drop his gun and stand where you can see him,' he whispered.

She nodded and stepped forward and called 'Milo'.

Craig saw the Russian jump out of sight into the shadow of the wall. He waved the girl back as she went nearer to the window, and pointed downwards to show where the man had gone.

She called again, 'Milo, where are you?'

'Open the gate, Amanda,' said a voice from below. It was calm and friendly, with a very slight foreign accent.

'Stand where I can see you,' she called, 'and drop that gun. I've got to talk to you.'

He must have moved along under the wall, because he was suddenly there, below the window. He ran a few yards out from the house and whirled round, his legs apart and bent at the knees, his right hand, with the gun in it, at the full extent of his arm and pointing at the ground, ready for the true gunman's straight-armed snap-shot. A classic stance, thought Craig appreciatively.

'You must drop it, Milo. Or I won't open the gate.' There was a most convincing tremble in the girl's voice.

'All right. I've got no time to argue.' He put the auto-matic down carefully on the ground in front of him and stood up, the moonlight, filtering through the trees, flicker-ing on his pale face. He was wearing, as far as Craig could see, a dark zipped-up jacket and dark trousers. The girl went forward to the window-sill, while Craig re-mained behind his curtain, watching.

'Well, darling,' said the man calmly. His smile was frank and oddly attractive. 'Let's have it.'

'You didn't have to kill Maria,' she said flatly.

'Oh yes, I did. I'm very sorry for your tender feelings. I had nothing against her but she had to go.'

'But why did you have to let her see Joao? The barn was locked.'

'She had another key. I saw her just as I was coming into the yard. She went in there to get something—I think it was paraffin for her lamp, because she had a can in her hand—and then she came out screaming. But I'm afraid she'd have had to be eliminated anyway.'

'No,' said Amanda sobbing, 'it's just that you're a killer. That's what I didn't know. I thought you were civilized, but you love killing.'

'Don't be a fool,' he said calmly. 'You've got a logical mind. Use it. Only she knew that you and Costa were here.'

'But she was loyal, she—'

'She might have been loyal to your boy-friend, but she'd have turned you in without a qualm. And in any case, once the PIDE got her—I assure you, I've saved her a lot of suffering.'

'Oh, don't be a hypocrite. I didn't think you were that.'

'For God's sake use your—what's that expression?—use your loaf. You know better than to let your womanly feelings dictate to your reason. All right, I killed her and Joao because they stood in our way, yours and mine. By tomorrow morning he'll be found a long way from here, and everything will point to an accident. I've thought of a good plan to explain your disappearance and you'll be in the clear. It's not what you deserve, after your foolish disobedience, but it's got to be like that for the sake of our plans. And those are more important than two little people, dead.' He took a step forward and looked up at her intently, trying to see her face. 'What had either of them got to look forward to? He was running head on into the arms of the PIDE—I only learned that today, but I assure you it's true—and he'd have finished up like Delgado, kicked to death and pushed over the Spanish frontier. And what was life worth to her, deaf, half-blind, without relatives who will take care of her—and half-crippled, she looked to me? You told me all that, remember? Well, they both died painlessly, because I did it that way, and suddenly, without any of the mental torture which is the fear of death—'

'And unshriven, Milo?'

He stopped short. Then he said slowly, 'Their religion foresees what happens in such cases.' Then he added angrily, 'But that's the last thing you would worry about, so stop wasting time. I've told you I killed them, and why, and that's enough for you. Now go down and open the gate. At once, Amanda.'

She backed away from the window, as if uncertain what to do. 'Let me think for a moment.'

'No,' he said angrily. 'Do what I say.'

'Oh be quiet, Milo. I must think.' She retreated out of his line of sight and looked quickly at Craig. He nodded. She waited until Janek called her again, and then went back slowly and looked down at him. 'All right,' she said wearily, 'I'll open it.'

'Good girl. You can trust me, you know that.'

Craig saw the Russian staring intently at the girl until she disappeared. Then he picked up the automatic and walked away towards the gateway.

Craig ran to the bed and started to pull off the sheets. 'That was a very good show,' he said in a low voice. 'You've won us several minutes before he comes back to ask what the hell you're doing.' He knotted the corners together and tested the knots. 'It's about twenty feet down from the edge of the battlements. We can get out there through the other window, can't we? We can't risk the side door; he may have someone watching it.'

'Yes, it's easy. We've been out there. I'll show you.' She went across the room and opened the wooden shutters, while Craig followed with his improvised rope. They were looking down the side of the house towards the farther tower. Between the stone castellations the roof was formed of small ridges, separated by valley gutters and covered with traditional tapered convex tiles. The slope of the nearest ridge came up to meet the wall of the tower below the window at which they were standing. Craig leaned out and twisted his head towards the left. He could see that the tower extended for about eighteen inches beyond the line of the battlements, and in the angle of the walls there was deep shadow. The moon was now shining on the tall trees of the garden and on the back of the house, but the part nearer the front was still in darkness.

'I'm going to get down into the gutter and have a look through the battlements. Put one end of the rope round your waist. I shan't pull hard on it, but I mustn't slip and make a row, and it'll help if I've got something to hold.'

She nodded and he climbed over the sill and lowered himself on to the sloping roof. Then he walked down it backwards, paying out the rope. Once in the valley gutter he could not be seen from below, and he went quickly to where it met the wall supporting the castellations, which were at head-level. He peered out between the stone blocks and could see down into the dense undergrowth which ran along the side of the house. To his left, where the corner of the tower projected, the gnarled trunk of an ancient wistaria had found its way upward to twine in and out of the battlements. He grunted with satisfaction, and looked back for the girl.

She had looped the rope around the projecting top of the hinge of the shutter and was lowering herself down the roof, her dress tucked up in a bundle around her waist and two long and strikingly well-shaped legs groping for footholds. She reached the gutter without making a sound and gathered in the rope with a neat twitch to clear it off the hinge. Then she joined him under the parapet.

'I'm going to let you down in the corner, so that you'll have the creeper to help you and you'll be in shadow. When you're down I'll drop the rope. Make a heap of it on the ground, so that I can jump on to it if I have to. But I think I can manage with the creeper.'

'What do we do then?'

'Take the rope with us, so that they don't find it and get away through the trees into the garden. You know your way from there?'

'Yes.' She was shivering slightly in the cool breeze.

'Are you all right, Amanda? You can manage the climb?'

'Of course,' she retorted scornfully. 'You forget I was up at Oxford. Any girl who couldn't climb in and out of men's colleges simply wasn't with it. This is old hat.'

'Proctors don't carry guns, as a rule.'

'Oh come on. I'll go first.' She was up the slope of the ridge and sitting on the parapet before he could reply. He followed.

She grasped the thick stem of wistaria with one hand and the rope with the other and vanished over the wall. Half-way down she must have lost her grip on the creeper, because Craig felt a sudden strain on the sheet he held in his hands. Although he had jammed one foot against the wall and was leaning backwards the jerk lifted his body until he could look clear over the battlements.

It was then that he saw something that set his heart leaping like a hooked salmon. Over to the right, where the bushes below joined the trees of the garden, there was a glint of light. A man, a dark shadow under the trees, was moving slowly towards the front of the house, and the moon had picked out the gun he held ready in his hand.

CHAPTER ELEVEN

The Siege

CRAIG was opening his mouth to shout to the girl when he realized that the man might not know he had been seen. Using all his force he hauled on the sheet, first with one arm and then the other, but steadily so that she would not lose her footing on the wall, until a swathe of pale hair appeared above the parapet, with Amanda's dimly seen face below. 'What the hell are you doing?' she whispered furiously. 'I'd nearly made it.'

'There's someone behind you. Over you come.'

She uttered a word that startled Craig and got one hand on the parapet. He hauled in the rest of the rope and seized her other hand. The man had broken cover and was crashing through the bushes. Craig gave a great heave and she jack-knifed over the parapet, her legs waving in the air. The gun was raised and pointing. The face above it had no features; there was a silken sheen around the man's head.

Craig caught the girl around the waist and fell backwards with her in his arms, rolling down the roof into the gutter. They lay there for a long moment, and he could feel the thump of her heart.

'If things weren't so dicey,' he said, 'I might even enjoy this.'

'Oh come off it! Has he got a gun? Was it Milo?'

'Yes, he has. And no, it wasn't Milo. Tall and loose-limbed, with a nylon stocking over his face.'

'A stocking? Whatever for? And why didn't he shoot?'

'Perhaps he's had orders. But I think it was the sight of those acres of bare Amanda. Stopped him in his tracks.'

'You do say the most charming things!' She rolled away from him and got on to her knees.

'Listen!' she whispered. They heard steps on the gravel, moving away at a run. 'Quick, before he comes back.'

She scurried like a cat up the slope and through the open window. Craig followed, snatching up the knotted sheets as he went.

Inside the room he threw them on the floor and closed the window and its shutters. Then he turned and saw the girl looking out on to the forecourt.

'They're both there,' she said in a voice that trembled slightly, 'Milo and a man with a stocking over his face. They're not running.'

'Can they see you?'

'Yes. The man's pointing.' Then: 'Milo's told him to put his gun away.'

'Listen, Amanda. Call out to him. Say, "Look out, he's armed." Say it *twice*.'

She turned a puzzled face. 'Go on. Do as I say.'

She turned back to the window, with Craig behind her, out of sight. He bent down and reached forward with his hand until he was almost touching her bare leg, just above the knee.

'Look out, Milo! He's armed! Look—' Her voice ended in a squawk of pain and she rounded on Craig furiously. He grabbed her round the waist and pulled her backwards. She slapped his face hard. 'You brute! You pinched me,' she spluttered through the fingers of the hand he had clapped over her mouth.

'That was perfect,' he said, rubbing his cheek. 'It was so beautifully natural. They'll think I'm holding you here by force.'

'You clever bastard! But they can't think that. He saw me on the rope.'

'He only saw me hauling you back, with you swearing at me. You were escaping from me, or trying to. At least, they'll be puzzled, and they'll think I've got a gun. So we've gained some time, anyway. You couldn't have done it better.'

She turned up the flame of the nearest lamp and twisted round to look at her leg. 'It's left a bloody great mark, you brute!'

'Oh, you *poor* thing!' said Craig with a derisive grin. 'Shall I kiss it better?'

'Not unless you want to start a fight. But it's all right. It's nothing to what I've had in the street in Lisbon, higher up.' She looked at him. 'What do we do now?'

'We just wait. Time's on our side, and they'll be cautious now about trying to get in.'

A voice called 'Amanda'.

'Don't answer,' said Craig in a low voice, and went to the window. 'What d'you want?'

The answer came from just below the window, out of sight. 'We're friends of Miss Harcourt. I want to talk to you.'

Craig moved forward cautiously. There was no one he could see on the spread of gravel below. They were evidently standing against the wall. He called out, 'Then stand where I can see you.'

There was a light laugh from below. 'No indeed. That would be too easy, wouldn't it?' Then, sharply, 'Who are you?'

'I'm a police officer, and I'm holding the young lady here until her parents can fetch her.'

But as he spoke his ear caught the sudden sound of movement underneath the window. As he sprang back he saw two figures running backwards on to the gravel, looking up at him with guns raised. The shots rang out simultaneously, and then again, and the thud of bullets seemed to be all round him. One hit the window hinge and ricocheted whining into the trees. Then there was another rush of footsteps and the same voice from below, a little breathless but quite calm. 'That's just to show you we mean business. Let the girl go. The same way, over the wall, if you like. One of us will catch her; the other will kill you if you try to interfere.'

Craig made no reply. Amanda rushed at him. 'You bloody fool! You might have been killed. Did they hit you?'

'Not a scratch. They knew they hadn't much chance. It was meant to be a lesson.' She was trembling violently and tears fell on his hands as he led her to a chair and pushed her into it gently. Then he went back and swung the heavy shutters across the window.

'We both need a drink. But first I'm going to check all the doors again.'

'Not without me,' she cried.

'All right. We'll do it together.'

They went down the stair to the half-landing, and Craig closed the round window lattice and worked the latch. At the bottom there was a door leading to the left-hand wing of the house, but it was already locked and bolted. Then they checked the bolts in the door giving on to the entrance.

'There!' said Craig encouragingly. 'Even if they get into the courtyard they won't get much farther. The windows are all barred on the outside.'

'But how *can* they get inside?'

'I don't know, unless they can get on to the roof somewhere and down into the courtyard. They looked agile enough. Your boy-friend's been well-trained, too. That was a neat little exercise—luring me to the window and then jumping out to get me in view.'

She shivered, and was silent until they had returned to the room in the tower. Then she shook herself. 'I'll get you that drink. Whisky?'

'Yes, please.' Craig sat down by the fire, coaxed some flames from the smouldering logs and pulled out his pipe. He looked around the room thoughtfully.

'Did Joao furnish this place alone?'

'Yes, with some help from me. He told his parents he wanted some place where he could be alone'—she half-smiled—'and write. They told him he could do what he liked here as long as he looked after Maria and got the factor to visit it every now and then to see to repairs. We chose the pieces of furniture from the rest of the house and brought other things from his flat in Lisbon. None of his friends knew about it, only me.' She paused. 'It was awful fun—while it lasted.'

'But his parents would know he might be here. I mean, when they find he's missing.'

'No. That was the first thing I thought of. But they're away—that's why he was staying at their house—and in any case they'd probably think he'd gone back to his flat. He was very secretive, you know.' She brought him a glass and sat down in the opposite chair.

'He'd have to be,' said Craig unguardedly.

She looked at him curiously. 'What *do* you know about Joao's group? You tried to fob me off before.'

Craig said nothing, and she cried out in exasperation: 'Don't just sit there smoking your pipe like one of those bloody TV advertisements. I know they're supposed to work on a girl's glands, but not on mine they don't! *What do you know about the group?*'

'Whatever I learned was given to me in confidence. I'm sorry, Amanda, it's no good looking at me like that. It's not my secret.'

'Secret and confidential Officer eyes only! Decipher yourself! What nonsense it all is.'

'That's what all spies say when they're trying to learn something they shouldn't.'

'Don't be insulting. I'm not a spy. I'm only curious about what you know.'

'No dice!' He paused. 'But Janek thinks you're one of his agents?'

'He thinks I'm his only agent; that's the point. And I am, I'm quite sure. But I haven't spied for him because that isn't what he wants me to do. I've told you all this already. He wants me to become a mature, well-trained

agent, in a position of access to important secret information, *before* I attempt to spy actively.'

'You sound as if you're quoting him.'

'His very words.'

'What sort of man is he? How did you meet him, to
start with?'

'I see. You'd like a nice cosy chat, while Milo and his
yobbo rampage around outside, trying to get in?'

'Informative chat,' agreed Craig, sipping his whisky.
'Yes please. I don't know what else we can do. We can't
telephone. There doesn't appear to be anyone within
miles—'

'There isn't. Not even a farm. It's all pine and eucalyptus plantations around here.'

'I thought so. Well, if we can't get out and can't
communicate with the outside what can we do but wait?
Charles Jenkins knows I'm here, and he'll have told your
father by now.'

She looked up in alarm. 'Old Charlie? I didn't know
any of this. They mustn't come; they'd get killed.'

'I don't think you need worry. Jenkins knows I haven't
got a car—he had to drop me off to get rid of a prowl-car
—and he won't expect me to turn up for quite a while.
But in the end they *will* get worried and I hope they'll tell
the police. In the meantime Jenkins and your father probably think I'm chasing after you somewhere and haven't
telephoned for security reasons.'

'What on earth are you talking about?'

'Oh, sorry. Your home telephone's tapped.' She looked
her bewilderment and he hurried on, 'I can't explain now.
The point is that unless the PIDE smell us out—because
they're on your track, too; what a popular girl you are!
—I doubt if anyone is going to turn up for some time. But
Janek doesn't know that. He must feel very pushed for
time now he knows about me, so either he'll just sling his
hook—'

'He won't. It'd ruin everything for him, as I told you.'

'Well then, he'll make a determined attempt to come in
and get us. And since, thanks to your splendid bit of theat-

ricals, he thinks I'm armed, he'll have to plan it very carefully. That,' he concluded, as he refilled her glass, 'is what
I imagine he's doing now.'

'I wish my nerves were as good as yours.'

'I've noticed nothing wrong with them so far,' he said
smiling. 'So let's fill in the time as I said—informatively.
It always helps. "Know your enemy" is what I was
taught. I know his name, but what is he?'

'He's a research student in international law at St
John's, Oxford. And he's supposed to be a Czech refugee.
I think it's true what he told me, that he was genuinely
reading classics and Roman law at Brno University and
graduated there, but how he posed as a Czech all that
time I don't know, unless perhaps his father was posted in
Czechoslovakia after the war, so that he could speak
the language fluently. And he must have been beautifully
documented and trained for the job by the GRU. But
then, when the balloon went up in Prague in 1968, he
became a resistance fighter, and afterwards he escaped
and was welcomed with open arms by the Czechs in
England. And they supported him and got him a place
at St John's and, believe it or not, a research scholarship.'

'Good Lord! It must have been a remarkable bit of
foresight by the GRU. I don't think anybody else knew
Dubcek was going to be forcibly stopped from carrying
out his reforms.'

'No. It wasn't like that. He never expected to be sent
to England at all; his job was to spy on the anti-Soviet
movement among the Czech students. And then when the
clash came it was too good a chance to miss. I'm guessing
a bit, but I do know for certain that the Czechs at Oxford
accepted him as one of themselves. And thought he'd been
a prominent freedom-fighter. That's how I met him.'

'But how did you get to *know* him?'

'Because I had an affair with him.'

Craig wriggled uncomfortably. 'It sounds the wrong way
round,' he said shortly.

'It's a permissive society at Oxford. You must know
that. To make it quite plain, *most* girls there have affairs

most of the time. Well, I was all for rebellion—any kind of rebellion—and mixed up with more movements than I can put a name to. And Milo—' she hesitated, 'Milo was rather glamorous and unapproachable, and my God he was intelligent. After Husak came to power and things got tougher and tougher in the CSR we used to have meetings, and you know what undergraduate speeches are supposed to be like, effervescent and witty and brilliant. Well, mostly they're not. They're fizzy but repetitious, an awful lot of bull, with no order in it. Well, Milo was never dull, and he could straighten people out without hurting their feelings, and while he talked sense—in terms of what was practicable—it was all very high-level and ideological. As I told you,' she added, 'he's a clever bastard. And extraordinarily well-read. He's always quoting Latin poets.'

'And you?'

'Well, I was becoming a bit bored with the ineffectiveness of so much of what we were doing, and with some of my friends. They were such show-offs, and class-ridden one way or the other and so *disorderly*.' She saw Craig smile, and frowned at him, but went on, 'They thought they were achieving something by growing their hair and not washing, and of course they smelled to Heaven. Which was all right as long as they didn't want to make love to you. So I became very interested in Milo—not in love with him, but interested in his ideas and because he seemed to know where he was going. And that's rather funny, if you think of it. Anyway, he didn't take any notice of me, which was a thing I wasn't used to. So then—then I made a real play for him. And got him,' she added with a sigh of satisfaction, 'and all my girl-friends were jealous.'

'So people knew?'

'Oh yes, at first. But afterwards we were most discreet —in the end it was part of my training—and he gradually got me to drop all the causes I was involved in. So we had more time.'

'And that's when he began to work on you—ideologically?'

'Yes. It was a slow process, and very subtly thought out,

I suppose. But he hadn't got far before I guessed that he was up to something.'

'So he wasn't as clever as all that? Or perhaps he met his match?'

She laughed. 'Perhaps he did. But you see, I was genuinely fascinated, for my own reasons, by the opportunity of studying a real live communist. That was his line—that he believed in communism but hated the Soviets. And it was his defence of communism which first struck me as phoney. The one subject on which he ought to have had all the arguments ready, and yet it sounded forced. So I began to help him out.'

'You did what?' And yet, he thought, it was all in keeping with the girl's evident belief that she could manipulate people as she wished.

'It was a game at first, but because I was pretending to be converting myself from an anarchist—or whatever I thought I'd been—to a communist, it made it easier for him. And then he realized that I really felt deeply about the Czechs, and that I might perhaps respect a Russian spy but never a Czech who double-crossed his own compatriots. So he hinted that he was Russian in origin, and I played up to that one, and then he told me the first bit of the truth.'

'He was taking the hell of a risk.'

'So did Lonsdale, when the time came. They've got to, or they don't get anywhere, and he was a bit pushed for time in the end. Milo was desperately anxious that I should get a first or a good second, and of course that's what I wanted, too, but I pretended to be rather blasé about it and he came clean. We agreed to see much less of each other in my last year, and I did get a first.'

'Did you indeed?'

'Yes. I knew I could if I tried, but it was a great strain because—well, we were fine as lovers, and by this time anybody else would have been a *sordid* anti-climax, and in addition I was burning with curiosity to know what he really had in mind for me, so it was awfully difficult to see so little of him.'

Craig drew a deep breath. 'It's the wrong moment,' he said, 'for me to feel sorry for this fellow outside. But I'm tempted. But wait a minute—damn it, what about Joao?'

'Oh, that just sort of happened, when I came out here in the long vac. I was curious about his political ideas, to start with, and then he was so sweet—' She broke off, and turned away.

'I think I'd better take a look outside,' said Craig.

'No, I will. They won't shoot at me.'

'You stay where you are. I'll only squint through the curtains.'

'Wait till I've turned the lamp down. Wait, Peter.'

He did as she said and then opened the curtains just enough to be able to look along the front of the house between the hinges of the shutters outside.

By this time the moonlight was bright on the gravel and on the tops of the trees beyond. He could hear nothing, and cautiously pressed forward until he could see more clearly. The whole of the forecourt was empty, but he could hear the sound of a car engine. He called to the girl, and she joined him. 'I think they may have decided to beat it,' he said in a low voice.

'Not Milo. He'll have some ploy—Oh look!' she added excitedly. The big Squire was coming out of the archway slowly, without lights. 'Peter! Why are they using Joao's car? They must have another one.'

'That's why,' said Craig grimly. 'And that's why he's got the retractable headlights tucked away. Oh God, I ought to have thought of it.' They could now see the estate car clearly, and the luggage rack on its roof and on top of that, held down with rope, the long slim trunk of a tree, projecting some way beyond the shining bonnet. The car made a sweeping turn and was steadied, facing the gateway of the main building. Then it moved forward and gathered speed. Craig turned to the girl.

'They'll be in the courtyard in no time,' he said urgently. 'We've got to think quickly.' There was a rending crash from below. He faced Amanda. 'If they're prepared to do that they won't be stopped from bashing in the windows

that give on to the roof. We could get out that way, as
we did before, but I'm sure it's what they'll expect us to
do, and one of them will be watching. And apart from that
—*all* the downstairs windows are barred, aren't they?'

'Yes. Oh God, we're trapped! No, wait. Where we used
to feed the swans.'

'What?'

'There's a sort of formal lake behind the house, facing
the *sala de visitas*. The windows there aren't barred. Thick
shutters on the inside, that's all.'

'Why aren't they barred?'

'The water reaches right up to the wall, and it's deep.
Oh Peter, I'm sorry. I ought to have thought of it before.'

'It wouldn't have been worth trying when we didn't
know where they were. But with one of them inside the
courtyard—at least one—and the other watching this roof,
we might get away with it. We can swim across and get
away through the trees, can't we?'

'I suppose so. I feel awfully scared.'

'You'll be fine. Come on, quick.'

He led the way, running down the stair and shining
the torch on the door leading to the unexplored side of
the house, which he unlocked.

The beam of the torch fell on shrouded furniture and
a double bed with gleaming brass rails and a mosquito net
looped up among the shadows. The light flickered on, and
found another door leading to a room beyond. It was a
bedroom, too, the furniture muffled and withdrawn and
two narrow beds misty beneath their nets. At the far
right hand corner the torch caught the rusty gleam of
panels of 'distressed' mirror in a pair of double doors.
Creaking gently they swung open to reveal the long *sala*
which took up the whole of the back of the house. There
were a number of tables and chairs, primly grouped. Dust
bags muffled the chandeliers and the heavy cabinets and
consoles shone dully through their coating of dust. Behind
the faded brocade curtains at the tall windows splinters
of moonlight showed through the closed wooden shutters.

Two shots rang out.

'The police!' cried Amanda excitedly.

'No. It was inside somewhere. Come on!' He ran to the window and opened the shutters, and then the long french windows.

They were looking out across a stretch of water. It was a square ornamental lake, bounded on three sides by a white stone balustrade while on the fourth, under their feet, the water lapped peacefully against the wall of the house. The moon shone down on the marble dome of a small circular folly which rose from the centre of the lake, its fluted columns mirrored, calm and ageless, in the smooth surface of the water. A swan was cruising on the far side, and catching sight of the open window came surging forward, silently, trailing a long V of silver ripples.

'He knows me,' she whispered, as she stripped her frock over her head. 'He won't attack. He'll think—he'll think you're Joao, I expect.'

Craig took her frock and shoes and made a bundle of them with his shirt and trousers. 'You in first,' he said quietly. 'I'll hold your hand.'

She stepped over the sill and he lowered her silently into the water. She pushed off and floated out on her back. The swan had come near and was circling, looking at her expectantly. Craig glanced for a split second at her smooth brown body in the water—and then all further thought was driven from his mind. The swan had turned, white feathers raised, towards the window and was hissing loudly. And something cold was pressing against the middle of Craig's back.

CHAPTER TWELVE

Janek in Action

FROM THE DARKNESS behind him a quiet, deadly voice was speaking.

'Put your hands on your head, Craig, and don't try anything. That's it. Now tell the girl to come back.'

'Swim for it—' he began, but a vicious jab took his breath away. He saw the look of horror on Amanda's face, but she stayed where she was, treading water.

'He won't shoot you,' gasped Craig, twisting sideways to avoid the second blow. Then it came, suddenly, aimed at his liver, and he doubled up in pain.

'I'll shoot *him*, though, Amanda,' said the quiet voice. 'You know I mean it. So come back.'

'Don't shoot! Don't shoot him, Milo! I'm coming.' She swam towards the window.

'Help her to get in. Go on, don't do anything brave and foolish. Give her your hand.'

Groaning, Craig leant over the low sill and helped her to climb back.

'Right. Now close the shutter and bolt it.'

Craig did as he was told, fumbling for the bolts. Then a torch was switched on and threw a pool of light over Craig, leaning against the shutter, massaging his liver, and the girl, standing wet and shivering in her bra and a pair of diminutive pants.

'You'll catch cold, Amanda,' said Janek mildly. 'You'd better get dressed.'

The bundle of clothes lay at Craig's feet and he bent down.

'Stop!' ordered the Russian. 'Don't touch it.' He thrust the revolver forward, so that the long barrel came into the torchlight. 'I warn you again. Don't make any move unless I tell you to. Otherwise I shall fire. Kick it over here. That's

better. It's where you've got your gun, of course.' He
went down on one knee and shook the bundle loose with
his left hand. There was a moment's pause; then his
voice rose dangerously. 'Come on, where is it?'

'I dropped it,' said Craig, quickly, before the girl could
speak. 'I had it in my hand when I was making the girl
get into the water. When you spoke I dropped it in the
water.'

'You did not. I could see both your hands. *Where is it?*'

'There never was a gun,' said Amanda. 'He told me to
tell you he was armed. That's all.'

The torch flickered over their two figures and searched
the floor by the window. 'I suppose it's possible—traditional, even, a British policeman without a gun. But I expect
you're both lying. You'll have to learn better. But first
—Amanda, take those things off and dry yourself on the
man's shirt. Get moving. I haven't time to waste.'

'You can't make her—' began Craig, but the Russian
broke in with a dry laugh.

'I can make her do what I like,' he said coldly. 'And
anyway, it won't be the first time I've seen her with nothing
on. You can close your eyes if you like, but if you think
I'm going to switch the light off this chaste Diana while
she changes you're a fool. And you're not that, I think.
Who are you, incidentally?'

'I told you. I'm a police officer, visiting Lisbon. The
Ambassador told me to find Miss Harcourt. I don't know,'
he added deliberately, for Amanda's ears, 'who the hell you
are, but you won't get away with this.'

'You don't know who I am? I wonder.' The light shone
on the girl's face. 'That'll do Amanda. Get your frock
on and push those clothes across slowly, with your foot, to
Mr Craig. All right, Craig. You can dress, too, and throw
me the wallet I felt in your hip pocket.' He jerked it open
and scattered the contents on the floor. 'Oh good! Visiting cards.' He stooped down quickly and picked one up.
'Well, that seems true, at least. "Police Adviser, Her
Majesty's Diplomatic Service." I wonder why you came to
Lisbon just now. But that can wait. We have a lot to

arrange.' He called out in English: 'Luiz! Come in with your lamp.'

The utter darkness from which he had been speaking, which had made Craig abandon his first idea of risking a grab for the revolver when the torch was on the contents of the wallet, began to dissipate. The light of an oil lamp grew in the doorway. The man with the nylon stocking over his face came into the room and set it down on one of the sheeted tables. For the first time Craig could see Janek's face properly, and the Smith and Wesson thirty-eight he held in his hand.

He catalogued the features quickly to file away in his memory: age 25-27, five foot nine, slim build, about ten stone, fair hair parted on the right-hand side—rather long at the back, light grey eyes—or could be blue), short straight nose, firm mouth—rather small, squarish chin, broad cheekbones, broad forehead, no visible distinguishing marks. Clothes: black polo sweater under a zipped jacket, charcoal trousers, desert boots—stripped for action, obviously.

The pale eyes looked into his for a moment, impassively, without either humour or menace. It wasn't a criminal's face or a killer's—a thinking face but wide-awake and wary. A soldier's face, that was it, the face of a first-class staff officer. He had no time to assess the man further, for Janek was issuing orders, and in English.

Then Craig remembered that the Russian probably knew no word of Portuguese, and the other would be a local man with no knowledge of Russian—a man whose identity had to be kept secret at any price. Hence the stocking over his face.

'Amanda, you go first, back to your love-nest in the tower. Move! Now you, Craig. Put your hands on her shoulders, where we can see them. Then you, Luiz. Put your gun in his back and hold the lamp high. And of course, shoot if necessary. That's it.'

The little procession passed through the rooms of the ground floor and up the spiral staircase. As he passed,

Craig turned to look at the window on the courtyard half-way up. It was open and the casement hung drunkenly on its hinges. He heard Janek's voice behind him, 'Yes, that's how we got in. Luiz got on to the roof of the car and shot the hinges off. He's a brave man. He thought you had a gun.' He heard Luiz chuckle, and the muzzle of the gun jabbed his spine.

The lamps were still burning in the tower room. Amanda moved over to the fire; she was still shivering uncontrollably. 'You can thaw yourself out getting us drinks,' said Janek lightly. 'Whisky all round. Craig, over there on the chair by the window. Luiz, keep him covered. Now listen. We're all going to drive away from here very soon. Where's Craig's coat—oh, there it is. Check the pockets, Luiz, please, and let him put it on. We don't want anything left around that belongs to either of them. Amanda, you're coming with me into the bathroom. Get some other things to put on. Something warm if you can find it. Come on, finish your drink. I want to talk to you.'

Some of the colour was coming back into her face. As she turned away from Janek to put down her glass she glanced at Craig and one of her eye-lids flickered almost imperceptibly. Then her face crumpled and she buried it in her hands.

'Don't try to start anything, Amanda,' said the Russian peremptorily. 'You aren't the crying sort.'

'I'm sorry, Milo,' she muttered, 'I can't help it. I've been such a *fool*. There's been so much violence, and you know I can't stand it.' She turned a distraught face towards him, and Craig could have sworn there were tears in her eyes. Then she moved towards the wardrobe, pulled out some things and went to the door. 'It's all right,' she said bravely, 'I'll go and do as you say.'

'If you do nothing but that,' said Janek in a milder tone, 'you'll come to no harm at all. Everything's going to be all right.'

He turned to look at Craig for a moment and then with a gesture to Luiz followed her out of the door. Luiz sat himself on the table several feet away from Craig and propped his automatic on his knees. He was a tall young man, for a Portuguese, long-haired, dressed in old jeans and a dark shirt. The finger-nails of his strong brown hands were broken and grimed with black. Grease, probably; he looked like a mechanic. It was a Browning automatic he held in his hand.

Craig stood up, and immediately the man was off the table and thrusting the gun towards him. 'You sit,' he cried angrily, 'you sit still.' Craig sat down again. The accent had sounded Portuguese, but he couldn't be sure. Perhaps it didn't matter.

Perhaps nothing did matter, as far as he himself was concerned. His chances of living to see the dawn, he thought, were very slim indeed. Amanda was up to something, that was obvious, but what was it? That little scene before she went out was intended to show that after all she was a weak woman whom a man could get to do his bidding. So she was probably trying to convince Janek that she had been bullied by Craig, first into saying that he was armed, and then later into the attempt to escape across the lake. But would he—could he, believe her? And could he further believe her protestations that she had said nothing to Craig about her recruitment as a spy? She would be trying that line, certainly, because if she had assessed Janek's motivations aright it was the one thing he would want to believe. But even if the Russian did believe her, and could go through with his plan—whatever it was —for somehow restoring the status quo, with Amanda as his sole and cherished agent and not a breath of suspicion, what then? God knew how he imagined he could fix it, although it was obvious that the man was no mean operator, but whatever plans he had, Craig would stand in the way. If he, Craig, was supposed not to know about Amanda's intelligence connections, where would he think Janek had sprung from? Who was he? What had he had to do with the girl's disappearance?

Then he remembered something which had struck an odd note, Amanda sobbing, 'I've been such a *fool*.' Not disloyal but foolish. It was a pretty tenuous hint, if it was one, but in Janek's eyes the only *foolish* thing she had done was to see Joao again. Everything had followed from that. Was she hinting that the whole thing could be played down, that she would say that she had only told Craig about her foolishness in getting mixed up in Joao's organization? The half-truth might carry conviction; a denial that she had told Craig *anything* about her secret activities would be certain to be disbelieved.

But again, Janek; where did he come in? An idea struck him. It was the one explanation the girl might say she had given him. If it worked, her life might be saved, so it was worth trying. He himself, he guessed, had been written off already, and so would Amanda be if Janek came to the conclusion that she had admitted to a police officer that she was working for the GRU. After that, he would never trust her again.

The door opened and they came back, Amanda wearing a man's slacks and shirt and a cardigan, positively demure; the Russian had lost some of his urbanity, he looked anxious and was watching the girl's face like a hawk. He brought her to the fire and made her sit down almost solicitously. But he took up a position facing Craig and with his back to Amanda, so that they could not see each other. 'Remember,' he said curtly over his shoulder, 'you are to be silent. Luiz will treat you roughly if you speak. You understand, Luiz?'

The faceless nylon head nodded, and the man slid off the table and sat on the arm of her chair, his gun glinting in the light of the fire.

'Now, Mr Craig. I have very little time, and I want you to answer my questions briefly, and stick to the point.'

'I want to know who you are, first.' That would give Amanda an idea of the line he was going to take. If only he could get a sign from her!

'I said *I* was going to ask the questions. What are you doing in Lisbon? Are you attached to the Embassy?'

'Good Lord, no. I'm just visiting.'

'Is your visit connected with this girl?'

'With Miss Harcourt? Again, no. I'm only here for this

one day. I went to the Embassy and they asked me to help
to find her.'

'What do you mean? Did they not ask you to come to
Lisbon because of her activities?'

'No,' said Craig, with an exaggerated show of patience.
'My ship called here today and leaves tomorrow for
Barcelona.'

'I wonder whether you're telling me the truth.'

'That's an insulting remark, which you wouldn't make
if you hadn't got a gun in your hand. But if you don't
believe me, tell your gorilla to look at the contents of my
wallet, which you spilled on the floor downstairs. He'll
find the landing-card. If he can read.'

'All right. I'll call that bluff, if it is one. Luiz, bring
all the papers up here, please.'

Now, thought Craig. While he's out of the way. Janek
had moved a little so that his back was no longer to the
girl and he could watch them both. But his main attention
was on Craig, who dared not look in the girl's direction.

'Now listen to me for a moment,' he began truculently,
'I knew nothing about what you called Miss Harcourt's
activities until she told me. The Embassy thought she'd
met with an accident. I discovered the address of this
place in her room, so I came here and found her crying
her eyes out over that young man's suicide.' He kept his
eyes on Janek's face, but just inside his field of vision
he could see Amanda's head nod emphatically. Now for it!
'I had to bully her a bit, but in the end she told me all
about you and Joao Costa, and your ridiculous movement
that she was involved with.' He almost felt the intensity of
Janek's cold stare. But the blur which was Amanda's head
was bobbing excitedly. He knew that he had guessed right.

'And what did she tell you about the movement?'

'You know very well,' said Craig impatiently, 'the plot to
discredit the Government, the rat-traps for distributing the
propaganda.' The pale eyes widened suddenly. That was
good. He was telling the man something he didn't know,
something that would deflect his attention from the main
story, perhaps. He followed up fast.

'Neither I nor, believe me, the Ambassador, is concerned with your movement. You may even have some right on your side. But what he will not allow is that anybody connected with the Embassy should have anything to do with it. The girl must leave Portugal and not come back; your precious group must get on without her. We shan't tell the Portuguese, I assure you.'

'Why not? A friendly act towards Britain's oldest ally?'

'How would we have found out, except through Miss Harcourt? She's known to be a former mistress of Joao Costa. The PIDE wouldn't stop until they got the truth. No. All we're concerned with is to get her out of the country. Fast.'

Janek turned his cold glance on the girl, who stared at him submissively. 'There, at least,' he said, 'our views seem to coincide.' Then he fired a question at Craig: 'And what did she tell you about me?'

'Oh, some nonsense about your being a Czech resistance fighter who couldn't get out of the habit of resisting. She said she'd met you in England. But how you got into Costa's group she didn't say, and I wasn't interested anyway. I suppose Costa hired you for your experience— you seem to be handy with a gun—or did you follow her out here?' He added in a disgusted tone, 'She seems to know you pretty well.'

He heard Luiz enter the room. Janek took the contents of Craig's wallet and riffled through them. Then he nodded and handed them back to Craig.

'*Claudia*? When does she sail? And where to, precisely?'

'Tomorrow at four p.m. Barcelona, Cannes, Genoa and Naples, where I get off.' He looked up at Janek. 'And now will you explain all this? And why in God's name did you have to kill that old woman?' Even as he spoke he knew he had made the fatal mistake.

'Because only she knew—' He stopped, frowning. Then he sprang forward and slapped Craig across the face. 'Why did you talk of Costa's suicide? You must have been here, behind Amanda, when I was talking to her from below.

You heard me explain why I killed them both. Why then did you pretend?'

'Because that's what she told me. That he shot himself because she wouldn't marry him.'

'Yes, that's what she told me, that she made you believe it was suicide. But later you knew better, didn't you? And so you're a liar. Perhaps the girl is, too, but that at least is a chance worth taking. As for you—'

He looked at Craig coldly, calculating, and then at Amanda, and Craig knew that if the girl were not in the room he would already be dead. But the Russian could not risk losing the girl's collaboration in the scheme he had in mind, and another violent death in her presence might make her useless. Craig's end was to be delayed until she had played her part, but an end it would be. As if to emphasize his decision he said to the Portuguese, casually, 'You're sweating under that mask, Luiz. You can take it off now.'

The young man hesitated, and Janek repeated impatiently, 'It's all right, I tell you. You can take it off.'

The face that emerged from under the nylon was pale olive, with a prominent nose between bold dark eyes, rather thick lips and a long lean jaw. The hair was almost black and hung low on his neck. He rubbed his face dry with the stocking and took up a stance near the door, watchful, his gun pointing towards the floor.

'We must now act fast,' said Janek in his staff-officer voice. 'Too much time has been wasted already. Luiz, collect the clothes the Senhorita left in the bathroom and anything else of hers—any women's things you can find, and make a bundle of them to go in the van. You'll find a plastic sack in the wardrobe. Put any silver ornaments and valuables in it—those silver candlesticks, the cigar box and so on—and add the fire-irons to make it sink.'

'I'll help him,' said Amanda, springing up.

'Good. You do that.' He turned to Craig. 'We are going to make it appear as if thieves had broken in here after killing the old woman. You will drive Costa's car, with me beside you and his body in the back. Luiz will take Amanda in his van. At a certain place, which I have reconnoitred already, we will stage an accident.'

'And the bullet in his heart?' asked Craig sardonically.

Janek glanced towards Amanda, who was collecting silver spoons from the sideboard. 'That will be taken care of,' he said in a low voice. Craig was impressed in spite of himself, but he tried again to needle him.

'And the old woman's body? Are you going to leave it where it lies?'

'I'm not stupid, Craig. If the thieves had found her there one of the doors would have been open and there would have been no need to break in. And the other question you were going to ask me is what we do with the luggage rack, which was badly damaged when we crashed the gate.'

'Yes,' said Craig, half-smiling, 'I *was* curious about that.'

'It will be disposed of on our way.'

'Why not here?' asked Amanda, who had come up while they were talking. 'In the lake. It's deep enough. I ought to know; I was out of my depth. And you could throw in all the loot as well.'

Craig thought, she's doing fine; not overdoing it, just showing she's on their side.

'You're being very helpful, Amanda,' said Janek, with a touch of suspicion in his voice. 'I don't see why not. Now Craig, sit still and put your hands behind your back. Luiz, tie them with the telephone wire. He's got to be able to drive, so don't stop his circulation. Leave his feet free. Right, now we go down to the gate. Same order as before. Amanda, carry the bundle of clothes. I'll take the bag.'

He went round the room extinguishing the lights. At the drinks table he stopped, picked up the four glasses from which they had drunk and pushed them into the open sack. Then he tipped the table over; there was a splintering crash of broken bottles and a small river of mixed tipple spread over the floor. Luiz pulled out drawers and spilled the contents on the floor. When they left the room, lit now only by the light of the dying fire, it looked as if it had been the scene of a fight between drunks.

At the bottom of the stairs he made Craig and Amanda wait, under Luiz's watchful eye, while he went off to the *sala de visitas* with the sack on his shoulder. In two minutes he was back, and they all went along the passage and out into the entrance by the gateway. The estate-car was still standing in the courtyard, underneath the window through which Luiz had made his entrance. The moon was high, and the marble fountain shone whitely in the centre of the courtyard. Under the gateway it was dark, but Craig could make out the gates, twisted and thrown back against the walls, and the tree trunk and the roof-rack, which had telescoped with the shock of the impact, lying on the ground. Luiz was told to get rid of the rack in the lake and then drive the Squire to the garage. Janek took the other two along the wall of the house towards the stables. Suddenly Amanda stopped in her tracks.

'You're not going to do anything to old Maria?' she demanded.

'I'm afraid so, but you needn't look. There's enough light now to see what we're doing. But you may only turn your back; you're to stay with us.'

They found the body lying on the cobbles of the yard where it had fallen. (It seemed to Craig that years had passed since then; but it was only two hours.) Janek stuck the torch in his pocket and untwisted the wire from around Craig's wrists. 'I'm taking no risks, Craig,' he said harshly. 'You will carry the body to the gateway and leave it just inside.'

'I can't carry her alone.'

'Then Amanda must help you.'

Craig hesitated, then bent down and gently gathered up the old woman's body. There was little sign of blood, and none left on the stones, as far as he could see. He walked slowly towards the gates and laid her down by the passage door. Amanda was weeping, and genuinely now; he could see the tears on her face as she came up to him. 'That was

kind of you, Mr Craig,' she said—they could both feel
Janek's eyes on them—'I'm sorry to have got you mixed
up in this.'

'It's my job,' he said gruffly. 'It's your parents you
ought to be sorry for.' But his eyes, which Janek could not
see, lingered on hers encouragingly. Then he turned away.
'What happens now?'

Luiz was bringing the Squire through the entrance now,
and turning towards the stables. Janek signed to the other
two to follow. There was a small closed van in the yard,
which Craig had noticed when he was fetching Maria's
body. When they came up Luiz had opened the back
and was pulling out a large empty crate, which he carried
across to the garage, where he had parked the Squire.

Janek reached into the front of the van, removed the
ignition key and made Amanda sit inside. Then he signalled to Craig and they joined Luiz, who had brought
Costa's body out into the yard and was lifting it into
the crate, awkwardly, cramming the stiff limbs together
by sheer force to fit them in. There was a pile of heavy
stones ready on the floor of the barn, and he pushed them
into the crate around the body. Then he put the top on
and drove in a few nails to keep it in place.

A scheme was forming in Craig's mind as he looked at the
big American Ford. He knew something about the car, and
the power of the optional seven litre V-8 engine which
Joao had chosen for it. Even for its size the Ford Country
Squire was overpowered for the Portuguese roads, the
front disc brakes were servo-controlled and the huge tyres
belted with fibre-glass. What a car! And he noted with
approval that the passenger seat in the front was inde-
pendent and 'fully reclining'. As he expected, Janek told
him to take one end of the crate, with Luiz at the other.
Then he looked perplexedly at the tail-gate and the keys
in the ignition lock.

'Electric,' said Luiz with a touch of professional pride,
'operated from inside.' The Russian found the button, and
with a whine the tail-gate swung outward, like a door.
The rear seat had already been turned down, pre-

sumably by Costa, and there were eight feet of loading platform. Craig carried his end of the crate to the right-hand side of the platform and Luiz pushed it forward. As soon as the gate would close Craig pushed it home and it locked automatically. Then he turned quickly to Janek.

'You want me to drive?' he said, moving towards the left-hand side.

'Yes. But wait.' He took a length of string from his pocket and made a running noose at one end. He put this round Craig's neck and told him to get in. Then he opened the passenger door, got in and picked up the free end of the string, which he tied round his wrist. 'Just so that you don't try to throw yourself out,' he said mildly. He settled himself against the passenger door, well away from Craig, with his gun-hand holding the revolver in his lap.

'Is this car safe to drive?' asked Craig, clipping on his safety-belt. 'What about the crash?'

'By the time the radiator reached the gates they were open,' said the Russian proudly. 'The shock was bad, but all taken by the tree and the roof-rack. The only other damage was to the wing-mirrors, as you see, and some scratching of the roof.' He smiled. 'What were you hoping for, Craig, a punctured radiator?'

'Yes,' said Craig blandly, as he ran his eye over the controls.

'No luck, we checked. You can start now. Turn right at the main road. After that I'll tell you. And don't go fast, understand? Keep two hundred yards in front of the van, no more.'

Craig operated the control which brought the hide-away headlights up into position and switched them on. Then he started the engine and gave a quick tug to tighten his seat-belt.

'What's the idea of that?' asked Janek suspiciously. 'We aren't going far and I told you *not* to drive fast.'

'What d'you mean? Oh, this thing? I always do that automatically—police training, I suppose.'

'Don't try anything on, Craig. You'll be dead if you do.'

'I'm not a fool,' said Craig shortly, and slipped the automatic transmission lever into position.

He drove slowly out through the archway and across the gravel of the forecourt. As he swung round to enter the avenue he glanced over his shoulder at the house, which when he had come to it had looked so impregnable, and which now stood in the full light of the moon, ravished and brooding on its wrongs. He wondered what the swan was thinking of the shining things that now lay under the water where only fish and weeds and mud had been before.

CHAPTER THIRTEEN

The Arrábida Road

ONE THING was certain, it was a honey of a car to drive. It flowed smoothly over the broken surface of the drive and the sandy track beyond the gates. In the rear mirror at the top of the windscreen Craig could see the lights of the van following. He took the sharp turn into the narrow side-road slowly, getting the feel of the power-steering and the turning-lock. Then he gently pressed on the accelerator and felt the seat pushing his back. He slowed down at once. 'That wasn't intentional, Janek,' he said quietly, 'so don't worry. It takes a bit of getting used to, this car.'

Janek grunted. He was watching Craig with complete attention, but sitting relaxed in his corner. 'I'm not worried, Craig.'

There was no sign of life until just before the junction with the road from Sesimbra to Setubal, when a man in uniform came trudging towards them and turned to stare at the car as it passed. It was hopeless to try anything with him, Craig decided, and turned right as instructed, going in the direction of Setubal and Azeitao.

The road soon left the pine woods and wound through fields bounded by stone walls, with a few white-washed cottages scattered among them. There were no villages; and no place at all where his desperate plan could be put into effect.

He thought he had a twenty per cent chance, and at that it was worth it, because he guessed that to Janek he was already a corpse on the hoof, allowed to live only as long as he could be useful and able if necessary to walk to a place of execution. All he had succeeded in doing, with his play-acting, was to persuade Janek that *perhaps* Amanda was still worth salvaging. For himself, he had no illusions. So it was worth trying, but only if he could find the right place and above all some way of diverting the Russian's attention for just a few seconds. That was all he needed. *All*, he added to himself wryly; he had no doubts about the man's lightning-fast reflexes. It was a tough condition he had set himself. As he drove on, decorously, along the winding road, his thoughts turned to an examination of his enemy.

This was no psychopathic killer. He had shown no compulsion to kill, no joy in killing. That business of closing the eyes of people he had just killed in cold blood—was it so strange? It showed perhaps that the man had feelings for what was due to the dead, feelings quite outside and apart from the grim professionalism of his trade. For there was no doubt about it, he was a professional to his finger-tips, dedicated, ruthless and supremely confident. He had scarcely raised his voice, had hardly had to threaten, but he demanded and got instant obedience. Luiz, who had probably never seen him before, followed his quiet-spoken commands like a well-trained dog. Even Amanda, who seemed to have succeeded in pulling the wool over his eyes, still respected him, although any affection she might have had for him had died when he put the bullet through Joao's heart.

She said he read the classics, and liked quoting Latin poets. What had he muttered over Maria's body—some Virgilian tag? Or was it a prayer? Could a GRU officer have religious beliefs? Was there some vulnerable spot which Craig could work on, to get those precious few seconds he needed so desperately? A glimmer of an idea came to him, but it still depended on finding the right place on the road. He mulled the problem over in his mind, and both men were silent until Janek spoke.

'You're coming to a T-junction soon. Turn right.'

The signpost said left to Azeitao, right to Setubal. The road began to rise between evergreen oaks towards the dark hump of the Arrabida range which was growing higher and more menacing as they approached. The van was still two hundred yards behind. He began to apply a little more pressure on the accelerator, using the silent power of the big engine to draw away imperceptibly from the car behind.

On the left, they passed two stone pillars at the end of a straggly avenue of trees leading to another *quinta*. Then a thin line of poplars, pale in the moonlight, and a road sign marking a hamlet—Casais da Serra. But the few white-washed cottages were shuttered and silent. Only a dog howled dismally as the car swept by.

The road was becoming more exposed now, rising in loops between rolling stunted maquis. Craig could see on the right the broken line of the cliffs, and in one place a glimpse of the shimmering sea beyond. Janek said, 'Turn left at the fork.'

He took again the turning marked for Setubal, and left the little road to Portinho de Arrábida dipping sharply to the right into a forested hollow. So much for any remaining hope of contact with Jenkins, even if he was still waiting at the Santa Maria restaurant.

They were now high above the sea, curling round shoulders of the range which towered above them. As they swung round a dizzy turn, with the ground on the right dropping out of sight and a precipitous curtain wall of rock reaching up on the other side he saw the whole glistening expanse of the Sado estuary. And there, true enough, was what he had only seen on the map—the great sandy spit of land which reached out from the other side to within a few hundred yards of the unseen cliffs below. It was an

eerie sight, thrusting out like a curling black finger across
the bright sea. But it was part of his plan.

As the road wound steadily upwards every curve was
edged with spaced-out granite blocks as a protection against
the sheer drop on the right-hand side. The blocks reflected
the noise of the engine in a rhythmic putt-putting noise as
the car rushed past. One curve after another, interminably.
And still upwards. He could do nothing until they began
to go downhill.

The moonlight was so bright now that colours showed,
bleached like a faded photograph. The scrubby maquis
was beginning to wear thin, and great ribs of granite shone
like old bones in the sweep of the headlights. They were
coming out on to the top of the range now, a hog's back
from which Craig could look down on both sides, over
his left shoulder to the glow of Lisbon twenty miles away,
and on the other side the estuary, with the fire-fly glitter
of the fishing boats and that same dark finger of the Troia
peninsula. The point where it came nearest to the hither
bank must be only a few miles ahead. The lights of
Setubal were still hidden by the rising ground.

Now they were on the last upward stretch, and the van
was a good four hundred yards behind. Janek had checked
once or twice, turning his head, but he was still watching
Craig with close attention and could not keep the other
car constantly in view. Craig could now feel rising tension
in the man beside him; Janek wanted to get the job over,
whatever it was. Perhaps there was some place before
Setubal, where the road ran close to the water and men
would be waiting for him with a boat. There could be no
other explanation for the heavy stones Luiz had put in the
crate. Or was it possible to drop something directly into
deep water? Craig forced his mind away from macabre
speculations; where Joao went, he would go too. He
accelerated up the slope to the shoulder, and maintained the
pressure as they went over the top.

It was a breath-taking view, because at last the whole
sweep of the Setubal coast was in sight, sparkling with

lights, spread in a majestic curve beyond that black finger of peninsula and the calm bright bay.

'My God!' exclaimed Craig. 'It's beautiful.'

'Yes. But keep your eyes on the road.'

'There's a Roman town at the end of that peninsula, where there are no lights,' remarked Craig, letting the car pick up speed on the downward slope. There was a warning sign ahead, a triangle edged in red, marking the left-hand turning. 'I can't remember its name.'

'It was Troia,' said Janek, 'but it's buried under the sea.'

'Good Lord!' said Craig conversationally, 'but that's where Catullus was born.' His voice was calm but his nerves were as taut as violin strings. He got the result he wanted.

'Nonsense!' exploded Janek scornfully. 'He was a Veronese; he never even came here. He was—Look out, you fool! Brake.'

'Sorry!' said Craig quickly, and jammed his foot on the power-brake. The disc brakes reacted smoothly but with implacable force. The screaming tyres held firm on the rough tarmac for three precious seconds before they skidded, and it was enough.

The heavy crate, pulled by the steep slope and the sudden check, slid forward across the loading floor and crashed into the back of Janek's seat. There was a loud 'ping' of breaking metal and the back of the bucket seat folded forward, pinning the Russian against the windscreen. His forehead hit it with a crack which Craig heard dimly as he strove to control the glide before the car was disembowelled by one of the granite blocks. It came to a standstill two feet away, and on the verge.

Craig unclipped the seat-belt which had held his body in place, and whipped round to see Janek, his face bleeding, groping down in the confined space for the gun he had dropped. Craig tried to stamp on his hand but the Russian changed his mind and seized the cord which dangled from Craig's neck and pulled on it with all his force. Craig's head was jerked sideways until he was staring into Janek's face as he tried with both hands to get rid of the thing round his neck which was throttling him. He knew he had only seconds before he blacked out and there was only one way. He threw himself sideways, smashing the rear-view mirror, and butted the other man in the face.

His head caught Janek on the point of the jaw and he saw his eyes close. He clawed at the thong around his neck and felt the dreadful tension relax, then pulled the noose over his head—it was still attached to the Russian's wrist—and drew a deep rattling breath. His head swam with vertigo as he bent down, as Janek had done, to grope for the gun, and he knew—the thought hammered in his brain—that he was too late. That last effort by the Russian had lost him the precious advantage he had gained on the other car.

There was a sudden squeal of brakes. The gun was still somewhere under Janek's legs and he twisted round to see the van halted beside him in the middle of the road, and Luiz leaning across Amanda's lap to thrust the door open and point an automatic at his head.

And he meant business. 'Hands on your head!' he shouted. 'And keep still.' Behind the muzzle of the gun Craig read murder in the dark eyes. He did not hesitate; he raised his hands.

Then he saw Luiz's head jerk backwards and heard him scream. The gun was wavering in his hand. Craig opened his own door violently and knocked it out of the man's hand, but the next moment the Portuguese had hit Amanda in the face with the back of his hand, and the pain made her lose her hold on his long hair. He slid over her legs like an eel, diving on to the road for the gun.

Craig threw himself through the door and rolled on top of him. He swung him away from the automatic and tried to get his hands on his throat, but Luiz's long arms were wrapped round him and they rolled between the cars, each trying to bring up his knee in the other's crotch. There was a moment when Craig saw Amanda's face above him, and the gun she was holding by the barrel as she peered down at the struggling mass on the ground looking for something to hit. That really scared him, and with a violent effort he broke Luiz's hold and lifted the man's head and banged it down on the road. The writhing body went suddenly still and Craig rolled over and got to his feet, gasping. He took the gun from the girl and pointed it at Luiz.

'Look at Janek,' he croaked.

'He's fainted,' she said. 'Or dead. He looks like it.'

'Not him. Watch his hand. There's a gun in there. If they move an inch, scream.'

The Portuguese got to his feet, staggering. He looked at the estate-car and saw Janek's face. '*E morto*,' he cried, and ignoring the gun sprang at Craig. But the muzzle of the automatic struck him on the breast-bone and brought him up short. Then Craig hit him on the side of the head with the barrel and he spun round and staggered back. The bumper of the Squire caught his leg and he fell backwards, his head hitting the road with a loud crack. He lay there, half in front of the estate-car, and did not move.

The girl shouted, 'Milo's waking up.'

Craig pushed her aside and gave her the gun. 'Stay away from Luiz but keep the gun on him.' He looked through the open door.

The lips were moving in the blood-streaked face and the eyes came round towards him and tried to focus.

'Get me out,' said the Russian indistinctly. 'Leg's broken.'

Craig didn't take his eyes off him, but groped in the glove pocket and got out the torch. One of Janek's knees was jammed against the fascia, and might have been fractured. But he was taking no chances. He shone the light on the floor and saw the other gun, and with one hand firmly holding Janek's neck he reached down and retrieved it. Then he shone the torch on the Russian's face.

It wasn't a pretty sight. The blood was welling in a deep cut on his forehead and flowing down his face on to the fascia. His body was still pinned by the pressure of the crate on the seat-back.

'Get me out,' whispered the Russian.

'All right,' said Craig. 'I'm coming round.' He stuffed

the gun into his pocket and backed out of the car. Luiz was still motionless, with Amanda watching him, both her hands holding the gun to stop them trembling. Craig kept clear of Luiz and went quickly round the back of the estate-car to the passenger door. As he did so he heard a movement inside the car, and when he reached the door it was locked. Inside he could just see Janek scrambling sideways into the driving seat. He snatched his gun out and then realized that Amanda was between the two cars, directly behind Janek's body. 'Amanda!' he shouted. 'Stop him! Luiz is—'

Through the roar of the engine he heard a pistol shot, but the car sprang forward with a convulsive leap as the Russian switched the selector to the drive position and the hydraulic transmission took up the strain and prevented the stall. As the car swung outward the off-side front wheel just missed Luiz's head, but the rear wheel, farther out from the verge and already moving fast, passed over his neck with scarcely a check to the car's career. It went forward, still accelerating, weaving from side to side, and skidded round the next curve in a cloud of dust.

CHAPTER FOURTEEN

The Trap

THE GIRL screamed wildly, and he found her kneeling by the body outstretched on the road. It twitched once, and then lay very still, the brown face distorted and the long arms half bent as if to push something away. Craig felt for a pulse beat but there was none, and he could see why. He looked at Amanda and shook his head.

She shrank back. 'Not *dead*—not him too?'

'I'm afraid so. The wheel went over his throat. It killed him instantly, without even waking him up.'

'But he moved afterwards!'

'He was already quite dead.'

She was on her feet now, looking down at the pistol she still held in her hand, and he could see the look of horror on her face. 'I too,' she said dully, 'I tried to kill Milo. To stop him. I *shot* at him—' Her voice was rising hysterically.

'You missed,' said Craig, 'that's the important thing. You're luckily a rotten shot at a yard's range. Don't worry, I've seen policemen do the same. Now come and help me. We've got to move the poor chap to the side of the road.'

But she was still standing frozen, petrified by shock. Then she turned her face towards him, slowly. 'Oh Peter,' she cried. 'When's it ever going to end?' Her eyes were wide open, staring at him appealingly.

He went to her and took her in his arms, holding her body tightly against his and stroking her hair and her wet cheeks as she sobbed and sniffed. She clung to him for some time and then turned and groped in the front of the car for her bag. Her voice came to him muffled by a handkerchief. 'There I go again! I think I'm so tough and bloody smart, and as soon as something goes bang I run to the nearest man and wrap myself round him.'

'Go ahead,' said Craig. 'Any time. Only I thought it was my initiative.'

'You'll know better next time. And anyway, I'll try to behave like Bonnie and Clyde in future. But it all happened so quickly. And what *did* happen? How did you—?'

'Listen, ducky. We've got to get away from here fast. A car could come along at any time. I'm still a bit groggy, so you'll have to help me. We can't leave him here.'

'All right. I'll keep my eyes shut.' She groped for Luiz's feet and between them they carried his body to the verge and laid him down.

'Keep the gun and get into the van,' ordered Craig. 'I've got to find out who he was.'

There was only an identity card and a driving licence, both made out in the name of Afonso Fonseca, both new-looking. Probably false, Craig thought. Luiz's masters had taken no chances when they loaned him to Janek. He put the papers back and turned towards the van—and stopped, frowning. A radio antenna was protruding from the wing.

He got in behind the wheel and drove down the road fast. The main thing was to get away. Then he turned to Amanda.

'That aerial wasn't showing when the van was at the *quinta*. Why did he raise it? Did he listen to bulletins or something?' He pointed to the radio set under the facia.

'He wound it up when we got to the first Setubal turning, and fiddled around in the shelf under the set, and he must have switched it on from there. He didn't touch the set, but it lit up. Then he pulled out a mike—isn't it there still?'

Craig reached down and found first a long torch and then, at the back, the little microphone with a cable attached. 'Go on. What did he do?'

'He didn't have to give a call-sign or anything, just started talking. All he said was "All OK, all OK"—everything twice and in Portuguese, of course—and then, "Both cars starting the climb now. About thirty-five minutes at this speed. See you then." Then he waited and I suppose someone spoke, because he said *"Está bom!"* and switched off.'

'You're sure that was all—it was just like that?'

'Yes. I remember it clearly because of the repetition. But what does it mean? Who on earth was at the other end?'

'The local boys. I thought Janek would need some help. They only allowed him one chap—Luiz—for the dirty work, but they were willing to dispose of the crate and the Squire. Thirty-five minutes? They'll be down on the coast somewhere, waiting, probably in a garage or warehouse. They won't get worried for a bit. We're only ten minutes late on schedule. I'm going to stop for a minute, so that we can talk.' He drew in to the side and switched off the engine.

He took the automatic from the girl, checked the magazine and gave it back. She shivered and pushed it away.

'I've got Janek's,' said Craig, who was examining the revolver as he spoke.

'For God's sake keep them both.'

'All right.' He put Luiz's gun in his other pocket. 'Amanda, I'm sorry about this but—when Janek shot Joao, what sort of gun did he use? Was it an automatic?'

'Yes. A little one. He had it somewhere under his arm.'

'And you're sure Joao had a revolver—this one?'

'Yes. You mean Milo's still got the little one wrapped up in the handkerchief?'

'It won't be wrapped up now. He used the revolver only because there was no longer any need to conceal it.'

'We're not going to meet him?' she asked in a tone of alarm.

'I don't suppose so,' said Craig slowly.

'Peter,' she said suddenly, 'how *did* you do that to the other car? Why did he let you? You were out of sight when it happened.'

He told her and she looked at him curiously. 'You mean you'd worked it all out—the position of the crate and making Milo show off his classical erudition?'

'As Dr Johnson said, it concentrates the mind wonderfully.'

'You mean—he was going to *kill* you?'

'But of course. He couldn't afford to let me go free.'

'I did realize it, I suppose. But I didn't want to believe it. I can't help thinking of him as a person, not as a sort of monster.'

'But you're right. He is a person, and a very cultivated and intelligent one, and that's why the trick worked. He couldn't resist correcting my ignorance—there's a donnish streak in him, isn't there?—and I only had to keep his mind away from the road for a few seconds, till the speed built up. All the same, I was lucky. Ninety-nine per cent of the time he's a single-minded professional IO, and that's what worries me. What's he doing now?'

'Oh God! Waiting to ambush us on the road, of course. Let's turn round and go back.' She pulled at his arm.

'Wait. I'm not so sure. If he blocked the road he'd know he'd be in for a scrap, and he knows I'm armed now. If he tried to pick me off as we pass he'd risk pranging

both the car and you, as well as me. And for all we know he
may still regard you as his most precious possession—he
doesn't know you saved my life by pulling Luiz's hair. That
was very resourceful, Amanda, and brave.'

'It was panic. But surely, Peter, he's too—I mean, you
saw how he was driving that car.'

'Yes. I *think* he's just gone to join his friends and get
reinforcements. He probably thinks we've got Luiz immobilized but doesn't know he's dead.'

'He could have seen what he'd done to Luiz in the rear
mirror.'

'No. That's just what he couldn't. I smashed it when
I butted him, and the wing mirrors didn't survive the
breaching of the gates. And he couldn't have looked back—
he could scarcely control the car as it was. So he may think
Luiz is alive, and seek help to try and rescue him. He'd do
a lot, and so would the Illegal Resident, whoever he is,
to stop us handing Luiz over to the PIDE. But—and this
is what I'm getting at—if he and his friends come chasing
back along this road, and we've already turned back, they'd
never catch us up on the corniche.'

'Well, then? It's obvious we go back. *Come on*, Peter!'

'Isn't there a direct road from Setubal to Azeitao?'

'Oh my God, yes! They'd go that way and cut us off;
it's only about ten miles, far shorter than the way we've
come—in time anyway. It's more or less flat.'

'That's what I thought. So you see—'

'No, listen. There's something we can do if we go on at
once. There's a side-road that links the one we're on with
the Setubal—Azeitao road on the other side of the ridge.
From here it's our shortest way to Azeitao in any case.
It leads off when we get down on to the plain, and they
couldn't possibly get to that turning before we do.'

'Good,' said Craig slowly, 'I suppose that's what we'd
better do.' He switched on the ignition.

She twisted in her seat to look at his face. 'But you
don't want to, do you?'

'I don't like letting murderers get off,' said Craig sourly,
'when there's still a faint chance of nabbing them. For all

we know he may have crashed, or stopped somewhere to get his wits back. And if we went on past the turning for a bit we might find him.'

'Oh for Heaven's sake, Peter, haven't you had enough for one night? You enjoy it, that's what it is—and don't laugh in that superior way. I saw the glint in your eyes when you were fighting.'

'What utter nonsense! It's just that—I'd like to have got it over with him. He's a public menace.'

'What you really mean is that your stupid manly pride is hurt when you run away.'

He laughed. 'I suppose you're right. And anyway, my first duty is to restore you to the bosom of your family. I agree; we run away.' He took the next corner fast. 'And you'd better be making up your mind what to say.'

'I don't know what story to tell yet. I've got to work it out, and you've got to help me.'

'Oh no! For once in your sweet life you'll tell the bloody truth, and no nonsense.'

'That sounds well, coming from a liar as accomplished as you are! All those smooth lies you told Milo with that down-to-earth honest look on your face—it was an eye-opener for me. But actually—' she paused, 'it was all to put me in the clear, wasn't it? You knew there wasn't hope for you?'

'It was pretty obvious, as I told you,' he said. 'But don't worry, Amanda. I've already told you the line you could take.'

'Oh yes, I forgot. All that jazz about my doing it all for MI5 and the Old Country. Well, I can't tell a bigger lie than that, so all you said just now about the truth was just temper?'

'Yes,' said Craig, defeated. 'But I will tell them about your half-scalping Luiz.'

'It was the way he was holding the gun. I hate these bloody guns.'

'So do I, like all good policemen. Now listen carefully. I want you for once to do exactly what I say; there'll be no time for argument. If by any chance Janek has turned

the car and we meet him before we get to the turning—
I can't be sure he won't try something crazy to rescue
Luiz—then I agree we run for it, straight ahead. He
won't be able to turn that big car again in a hurry and in
any case I'll keep the headlights full on so that he won't
be able to identify us until we've passed. He'd never catch
us up. Right. Now, if he's crashed we drive on two hundred
yards and stop. I might be able to do a bit of Boy Scout
stuff—cautiously.'

He overrode her protest. 'I know I said we'd run away,
but obviously if he's handed to me on a plate that's different. You'll take over the wheel and be ready to leave in a
hurry. If I can't get back to you within three minutes
you're to take off for home. I can always walk down to the
next house—look, there are some lights already—and cadge
a lift, but I can't have you and the van remaining on this
piece of road if there's any chance that the Russkies come
surging along. And I'm not going to get you into another
scrap. You've done enough already.'

'I'm not going to leave you like that—'

'Oh yes, you are, if you want me to help you with your
homework.'

'That's blackmail!'

'Do you promise?'

'Oh, all right.'

There were several lights ahead now, down to the right,
but still no houses on the road, and no cars.

'Do we wind down into that lot?'

'No, it's the Fortress of Outao, at sea level. There's a
road along this part of the coast, down below. And you see
those swirls of smoke in front of us? It's a cement works.
We cross through the works on a bridge, and there are some
houses, but then it gets lonely again for a bit until we
reach the turning to Azeitao.'

They rounded a curve and quite suddenly the cement
workings were in front of them. It was like a glimpse of
inferno, with great clouds of smoke, lit from beneath by
the muted glare of the furnaces, mushrooming upwards from
a canyon spanned by a misty web of giant cranes and aerial

conveyors, and throbbing with noise. The straggling road-side trees were pale grey with the acrid, suffocating dust, which chafed the rims of their eyes and filled their nostrils.

'If they ever have industries on the moon,' said Craig, 'that's what they'll look like. There's no sign of Janek; it looks as if he's made it.'

They passed through clusters of small houses, ghostly amongst the figs and olives, with the occasional clump of palms and oleanders all tainted with the dusty blight. Then they were through the last houses and the road ran down-hill between banks of trees. There was a U-bend ahead.

Amanda exclaimed. 'It's there,' she cried, 'there at the bend.'

The big Ford must have run forward at the curve, out of control, and ploughed its way into a thicket on the other side. As they came nearer the headlights shone on a litter of small trees and bushes which had been smashed down before the car had run full tilt into a big pine, whose top branches lay fallen on the roof. At the last moment, as Craig took the bend slowly, they saw the crate still lying against the folded passenger-seat, and something dark which concealed the steering wheel.

'I think that's it,' said Craig, 'but I want to make sure.' He heard the girl's breath coming in great gasps. 'It's better like this,' he said gently. 'He hadn't much future to look forward to.'

'That's what he said about Joao,' she said in a muffled voice. 'Drive on, Peter. I can't stand any more.'

He stopped the car a little way down the road. Around them was utter silence, but they could still hear the throbbing of the cement plant in the distance. 'You stay here,' he said. 'I can't leave him like that; he may be bleed-ing to death. Get into the driving seat and be ready to reverse back to the corner if I call. But don't move until I call. I don't trust him, even half-dead.'

She said nothing, but moved over as he got out. He took the automatic from his pocket and offered it to her, but she pushed it away and hid her face. He held the gun in one hand and took the long torch from under the fascia

board in the other. He switched it on and began to walk
quickly back along the side of the road under the trees. As
he approached the bend he went more slowly until, still
under cover, he was looking at the scene of the crash from
a few yards away. He shone the torch on the front of the
estate-car, but could see nothing for the tangle of bushes
and fallen branches which obscured the side-windows. He
hesitated for a moment, and then went forward, pointing
the torch with his left hand and pushing aside the branches
with the hand that held the gun until he could peer in at the
open window.

The light fell on the figure huddled over the wheel. But
the hair was dark. It was not Janek. It was Joao.

But it was Janek's face that he saw framed in the window
opposite, above the evil silver ring of the muzzle of his
automatic.

It was only the light of the torch, dazzling the man's
eyes, that saved Craig. As he threw himself to the left his
right arm crossed the window aperture and took the bullet
aimed at his head. He felt a hammer blow above his elbow
and his arm flung itself backwards. He spun round after
it and fell, dropping the gun into the bushes. Then the
pain came, unbearably, and he lay back on the ground
with a groan.

A torch shone on his face and he heard Janek's voice,
high-pitched and strained, through the dazzling light. 'I'm
not going to kill you Craig, not yet. Second thoughts. You
can help me. Call the girl. Go on, tell her to come here.'

'Too far away,' muttered Craig. 'Couldn't hear.' He
had to give her time to get away. She surely must have
heard the shot. And he still had the revolver—but in his
right-hand pocket, and his right hand was useless. He rolled
over as if trying to get up and deliberately let his right arm
swing against the side of the car. The shout of pain he
gave was quite genuine, and when he fell back with
eyes closed he felt he could not have staged a better faint.
If only Janek would believe it and go and look for the girl
he would get the other gun. But the other man didn't

move; only the light. It moved off his face and through slit-open eyes he could see it searching for the automatic he had dropped. It was only a foot away, caught in a clump of heather near his right arm—that useless bloody arm. He couldn't risk a grab with his other hand.

But neither could Janek; Craig's body lay between him and the gun. He kicked at Craig's ribs—and stubbed his toe on the hard shape in his pocket. The Russian grunted in surprise and pushed the muzzle of his automatic against Craig's teeth. Then he groped in the pocket and stared down at the second gun in his hand. He threw it away into the bushes, and said in a tired, deadly voice: 'That hope's gone, Craig, and don't pretend you can't hear me. Where are you hurt?'

'Right arm,' whispered Craig. The torch found the dark stain on the sleeve.

'Roll over towards me,' ordered Janek. 'I'm afraid it will hurt, so do it slowly. I don't want a real faint.' He held the gun pressing into Craig's body as he helped him to turn over so that he was again on his back, but out of reach of the fallen gun. It was a painful process, as he had said. 'On your feet. Come on, I'll take your other arm. But don't try any more of your tricks. It's no good this time.'

Craig let himself be helped slowly to his feet. The torch was switched off, and they stood in the moonlight, looking at each other. 'You've finished with her, Janek. You can't use her again. She'd never agree now. You must know that. Let her go.'

He heard the other man laugh shortly, and when he spoke there was again that strained high pitch to his voice. 'You're wrong. She'll do anything I tell her. I've told her what to expect if she doesn't.'

'I told her,' said Craig deliberately, 'that your threat to pin Joao's murder on her was boloney.'

'Yes, I thought that was how you got her to collaborate. But I know how to influence her. So get moving. Go out on the road and call her—or I'll shoot to *hurt*.'

'She must have heard the shot.'

'But who fired? If you call her she'll come.'

'You fool! She's not your property.' He could see
Janek's wild eyes glaring at him under the bandage he
had tied round his head.

'But she *is* my property,' shouted the Russian, 'and she'll
do as I say. Now move or I'll—'

'I'll tell you what you can do, you Bolshevik Soames
Forsyte,' said Craig warily, 'you can stuff it.' And he
elaborated this theme briefly, in coarse and picturesque
terms as he moved forward towards the Russian.

'I couldn't have put it better myself,' said Amanda's
voice from somewhere near at hand. Janek sprang between
Craig and the road.

Craig shouted, 'Run, you bloody fool. I told you—'

Janek laughed harshly. 'Now that you're here, Amanda,
that's all I want. You and that van. We don't need Craig,
do we?' He raised the gun.

'If you kill him, Milo,' she said in a voice that trembled
at first and then became as firm as a rock, 'I'll kill you.
Some time when you don't expect it I'll kill you—*Rogov*.'
Her voice was coming from behind the Russian.

He started violently and thrust himself back against the
side of the car. But his torch was still on Craig.

'Like you killed Luiz,' the cold hard voice went on re-
morselessly.

They heard Janek gasp, and the light switched on to
the figure of the girl, standing in the shadow of the trees by
the road. Craig groped for a branch with his left hand and
somehow thrust his right hand into his jacket pocket, out
of the way.

'You're lying,' Janek shouted.

But she was riding him now, lashing him with the whip
again and again. 'You must have felt the bump when you
drove over his neck,' she said, and heard him groan.
'But you didn't stop. Oh no, you went on running away.
Just like your father, at Minsk.'

'You whore!' he screamed. 'You lying—' but Craig had
launched himself at the silhouette he could see against the
glow of the torch, and his head hit the Russian in the middle

of the back. His arms flung out sideways and he tripped in the debris and fell at Amanda's feet. As Craig staggered forward and fell on his legs she turned round and sat with a solid thump on the Russian's head. Then she snatched off her shoe and as he lifted the automatic struck his hand savagely with the heel. He dropped the gun and she snatched it up and threw it into the middle of the road.

For a moment there was stalemate. Janek was immobilized, but so were they. Then Craig got the man's wrist with his left hand and twisted his arm behind his back. 'All right, get off him,' he shouted, and gave a savage jerk to the arm he was holding. As she got to her feet he let go the arm, seized the heavy torch and as Janek tried to get his arms under him hit him on the back of the head with all his remaining strength. He lay still, and Craig got shakily to his feet. Amanda was standing in the road, one hand to her mouth and the other holding the gun gingerly by the barrel. It was Janek's own gun—a small calibre Beretta. He took it from her and whipped round to look at Janek.

'Thank you,' he said over his shoulder. 'It was brilliant and more than I deserved after making such a fool of myself. I ought to have guessed he might set something up. Now listen. I'm afraid you'll have to help me. This arm's not what it was.'

He was standing near enough for her to see the blood dripping down his hand, which he had taken out of his pocket. She cried out.

'It looks bad, but it isn't.' He looked down at the automatic. 'It isn't a big bullet, and it must have missed both the bone and the artery, thank God. And it went through because here's the hole on the other side.' She was looking at his arm with round eyes, whimpering a little. 'I tell you it's all right. All I want you to do, while I go on watching the fallen, is to get my handkerchief out of my trouser pocket—that one—and tie it round the sleeve of my jacket, just there.' He pointed with the muzzle of the gun. 'Fairly tight. It'll slow down the bleeding and it'll stop very soon. I heal up fast.'

She pulled herself together and did the job neatly. Then she said, in a low voice, 'I acted like a vicious bitch. I said everything I knew would hurt him most.'

'But it worked—as I said, brilliantly.'

'But that's the awful thing. It only worked because he's a human being, with feelings. He's not *just* a spy.'

'Nobody's just a spy. Look, Amanda, we've been through all this before. The fact remains that he's the most dangerous man I'd care to meet, and I'm making bloody sure this time he goes inside.'

'We ought to get some water for your arm.'

'No, it's better as it is. It's bled nicely at both holes, as you see, and the only danger of infection is if some of the cloth has been carried in. But that can wait until we get to a doctor.' He pointed down at the Russian. 'Back to the subject, please. We can't take him with us in case we're stopped. So he's got to be tied up good and tight, and you'll have to do it.'

'All right.'

He went to the car. The tail-gate had been left ajar, and he shone the torch inside. The stones which had been inside the crate had been tumbled out and were lying on the ground behind the car. There was a coil of rope on the loading platform and he pulled it out quickly and slammed the gate shut, wondering what Janek had had in mind.

Perhaps he had blacked out and the crash had been unintentional, and he was planning to start a fire when he heard them coming. The trees all around would have caught and the whole copse would have gone up in flames, with the car, the crate and the body. That would explain why he had undertaken the arduous task of shifting Joao's body into the driving seat, and why he had thrown out the tell-tale stones, which had been intended for a sea operation. The man's stamina, his recovery after the earlier damage to his head and the final crash, were impressive. He looked again at the still body and called to Amanda.

She was standing in the road as if hypnotized, watching

him dully. 'Come on,' he called impatiently. He unhooked his belt and drew it out of the runners. 'Sorry, but you've got to do this. Take the belt and wind it round his ankles twice and knot it. Don't use the buckle. And make a granny knot; it's harder to untie. That's it. Now the rope. Can you make a running noose?'

She said nothing, but made it up. Craig was lifting Janek's body by the collar of his jacket. 'Pass it underneath and round his arms, at the elbows, and bring the end through the noose. Now give it to me.' He pulled the rope tight, put his foot on it to stop it running and made her knot it securely. Then he passed the end through the tight loop of leather which held the ankles together and hauled on it until the lower legs were drawn up. He put his foot on the rope. 'Now pass it round his neck and through the noose again. That'll hold it in place. Good. Knot it. Now the rest of the rope round his lower arms—it'll go twice— and a final knot. Good girl. That'll keep him quiet for a bit when he wakes up.'

'It's horrible,' she said disgustedly.

'But it's necessary, I assure you. I wouldn't trust him not to get free if he has time. That's what he's been trained to do. But I'll see he doesn't get time. Don't spare any sympathy for him. He can breathe. I'll turn him on his side, so that he doesn't choke. Go back to the van. You don't want to look at his face, do you?'

She shuddered. 'No—no, I don't.'

It was just as well, thought Craig. Janek's face, when he turned him over, was a ghastly mess of scratches and bruises and dried blood. But there was no deep wound apart from the one in his forehead, and the bandage showed that that had stopped bleeding. The rest had been caused mostly by the twigs underneath him. The man still lay quite unconscious, breathing stertorously. His body was giving itself the rest Janek had refused it.

The girl was twenty yards away, not looking back. Craig felt in the pockets and found a British passport in the name of Miles Hawkins. Another forgery, provided no doubt by the London Residency. He took out his pen and wrote in big letters across the first blank page—clumsily, with his left hand—'*Sou espiao russo*!' and stuck the open passport inside the bonds where they were tightest. That, he thought, would make sure that when the police arrived they wouldn't untie him in a hurry. Self-confessed Russian spies, he thought with a twisted grin, must be rather rare in Portugal. As an afterthought he rescued the automatic from where it had fallen and pushed the Beretta, the little gun that had killed both Joao and Maria and caused his own wound, into Janek's pocket, bullets and all. He couldn't disarm it with his one good hand but he rubbed the butt through the cloth of the pocket to remove his fingerprints.

CHAPTER FIFTEEN

The Road Home

CRAIG caught up Amanda. Her shoulders were shaking, but he had more sense than to touch her. 'He'll live, you know,' he said.

'I don't care if he doesn't—in a way. It was all that fighting and—and leaving him trussed like a chicken for some rustic policeman to laugh at. I was nearly sick.'

'But you weren't. You're the second guttiest girl I know. Thank God you didn't do as I ordered and leave me to it. If you had I should be dead. You saw what he was going to do?'

'Yes,' she said, sobbing.

'Well, there you are. I don't seem to be able to take on anybody without you to pull his hair or sit on his head like a broody hen. *That* bit was the instinctive move of a born fighter.'

'But I'm not,' she cried. 'I hate it and I'm a coward. I was *quaking*. I've never been so disgusted with myself.'

'I've no doubt your father was quaking, too, when he crawled into a shell-hole to save Charles Jenkins.'

Her head jerked up. 'He never told me.'

'No, he wouldn't. But that's how he got his MC. And if he'd seen your hen act he'd have been very proud of you.'

She laughed. 'Not Daddy—or would he? I wonder.' Then she looked at Craig. 'All right, Peter. Your morale-raising exercise is over. What do we do now?' She started. 'For Heaven's sake, are you all right?'

'Lord, yes. Get in. You'll have to drive. We've got to reach that turning fast.' Then he turned his head. 'Oh hell! Listen.'

In the distance there was the scream of a siren, rising and falling like an air-raid signal. Craig ran to the van and scrambled in. The engine was running before he could close his door.

She drove fast and well. As they raced down the road Craig looked up at the stretch above them, beyond the U-bend. He could see a glimmer of headlights behind the trees. 'Dim your headlights, quick,' he ordered. 'We don't want them to know that there's another car on the road. Drive without them if you can.'

She flicked the lever to parking lights, and found that as soon as her eyes got used to the moonlight she could drive without much difficulty. Craig saw the headlights of the police directly above them; then she drove round a corner and they were lost to view.

They were running down more gently, between olive-groves. He said, 'Can you still hear the siren? It's on your side now.'

She lowered the window and listened, and then glanced quickly up to the left. 'It's still going, but I'm pretty certain the lights aren't moving. They've stopped.'

'Yes, I think you're right. They couldn't have driven past; it was so obvious, right on the bend where they'd have to slow down anyway. Good. How far to the side-road?'

'Not far. When we come to the bottom of the hill. You think they were following us?'

'I don't know. They might have been. I told you the PIDE might tumble to it in the end. They knew I was somewhere in those parts. And if they got to the *quinta*—

no, I still don't understand how they knew we'd come this way. There was no one on the road except that soldier —'

'O God, I forgot Roberto. I meant to tell you.'

'What's that?'

'Roberto, the soldier. The one who was on the road. I tried to attract his attention, but he was staring after your car.'

'*But who is he?*'

'Maria's grandson, who's doing his military service. He must have got leave, but I'm sure the old girl didn't know or she'd have told me. He's the one who saws up the logs.'

'Then you know him?'

'Of course. He's been there once or twice when Joao and I were staying in the house.'

'For Heaven's sake, Amanda, don't you see—? You mean he knew about you and Joao?'

'But yes, of course. Does it matter?'

'Does it—? Yes,' he continued gently, 'it matters quite a lot. But let's get this clear. He knows Joao's car, and he recognizes it—that's why he was staring—and he sees a stranger, me, driving it. He's puzzled, but he goes on to the *quinta*—did he stay with Maria when he was on leave?'

'Yes.'

'Well, there it is. He finds her dead, and your room in a mess, and things stolen. What does he do? I know exactly what he'd do—run for the police or a telephone before anyone can accuse *him* of having done it.'

'He's a decent boy,' she cried indignantly.

'He's a peasant. And all peasants are scared of the police, everywhere. And anyway, it was the right thing to do. I only meant he wouldn't waste time. And he'd report that he'd seen two cars going this way.'

'But the cars might have gone back to Lisbon through Azeitao.'

'It wasn't so late then, and there'd be people in the streets in Azeitao who'd say they hadn't passed through. So it's the Setubal road, or the one to Portinho, and that comes to a dead-end, doesn't it?'

'Yes.'

'Well, there you are. They'd whistle up the first squad car and send it this way.'

'But Peter, if they'd caught up with us it wouldn't have been *so* bad. After all, we didn't kill anybody.'

'I told your father I'd keep you out of the clutches of the PIDE and I'll do that or bust. Look out, there's a car coming. Put your main headlights on.' The approaching lights were still only a glimmer in the trees.

'What did you mean when you said it mattered a lot that Roberto knew about me and Joao?'

'If it weren't for that the case against you at this moment wouldn't be strong at all. But if they know you were often there with Joao they'll find evidence that you were there last night—fair hairs in the waste traps, lipstick on the pillows and cleaning tissues—'

'How perfectly revolting! And I *never* wear lipstick in bed!'

Craig grinned. 'You've given me no chance to find out, have you? But believe me, Amanda, we both left traces all over the place, not to mention fingerprints. We just mustn't give them time before we produce our story and make it stick. What *is* that car? It could be the Russkies.'

'You mean the other lot? Oh Lord yes, it's way after the time Luiz gave them and they must be getting worried. And of course Milo couldn't have warned them, without his little transmitter. They'll recognize the van, Peter.'

'Only when we've passed them. Here they come. But I think it's all right; look at the size of the thing.'

A big covered van went by in a cloud of dust and a rattle of gravel. Craig turned in his seat. 'I can't see it for the dust, but it looked enormous. Keep going fast.' The little van was bumping madly at nearly sixty, and Craig's arm was hurting like fire.

'They've stopped, Peter,' she cried, glancing in the mirror.

'Blast them! They must have a passion for vans, unless —oh yes, that's it. They were going to put the whole estate-car inside and whisk it off somewhere miles away. Clever! How far to the turning?'

'Round the next bend, on the flat.' They careered down the last slope and saw the sign on the left—'Azeitao'. 'The side road's better,' she added. 'No dust.'

'Thank God! That was one break we needed badly. They may jump to the right conclusion but don't let's help them. Switch your headlights off. It's going to take them a hell of a time to turn that pantechnicon round, so you can take it quietly.'

She made the turn and drove gently along the smooth asphalted road which sloped up the bed of a little valley. She soon found that she could cut even the parking lights, for the asphalt was held between two rows of pale concrete slabs which showed up well in the moonlight. They were still in full view of the road they had left, but the large van had not re-appeared. Then, to their relief, they saw the pale track ahead swing round the shoulder of a hill, and they were out of sight.

On the other side of the crest she switched off the engine and coasted downhill. Craig nodded approvingly. They could now hear some of the sounds of the country-side through the open windows—the howl of a dog, and the whine and rattle of a windmill pumping water from a well near the road. The rolling hills closed darkly round the car but here and there a farmhouse gleamed bright under the moon among the patches of eucalyptus trees, whose torn bark glistened like shredded silver in the rustling foliage.

'We've got away, I think, but they may have had to go on to find a place to turn round. I suppose the main road, when we get to it, is good.'

'Very good—and fast.'

'Yes, that's what I'm afraid of. Any ideas?'

'Did you say we'd have to ditch this van?'

'Yes. It's more important than ever, because your friend Roberto may have given a description of it. Where can we do it?'

'Not on this road, obviously. But there's a sort of short cut not far ahead. This road turns sharply to the right and goes on to meet the Setubal road in a T-junction. But at the bend there's a small turning which leads to Azeitao, round the back, so to speak. The surface is rotten and it's very lonely except in summer, when there are people in the villas.'

'That's it, then?' His arm was giving him hell, and he was glad to let the girl make the decisions. She glanced at his white face.

'Yes. But it's going to be tough on your arm, Peter.'

'I'll wedge myself in. Go on. Take that way you said.'

She slowed at the bend and entered the rough lane carefully. It had a stone core in the middle but the sides were dried mud and there were many potholes. It rose steadily between fields and half-tended vines, a neglected countryside with trees straggling along the sides of the road bearing notices forbidding fishing and shooting. On the crest of the hill Craig looked back.

'Still no lights,' he said. 'You'd better bash on regardless. Put your lights on and go as fast as you can.' He braced himself to protect his arm.

The surface was becoming very bad, scored by rains and covered with loose stones, some big enough to make the little van bounce and lurch as it gathered speed. Villas appeared, all closed for the winter.

'Don't talk to me now,' she said jerkily, pulling on the wheel to avoid a rock which would have cracked the sump. 'I'd just—like to see—that bloody van catch us up on this.' Craig had no wish to talk. The fiery pain had eased suddenly and he guessed that the wound had opened—one of them anyway.

The track grew narrower. The lights of Azeitao were visible now, slightly to the right. Then they were running between stone walls above the village, and she slowed down. They passed under an arch between the two halves of a ruined *quinta* and found a broad lane on the right which appeared to run straight towards the village. It was bordered by villas with neat gardens. 'There's no cover there,' she decided. 'We'll go a bit farther. We've got to stash this thing somewhere.' She came to an opening in the stone wall on the left and stopped the car. 'What about that?'

Craig got out slowly and went to look. It was a good place, a narrow opening into a peach orchard, with grass underfoot, and the wall was high enough to hide the van. He helped her to reverse the car through the opening and park against the wall. There was no track leading through the gap and Craig thought that with any luck the van would escape attention. But he wanted it to stay put. He opened the bonnet with his left hand and called the girl. 'Do you know what a rotor head is?'

She looked at him scornfully and reached in to detach it. She took her handbag from the seat and put the rotor inside. 'Now what?'

'Your clothes.'

She opened the back of the van and shone the torch inside. The bundle had come undone from the battering the car had received, and her shimmering dress, a brassiere and a diminutive pair of pants were scattered around on the dusty floor. Nothing else was there. She crammed the underclothes into her handbag and held up the dress, looking at it ruefully. 'That was supposed to be an exclusive model,' she said ruefully.

'We could bury it somewhere,' suggested Craig helpfully.

'*Bury* it? Not on your life. I'll resurrect it somehow.' She rolled it up carefully and put it under her arm. 'What about all those bloody guns?'

'There's only one—Luiz's automatic. That was in front of me, under the fascia. Could you get it out, please?' He showed her how to release the magazine and take out the bullets. 'Right. Throw those away into the grass as far as you can—into those bushes by the wall, that's it. Now put the magazine and the gun into the van where they can be seen.'

'What about the other two?'

'Janek threw the revolver away and I left his Beretta there.'

She looked at him suspiciously. 'Why?'

'Oh never mind,' he said irritably. She looked at him and exclaimed.

'You don't look so good, Peter. It must have been hurting very badly. Let me have a look.'

'No.'

'You can't go around with that bandage on.'

'It's painful, that's all. But you'd better take it off.'

She put the torch on the ground and gently undid the bandage. Then she drew his hand out of his pocket, picked up the torch and yelped with horror. His hand was crusted with dried blood and the shirt cuff was soaked and still damp.

'It's all right,' said Craig impatiently, 'it's stopped bleeding, I think.' He was feeling tired and almost past caring.

'Come on,' she said firmly, 'we've got to clean you up. There's a water trough the other side of the lane. We'll go there.'

She put his hand back into his pocket and took him by the other arm. When they reached the trough she carefully pealed off his jacket and washed his hand and the lower part of his arm. Then she gently bound the handkerchief over the wounds, on top of the shirt-sleeve, as Craig directed, and made him sit down against the wall while she did her best to clean the jacket, drying it with some grass. The pocket was stiff and sticky with blood, but showed little on the outside. She helped him into the coat, brushed him down and collected the torch and her rolled-up dress.

'There,' she said, 'we're reasonably respectable, except that these slacks look a bit odd and I'm not wearing a bra. But there's no time to put it on and I can always walk a bit round-shouldered. Are you feeling better?'

'Very much, thanks.' And odd though it was he did. The cool air and the fresh feel of the damp coat-sleeve against his inflamed arm made a lot of difference, and he felt he could think ahead again. 'Now listen. When we leave here, with no GRU van, no guns and our honest faces, we're two ordinary people. Janek's colleagues don't know us by sight. We just walk into the village and get a taxi, if there is one.'

'I don't suppose there'll be one, but there are buses all night on the Lisbon road. But they go to Cacilhas, not over the bridge.'

'Is that where the ferry is?'

'Yes.' She looked at her watch. 'It's nearly eleven, so they won't be running to the Praca do Comercio, but there are still ferries to the Cais do Sodre, even if we don't get there till midnight. But look, can't we telephone from here— the cafe's still bound to be open—and get Daddy to pick us up? Then you can rest properly.'

He was much tempted but he shook his head. 'It's that blasted telephone. As soon as the PIDE knew where we were telephoning from they'd send a police car along before your father could hope to get here. And I don't like the idea of a taxi either, even if we could get one. We'd attract too much notice. No, we'll telephone him from the other side of the Tagus.'

They were walking down the lane, and it brought them out on to the main road at the edge of the village. At this point the road swung away from Azeitao towards Lisbon, and although a few cars came past they did not turn into the village, which appeared empty of people and traffic. As Amanda had said, the cafe was still lit up, but there was no one at the petrol station or in the cobbled square, bordered with pollarded limes, which sloped up from the street to the entrance of the Tavora *quinta*.

'The bus stops over there,' said the girl, 'in front of the cafe, but I think we'd better wait under the trees. We do look a bit odd, as I said. And we can see the bus coming in plenty of time.'

They walked slowly over the cobbles and found a seat under the limes. It was very peaceful in the darkness heavy with the scent of the blossoms, with an occasional whiff of the wine bodega a few yards down the street, and they sat contentedly, without speaking. They had to readjust themselves to such somnolent calm, after the night-mares of the mountain road and the noisy bucketing of the van.

Then Amanda said suddenly, 'Peter, who's the other girl?'

'What d'you mean?' he asked sleepily.

'When you passed me all that flannel about being the second guttiest girl you knew.'

Craig started. 'Did I say that? How ungallant! I thought you were magnificent. I mean, the way you—'

'Who is she, Peter?'

'Oh, a girl I know. Not like you at all.'

'Not like me?' She thought it out. 'I think I can see her —pretty, isn't she, with such trusting eyes, and about knee-high.'

'Oh don't be cheap, Amanda. And incidentally, she's nearly as tall as you are.'

'A big girl, is she? And gutty. Some heavy from the hunting counties? Takes her fences straight and keeps a stiff upper lip?' She glanced sideways at his furious face and gave a delighted laugh. 'My God, I've got near it, haven't I? She does ride a horse. And what a wonderful seat she's got—for a horse, I mean. Where—'

'Amanda,' said Craig sombrely, 'my right hand may be a bit dicky, but I could still catch you a dirty great wallop with my left.'

She jumped up and stood away from him. 'Oh my man,' she breathed ecstatically, 'the things you do to me! If only—Look out! There's the bus.' She began to run towards the cafe, everything else forgotten. 'We'll pretend we're lovers,' she called over her shoulder, 'then people won't be curious.' Craig grinned and got to his feet.

Three or four people were erupting from the cafe at the sound of the horn, followed by a smaller group who came to see them off. The bus was half full of sleepy passengers from Setubal. Amanda pulled Craig into the bunch of country people crowding around the step, and in the jostling for position nobody seemed to notice them. The

girl paid the driver and found seats at the rear. She
pushed Craig towards the window, so that his arm would
be protected, and sat close, looking up into his face ador-
ingly. He played his part, put his arm around her and
settled her head on his shoulder. Then he told her firmly
to go to sleep.

Which, surprisingly, she did. Not at first, but slowly. In
the thick warm atmosphere of the bus, her head grew heavy
and her breathing slow and regular. He felt a sudden rush
of tenderness, which was something new. He had respected
her courage and her intelligence but had been really shocked
—there was no other word for it—by her frightening lack
of responsibility, and completely baffled by her motivations.
And he couldn't forget the hurt and dismay on her
father's face when he had learnt about her involvement
with Costa and his group. She had really seemed to go
out of her way to flout every article of the code of
loyalties and conduct which was the essence of her parents'
lives.

The bus squealed to a stop as it came alongside a cafe
on the road. The girl started violently and opened her
eyes, terrified. Then she turned and looked up at him with
a contented smile. She kissed his cheek and was asleep
again, her face snuggled into his neck, before the bus
began to move.

It was that captivating warmth of personality, he thought,
as well as her looks, which must have driven young Costa
crazy and deceived Janek. There was no equation which
fitted that warmth and also the ruthlessness, the histrionics
and the reckless playing with fire. Yet she seemed to know
her own mind; that extraordinary story of planning and
scheming to become—of all things—a Russian spy didn't
make sense, but at least it seemed to have succeeded. Even
right up to the end Janek had believed that it was he who
could call the tune, when all the time she was planning to
use him as a pawn in some weird ploy of her own. He
looked down at the gleam of the sun-bleached strands in
her hair and the smooth line of her cheek, and wondered.
Then he, too, fell asleep.

When he awoke the bus was running smoothly on the short stretch of motorway, and just when the lights of the bridge came into view they turned off to the right towards the ferry, which was some way upstream. Shortly afterwards the bus rattled through the streets of Cacilhas and out on to the quays, and people were starting to chatter again and gather up their parcels. He shook the girl and she sat up, yawning, and blinking at the lights. Then she struggled to her feet.

'Come on, Peter, we're there.' She smoothed down her slacks and looked at them. 'They're not as tight as I thought they'd be, but they're four inches short and I shall look a fright. Poor little Joao, he hated being shorter than me.' (So much, thought Craig, for the man she had seen dead and stuffed into the driving seat of the Squire like a dummy.) She went on, 'I'm getting hungry. How's your arm?'

'It's easier. I slept. Come on.'

They climbed down and walked across the cobbles to the ticket office. The air was fresh and clear, and the lights of Lisbon sparkled over the water. She bought the tickets and they took their places in the queue of people waiting for the barrier to go up. The ferry boat, carrying a lot of passenger cars on deck, came swirling alongside and within a minute the first cars were beginning to come ashore.

CHAPTER SIXTEEN

The Ferry

CRAIG LOOKED AROUND. He could see no signs of a police check, nor anyone interested in the girl or himself. He wondered where the big van had got to. Perhaps it hadn't contained baddies at all; perhaps Janek had had no support but Luiz. But it seemed very unlikely—and then he remembered the transmitter. There *was* a supporting team, somewhere. But what did they know, and what were they planning?

The crowd surged forward suddenly, crossed the pontoon and swarmed on to the open deck, where a handful of Lisbon-bound cars had already been parked. Craig and Amanda found a place on the rails between two cars, and looked across the agitated water. There was still traffic moving on the broad bosom of the Tagus and downstream they could see the suspension bridge outlined in lights, and this side of it, against the far bank, the *Claudia*, lit up from stem to stern. He pointed.

'That's where I'm supposed to be, drinking a thoughtful scotch and water before going to bed.'

'Poor Peter. She looks pretty, doesn't she? But you can still get there, as soon as we've got home.'

'Not a chance, ducky. There'll still be a lot to do.'

The engine-room bell rang loudly and the shore-hands cast off the ropes. The tubby little ship swung out from her mooring and the deck beneath their feet began to tremble as the blunt bows pushed their way through the water.

'When we get to the terminal,' said Craig, 'we'll ring your people. I don't know what the PIDE may have been doing since Joao's body was found, and it's just conceivable that you ought to go straight to the Chancery building and not to your flat. And anyway, the sooner we let your mother know you're safe the better.'

'Poor Mummy. I'll ring her.'

'You do that, and I'll ring the PIDE.'

'Good Heavens, them? Why on earth?'

'I want to switch their attention on to Janek. I'll make a statement for Ferreira, a PIDE officer I can trust—'

She laughed scornfully. 'You must be more gullible than I thought, Peter. Joao said they'd rape their grandmothers. And can't you leave Milo alone?'

'No I can't. And don't be so damned forgiving. We want him safely inside—not just in some country nick—and his friends on the run. Otherwise they can still make a load of trouble for you. For God's sake don't underestimate them. I'll call the duty officer and dictate a statement for Ferreira, saying who Janek is and adding that I've got you with me and will report to him tomorrow. I shan't say anything else—just enough to make the DO feel he's got to play the tape to Ferreira over the telephone and get him out of bed so that he can take care of Janek.'

'Loyal collaboration with the PIDE?'

'That's it. And high time, too. The sooner I can make that gesture the better I'll be pleased. Now we've got to decide what we tell everybody.'

'You were a bit cagey about that, but I gather you wanted me to tell the truth but not the whole truth. But not to the PIDE surely; that's going too far.'

'But it's necessary. They know such a lot about the part you played in Joao's group—'

'But how could they?'

'They probably followed you and saw you attend meetings. But take it from me. They do. What we'll say is that you broke with Joao because you were getting too involved.'

'But I didn't. I *believed* in what they were doing; in fact I—' She stopped. 'Anyway it was Milo who insisted I should leave them.'

'I know that,' said Craig impatiently, 'but when Milo did that he happened to be acting in the best interests of Her Majesty's Government. As far as the PIDE is concerned we've got to credit you, although you don't deserve it, with enough common sense to have realized that you were going to create a hell of a lot of trouble for the Embassy if it came out. So you decided you couldn't risk it, and for *that* reason—and no other—you dropped the group last Christmas.'

'There was no risk,' she said sullenly. 'We were very careful.'

'You weren't careful enough. The PIDE knew. I can't tell you any more. Just get the story into your obstinate head : you were no longer involved because you had decided it was unwise, and you agreed to meet Joao solely to tell him that your affair with him was at an end—we can't conceal that part of it, with young Roberto around. Right. So what was Janek doing? He was muscling in on a dissident movement, to subvert it to Soviet ends. The

PIDE will be prepared to believe that; they always said General Delgado had communist backing in Algiers, didn't they? Well, that gives them grounds for a long hard look at Janek. Alias Rogov.'

'But he'd never have——' she began to protest.

'Oh shut up, Amanda!' His arm was aching again. 'I'd much rather leave you to it and get back to my comfortable ship, but it's your parents and the Embassy I'm thinking of. How else *can* you explain Janek's intervention?'

She thought it over. 'But it's such a lousy thing to do.'

'Oh give me strength! Wasn't it a lousy thing to tell Marshal Rogov's son that his father ran away?'

'Yes, it was horrible. But I had to. If he hadn't lost his temper he'd have killed you.' She looked out over the water at the farther shore, and said slowly, 'Yes, I see what you mean. I agree there's no alternative.'

'What I still don't understand is why Rogov told you about his father. It's the last thing he should have done.'

'Well—you're not going to like this, I expect, but it serves you right. There was a place Milo and I used to meet at weekends, during term. We were keeping it all very quiet—part of my training, he called it. A quiet pub on the Thames, near Reading. Most people at Oxford who want a dirty weekend go somewhere nearer. Anyway, we didn't eat downstairs much. There were two single rooms with a connecting door. All very proper.'

'It sounds like it!'

'Peter, I warned you. Well. One evening we arrived there separately, as usual, and I went up to my room and got out some iced vodka I'd brought in a vacuum flask, and some smoked salmon—lots of it because we both liked it. And then I went and opened the door into the next room, and there was Milo lying on the bed with a newspaper on the floor beside him. And he was crying.'

'He was *what*? I wouldn't have thought he could have squeezed out a single tear.'

'Well, he was. He was shattered. He told me his father had died, and he'd just heard about it. Through a friend, he said as a sort of afterthought. And then—I suppose I didn't know what to say, and I picked the paper up—it looked untidy on the floor. And he snatched it out of my hand, but not before I'd seen the headline. Marshal Rogov, Hero of the Soviet Union, had died after a short illness.'

'I remember,' said Craig thoughtfully. 'A lot of Soviet generals died last year—and all after a short illness. There was speculation about it.'

'Milo was convinced he'd been liquidated, and was— you must believe me—he was distraught with grief.' She stopped for a moment. 'I know it's the same man we saw kill Maria, like swatting a fly—that was the worst thing, the unforgivable thing he did—but what I'm telling you is part of him, too. That's why I can only see him as a person, and why I still say things that you think are just sentimental. Do you understand, Peter?'

'Yes. Yes, I think I do.'

'You see, his love for his father and his pride in the Soviet Army were the main things in his life. He must have been brought up in what passes for luxury in Russia— servants, good food, the General's quarters, the military clubs, the dacha in the country, all that—but it was the discipline and traditions of the Army that meant most.'

'As they might have for you, if you'd been born a boy.'

'Oh no, not me. But you're right in a way. That background was a sort of bond between us. He was curiously respectful when he spoke of my father.'

'But why did he join the GRU?'

'Well, it's staffed from the Army, I think, and I imagine they just posted him. He was young and brainy, and they wanted someone to train as an expert on student resistance in the satellites. So he took a genuine degree in Roman Law at Brno, and when the crisis came he was already a leader in the resistance. And then they saw the possibility of getting him into England under natural cover. He was a cinch for the generous people doling out scholarships to deserving refugees. But he had to prove himself, and more than ever after his father had been liquidated. If he could establish one long-term, really high-level agent like Philby or Maclean he'd be in the clear. If not, he'd have failed, and all the pride and panache would have gone out of his life.'

'Don't get *too* poetic about it, Amanda. Aren't those just the things you most object to—the loyalties and the hierarchy and even national pride?'

'Of course. I told you, they're rotten; they're at the root of half our troubles. But I *can* understand how people come to depend on them. It's what I've been brought up on —the Regiment, the battle honours, the turn-out that's always better than the next-door lot of chaps, "the type of young officer we're getting" '—she was imitating her father's clear, precise tones—'plenty of dash and zip, bags of initiative—'

Craig was infuriated. 'But damn it, you silly girl, those qualities are worthwhile. You don't come by them easily. That's what the traditions of a regiment are about, to attract the best men.' He glared at her. 'And take that motherly grin off your face. It's like patting me on the head.'

'You see, you're one of them. I wouldn't like you so much if you weren't.'

'And that's a fine bit of logic. Let's get back to your precious Milo. And let me make this clear. I'm not sorry for him. He's a murderer and a spy. And spies may have their ideals and they may be fine as fathers of families or— as you tell me—in bed, but they're still spies. Termites. If you can't exterminate them you stand the legs of your chair in saucers of water. That's security.'

'And you forget to top the water up,' she jeered, 'and your comfortable chair crumbles into dust. And a damned good job, too.'

'You're an anarchist. But one thing's certain. You are never going to be a spy. I can see to that and I will. And anyway, how were you going to become what you modestly called a high-level agent as an interpreter? You'd never see the pay-dirt.'

'Oh,' she said casually, 'that was to be just the beginning. You meet all the top people who go abroad on missions.

Milo was determined that I should finish up as PA to somebody in the Cabinet. He had it all worked out.'

'And you?'

'Oh well, I'd have shaken myself loose from Milo in the end. Told MI5 and got them to push him out of the country, I suppose, before it became too serious. I wasn't looking forward to that.'

'I'm not surprised. You probably wouldn't have survived. But what did you want to be—a political leader, another Bernadette Devlin?'

'Well, she didn't do too badly. She was an MP at twenty-one. I've started more slowly, but then I want to understand all the strings of power before I start pulling, and with luck I'll go further.' She turned to look at him appraisingly. 'It's no good, Peter. You wouldn't understand.'

'Let me try.'

'All right, but look, the other boat hasn't left.' They could see the bulky shape of the other ferry against the lights of the Cais do Sodre, and their own boat had slowed to a standstill.

'Good,' said Craig. 'The longer we wait here the better. I must get to the bottom of this, for my own satisfaction.'

'Well, as everybody knows, all of us—the young, I mean —are fed up to the teeth with the mess our elders have made of the world. It's not only two useless world wars, but what's happening now. They go on making the wrong decisions over and over again. They never learn. They just spend their time explaining, and in the end there *will* be a holocaust, and it's we who'll be left to carry the can. It makes you want to vomit.'

'I agree, but there's nothing new in all that. I can't do anything about it, so I get on with my job.'

'All you're doing,' she said bitingly, 'is keep the leaves shiny on the biggest aspidistra in the world.'

'And what's your alternative? Anarchy?'

'There's a lot to be said for anarchy,' she said judiciously. 'The trouble with political parties is that the scum comes to the top.'

'It's supposed to be the cream.'

'Oh, don't quibble, Peter. The point is that it's the wrong process. By the time they get to the top they're tired men, and chained to their parties.'

'They don't all look tired,' said Craig mildly.

'None of them has the imagination or the energy or even the intelligence they had at thirty. It stands to sense. What we want is people who become leaders first, and make their own parties. And the media we've got now make a nonsense of parliamentary democracy, anyway. That's what a lot of the revolt is about, people learning to influence and lead other people. They don't necessarily believe in all these sit-ins and strikes and demonstrations, but by God they believe in themselves. And they get their ideas known on the telly; that's where the real power is, and the parties have to toe the line.'

'But the mass of the people who demonstrate and strike aren't trying to be leaders?'

'Oh no, they're genuinely protesting. Why should they be kept in their little boxes like battery hens? So what happens? They break out and scratch around in deep litter. And love it,' she added scornfully.

'And what are you—a bird that likes to range free?'

'I think that's rather a good description, one way and another.'

'Well just remember that someone, sometime, is going to wring your pretty neck. I've wanted to do it myself several times in the last few hours.' He paused. 'So that is what you're trying to make of yourself—a leader? Someone who can form public opinion?'

'Yes. And that's why my friends and I, in England and abroad, have got to get all the experience we can. And my job is to be an expert on intelligence. The techniques, targets, personalities—everything I can find out.'

'Good God! You mean you planned to work for the Russians, and then double-cross them and learn something about MI5, and put your acquired knowledge into the kitty?'

'More or less.'

'But did you really imagine,' said Craig, his mind reeling, 'that both services were going to lie down and let you walk over them?'

'They'd never have known if all this hadn't happened. I've got to start all over again now, and the awful thing is I may not have much time.'

'Before your neck gets wrung? You're darned right.'

'No. That's just a professional hazard. It's just—I ought to know better than tell you, but it's so worrying—it's this nightmare I have sometimes. I meet this goon who *really* sends me, and I go all womanly and want to have babies by him, and get married and spoil everything. I wake up in a muck sweat.' She looked at him appealingly.

He tried to keep his face straight, but couldn't make it. He put his arm round her shoulders and burst out laughing. 'I'm awfully sorry,' he gasped, 'but I can't help it. All that stratospheric ambition and calculated unscrupulousness—I know how seriously you feel about it—all going to pot because—'

She shook herself free. 'It's not funny,' she said coldly, 'it's a serious hazard. Haven't you learned any history?'

'I read it at Cambridge.'

'Oh, *there*,' she snapped bitchily, 'well, even there they must have taught you something about Mark Antony and all the others who mucked everything up because of some floozy.'

'But damn it, they were men!'

She gave a triumphant laugh. 'Oh Peter, you fell flop into that one. You can only mean that women ought to be tougher.'

'I could mention some—'

'Yes,' she said more quietly, 'you're right. I *am* tough. But I'll have to be even tougher. All this happened, and three people died, because I tried to be kind to Joao Costa. I can't forget that. I never will.'

CHAPTER SEVENTEEN

Hide Out

THE BEAT of the propellers stopped and the ferry-boat swung gently against the wooden pontoon. It was well-lit and Craig could see clearly the small throng of people waiting to take the boat back to Cacilhas. There seemed to be no control apart from the ticket-collectors at the barrier, but then he stiffened and moved behind the deck house, pulling the girl after him.

'What's the matter?' asked Amanda. 'You're pointing, Peter, like a gun-dog. I can't see anything.'

'Those two men there in front of the crowd. I can't show you. The bulges in their suits, gun in the hip pocket and transceiver at the left breast. We won't leave together; you go a few yards ahead. Where can we telephone?'

'There's a cafe on the right-hand side of the square with a public telephone. I've been there.'

'OK, we'll meet there. Try and pick up another woman as you go ashore and start chatting to her in Portuguese. It *might* put them off, but you can't hide those bloody long legs and your hair.'

He watched her walk forward quickly and push into the crowd against the rail. She apparently succeeded in losing a shoe, because he saw her holding on to another girl of her own age and pointing downwards. Someone good-naturedly cleared a space between the jostling bodies and found the shoe. She thanked him and put it on, still holding on to the girl and chattering loudly in Portuguese. There was a roar of laughter at something she had said, but the next moment the rail was slid back and the whole crowd charged forward, with Amanda lost amongst them.

Craig followed more slowly, breathing the smells of engine oil and fish, cigars and roasting coffee, which drifted on the night air. She was still talking to the other girl when they passed the barrier and Craig saw one of the plainclothes men look at her uncertainly. But then he saw Craig's tall broad-shouldered figure coming towards him, the face unmistakably British, the arm thrust stiffly into the side pocket. ('Good Lord, thought Craig, he'll think I've got a gun there.) He couldn't draw his hand out easily because his arm was very stiff, so he let it stay. The man, rather to Craig's surprise, let him pass, but he could sense that he was being followed as he skirted the open space by the water and crossed into the square.

On the opposite side of the *praça* he could see Amanda taking leave of her friend, who insisted on shaking hands, and turning to cross the square. By the time she reached the café he was already on the telephone. He got through to Harcourt at once.

'Craig here. It's all right, she's with me. We'll—'

Harcourt's precise clear voice interrupted him. He spoke fast. 'Listen, Craig. There's a warrant out for her arrest and they're insisting we waive immunity. A PIDE officer's here now. Costa's been murdered. Keep her away. We're getting a legal chap from London. Keep—' There was a high-pitched buzz which made Craig's ears tingle. The monitor had jammed the line.

He joined the girl, who was sitting in front of two large brandies. She passed him one and he took a quick drink. Then he looked around, but the agent must have been waiting outside.

'Thanks,' he said. 'I really needed that.'

She looked at his face. 'You look very dicky, Peter. Let's get a taxi. Is Daddy all right?'

'Yes. But we aren't. We've got to go into hiding, for the night at least. They've got a warrant out for your arrest.'

She put down her glass with a jerk and stared at him. 'Me? How did they work that out?'

'It's what I was afraid of, as soon as you told me about Roberto. They've good reason to suspect you were with Joao—I told you they'd find traces—and you've disappeared, so they think you're responsible. They don't know anything about the others, and there's the break-in to explain, but they'll still go for the obvious suspect. The Embassy's getting a Foreign Office lawyer and they want me to keep you away from home until they know where they stand.'

'Oh, *poor* Daddy!'

Craig smiled involuntarily. The girl never ceased to surprise him. 'It's you I'm worried about. We've got to hole up somewhere. And there's a man outside who picked me up as I left the boat, and of course he's seen you now. Come on—ideas! No hotel's any good. Charles Jenkins will be blown by now. *Where?*'

She finished her glass, frowning, then jumped to her feet. 'Jack Davies. He'd play. He's—'

'Your quondam boy-friend. Lives in the Alfama. Yes, that's a good thought. I rather liked him.'

'How on earth—?'

'Tell you afterwards. We've got to get rid of that tail first. If I can hold him up for a bit you can slip away and take a taxi to the Alfama. I'll come along as soon as I can.'

She looked at his pale face. 'No violence, Peter. They're awfully tough, and look at you, practically rocking on your feet. Thank God you haven't got that gun any longer.'

'I told you I don't like guns, but I think I've got a chance. You've been trained to isolate someone following you, if Janek did his stuff. Where can we do it?'

'I know a perfect place, only a few yards away. Come on, I'll show you how we do it in the GRU.' She looked at him with an impish grin on her face. Then she led the way to the door.

They stepped out into the square. A small yellow tram was racing round the central flower beds and rocked over the points to tackle the steep slope of the Rua Alecrim on their right. On his tall pedestal the Duque de Teixeira, in all his petrified Victorian dignity, glowered darkly down. Under a nearby tree another dark figure was staring at the entrance to the cafe.

'Come.' Seizing Craig's hand she drew him across a street into a narrow passage which skirted the abrupt rise of the Rua Alecrim and led down to a small street that tunnelled beneath it. They heard steps behind them. The passage was almost completely dark; it smelt of tomcats.

'Good,' muttered Craig. 'Just the job.' He gave her a little push. 'Go on, and as soon as you get to the bottom run for it. I can hold him for a bit.'

Opposite the end of the passage, on the other side of the narrow street, was a dimly-lit cafe, but otherwise there was emptiness, and the black shadow of the bridge carrying the Rua Alecrim above their heads. Amanda slipped away into the shadows, and Craig turned back to face the man whose footsteps he could hear behind him in the passage. As the plainclothes man stopped in his tracks Craig went up to him with the hand in his right pocket pushing forward. The pain of straining his arm made him look ferocious in the dim light, and his voice was hard and threatening.

'Keep still, Senhor,' he said, as the man tried to dodge round him after Amanda. 'You are molesting the *mocinha* and me.' He made a threatening gesture. 'Turn round and go.'

The policeman stood his ground, but his frightened eyes were on the pocket. Then he made up his mind and prepared to make an arrest. '*Sou agente de policia*—' he began. But the edge of Craig's left hand struck down savagely at the side of his neck. He dropped to the pavement, just inside the passage.

A tram roared overhead, breaking the silence and splashing the small street with light. Craig stepped into the darkness beneath the bridge. His left arm was gripped and Amanda whispered urgently, 'Has he gone?'

'He's out,' muttered Craig, and dragged her into the parallel passage that led back to the square. 'You idiot! I told you—'

'There should be taxis in the square; there's a rank by the station.'

They emerged into the lights of the square, which was deserted except for a few people straggling from the ferry towards the station. There was no sound behind them from the shadows under the Rua Alecrim. As they crossed the wide road which led to the docks Craig felt the hair on the nape of his neck prickle; someone was coming across the square, under the trees. He had forgotten the second agent.

The rank beside the station was empty and no taxi was in sight. Far down the road from the docks a tram was approaching, bucketing along the empty street. The stop was within a few yards of where they were standing.

The man had paused in the shadow of a tree and had pulled something out of his pocket. Craig saw a glimmer of hope; the tram was coming nearer, but still no taxi. 'We'll take the tram. But go on pretending to look for a taxi.' The tram stopped.

'Wait till just before it leaves.' He glanced at the plain-clothes man, who had finished the message on his trans-mitter and was walking across towards them, with an occasional worried look over his shoulder at the entrance to the passage. He could not think what had happened to his chum.

The tram's bell clanged sharply. Craig ran and grabbed the handrail and swung himself on, with Amanda in front of him. The man had started running, but he was too late.

'He'll probably look for his side-kick before he reports,' said Craig, 'which might give us a few moments' start. Where does this tram go?'

'It's a good one. Along the river through the Praca do Comercio and then there's a stop at the Arco do Rosario, which is what we want. But won't they follow?'

'It's not so easy,' said Craig. They were sitting in the almost empty tram, which was travelling fast, with no traffic to stop it. 'He can't chase us on foot especially if as I said he's gone to look for his pal, and it won't be so easy to find a prowl-car at this time of night. I think we've got quite a chance to get away with it.'

A low archway tunnelling through the thickness of the

houses opened on to a small *praça*, deep as a well between
the tall old buildings and the Visigothic wall at the far
end. A fountain dripped into its carved basin, and the
light of a single lamp glinted on a tangle of cats.

Craig stumbled on the uneven paving. Each of his feet
was a separate burden and only the pain in his arm felt
fresh and fiery. They climbed a flight of steep steps, and
he longed to sit down and fall asleep to the soothing sound
of the dripping water

The girl pulled at his arm. 'I know you're desperately
tired, but it's not far now. Only steep, all the way.' She
put her strong arm under his elbow.

'Tired yourself,' mumbled Craig. They came out into
the little square with the baroque church, now locked
and silent, turning blind windows to the moon, like the
houses which crowded around. Cats were slipping, dream-
like and intent, towards the alleys that led down to the fishy
cobbled streets of the market.

They crossed the tilted pavement of the square and into
the little cul-de-sac. From one house came the sad wail
of a fado, and through the faint cracks of light around
the shutters they heard the throb of a guitar. 'At least someone is awake besides the cats,' Craig muttered. 'I hope
Davies isn't on the tiles, too.'

She hauled him up the steps of the little house and rang
the bell. There was a long silence, and then the window
opened and the bearded face appeared, addressing them
pungently in fishwife Portuguese.

'It's me, Jack. I've got somebody with me. Let us in
quick; we're in a jam.'

'Great Jesus, Amanda! Tell the boy-friend to muck off.
We don't want him, do we?'

'He's hurt, you fool. There's been a scrap.'

'Jeeze-us! Hold it, I'm coming.'

They heard his big feet thumping towards the door and
it opened. He seized the girl by the neck and kissed her
lavishly. Then he pulled them inside and turned to Craig,
who was standing under the light in the passage. 'It's you

again. So you found her. My word, cobber, you do look crook.'

Then he turned suddenly to the girl. 'Where were you hiding?'

'Oh, in the country. But it doesn't matter—'

'But how did he find you?' asked Davies, with a suspicious glance at Craig.

'Oh for Heaven's sake, Jack, I don't know. He wouldn't tell me.'

Davies's face split in an enormous grin of relief. 'Well, come along in.' He led the way into his studio. 'Now then, what's wrong?'

'It's Peter; he's been shot.'

'Good old Amanda, always bring trouble, don't you? Oh, it's his arm, is it? Sit down, friend, and let me have a look.'

He eased off the jacket. 'The shirt's stuck. Hang on a moment. I'll get some things.' He ran down the passage to the bathroom and came back with some bandages, a pair of scissors and a packet of sulphonamide powder. 'Go and get us some drinks, beaut; he'll need his. But bring the gin first.'

He had Craig sitting in the armchair, and was cutting the shirt away from the wound. 'Did it go through?'

'Yes,' said Craig, his teeth chattering as he drank from the glass Amanda was offering him.

Davies poured some gin on to a pad of lint and began to clean the blood away. He had left two patches of shirt over the wounds, but the skin as it emerged to view was red and angry.

The girl looked on, worried. 'Do you know about this sort of thing, Jack? If you touch him with anything from here it'll go septic.' She cast a disgusted look around the chaos in the studio.

'Yes, love. I was an ambulance chap once. Nights only, so's I could paint during the day. Come on, my beaut sheila, make him finish his snort.'

'Oh talk proper, Jack darling! You overdo this *rive*

gauche lark. Just look at your pad. I thought I'd taught you—'

'When you left me,' he said cheerfully, as he gently dabbed gin on the patches of shirt, 'I reverted to type. I couldn't see a clean plate without thinking of my lost one. It may look a bit disordered, but it's functional. You know you were lucky, Pete. It only missed the artery by the skin of its little lead nose. Have you had a tetanus shot recently?'

'Yes. A few months ago, before I went to South America.'

'Good. Now I'm going to hurt a bit. The scraps of cloth I left over the holes have loosened up, so I'll pick them off. Right. Now I'm going to wash the wounds very gently in gin and then put the powder on. That's all I can do. Ready?'

The sting of the alcohol was not as bad as Craig had expected. Both wounds were almost entirely plugged with dried blood. He lay back in the chair and let Davies finish the job with the powder and a neat bandage. The Portuguese brandy was warming him already and he felt better. Davies went off again and came back with some aspirin.

'Amanda will give you some of these before you go to sleep. You'll have to doss down here, of course. You've had it for the time being.'

'Oh, thanks, Jack darling.' Amanda patted his hairy cheek. 'Isn't he a doll?' she said to Craig proudly.

'Oh, he's a doll all right,' said Craig sleepily. 'And thanks, Jack, we'd like to. I've got to get moving first thing tomorrow, though.'

'It's tomorrow already.' He looked at Amanda. 'You're a bit peaky, too, love. When did you last eat?'

'Lunch. And Peter too, I suppose. We could both toy with some food now. But have you got anything?'

'Plenty of eggs and bread and butter. I'm hungry, too. Can you cope, Amanda?' He was busy making a sling out of two large handkerchiefs.

'Yes, darling.' She disappeared into the passage.

'Now, Peter, what's it all about?'

'I told you she was mixed up with a resistance group led by her boy-friend Joao Costa.' He could hear Amanda coming back through the door, and raised his voice. 'She and Costa were at a *quinta* near Azeitao and some other people turned up who were involved in the same movement —I don't know the details—and there was a fight. Joao Costa was killed.'

'Killed? Good God!' He turned to Amanda, who was standing in the doorway. 'I'm very sorry, girl.'

'It's all right, Jack. But they got Peter in the arm, too. We ran away, but it took us several hours to get transport and when we arrived back in Lisbon Peter telephoned Daddy. But he said there was a warrant for my arrest, and to keep me away for the time being until the Embassy can straighten it out.'

'But you're a diplomat's daughter. They can't hold you.'

'They'd have a damned good try,' said Craig. 'In a murder case our Government might have to waive immunity. So it's essential for her to go to ground until I can convince the PIDE that they haven't got a case at all. I think I can, but it's a bit tricky.'

'You're durned right it's tricky. If they believe that load of codswallop you've both just told me I'm a Dutchman.'

'It's *almost* all true, darling, every word we said.'

'Then you missed out a hell of a lot. Why couldn't you ring up for a car?'

'The telephone had been broken,' said Craig stolidly.

'Oh fine!' said Davies scornfully, turning to Amanda. 'I'd have thought *you* could have trusted me.'

'It's all too complicated,' she said firmly. 'And really, love, it's better you don't know the whole thing. But I'll tell you something he missed out. He slugged a cop. We couldn't have got here if he hadn't.'

Davies roared with laughter. 'Now that's the sort of thing I like to hear. Cop-slugging used to be a pastime of mine, but these days—' he grinned ruefully at Craig, 'my hand seems to have lost its cunning.'

Amanda looked at them both suspiciously. 'What's all this "not before the little woman" stuff?' she demanded.

'Darling,' said Davies, 'no one could call you that.' He put an arm round her appreciatively. 'Oh all right. I'll buy it. Now what about that grub? Go back to your kitchen, lovely.' He began to clear a section of the crowded table and put out cutlery and glasses. 'I've got some good Dao wine, and there's always the Aussie beer and the brandy. You don't want to get up too early, do you?' Sounds of cooking were coming from down the passage.

'About half past eight. That'll give me time to clean myself up and get round to the Embassy by the time they open.' He lowered his voice. 'Look, Jack, I think you ought to know. Amanda's in a real jam. Whatever happens I'm afraid she'll have to leave for England tomorrow or the day after. And not come back.'

Davies turned his head away. 'Thanks, chum. It stops me making a fool of myself again. I didn't really think she was going to come back to me, anyway.' He paused. 'Now let's make you comfortable.'

Amanda had found some garlic and herbs and made an enormous omelette, which she brought in triumphantly. Then she took off the towel she had tied round her waist, put her arms round Davies's neck and kissed him. 'Beneath all this rugged exterior,' she told him lovingly, 'you're a dolly angel. I knew we could count on you.'

He patted her face. 'I think you've stuck my angelic head into a beehive,' he said, 'but I do like honey. Anyway, you've both had it for today.' He picked up his fork. 'After we've eaten we'll put Pete up on the sofa,' he added, pointing to a vast shabby couch at the other end of the studio, 'and you can sleep with me on the divan. And darling, I mean *sleep*.'

CHAPTER EIGHTEEN

PIDE Headquarters

PETER CRAIG awoke. It was broad daylight, and through the open window he could hear cheerful sounds from below. His arm was easier, and only hurt when he moved it. He got up slowly and looked across at the divan. They were still fast asleep, Amanda's head on the man's shoulder and her arm flung across his chest. He went quietly into the bathroom and shut the door.

A bath, which he yearned for, would be too complicated, but he washed and then shaved himself with Davies's razor. Then he found his jacket, which the girl had cleaned very competently and hung by the geyser to dry, and managed to get it on and fit the sling for his arm. He looked at himself in the glass. His shirt was not too bad and at least he looked respectable. He went into the little kitchen next door and made himself a strong mug of coffee, which he drank while he heated more water. He looked at his watch. It was nearly nine o'clock. He made two more cups of coffee and took them into the studio on a tray.

They looked very young, both of them, sleeping with total abandon, and he was loth to disturb them, but during a long wakeful period in the middle of the night he had put his plans in order and he had to tell Amanda what he had decided. 'Wake up, love-birds,' he said, shaking the girl's shoulder. 'Coffee.'

It was a long job, but in the end he had them sitting up with their arms round each other's shoulders, blinking and yawning. He served them with coffee and sat down beside them.

'Now listen, Jack. I don't think for a moment there can be anyone on to us here, and I'll get away all right. But I don't want Amanda to go out on any account. She's far too conspicuous. I'm going to the Embassy and I hope to get the PIDE man I know to meet me there. If he won't play I'll have to go to his office, and that'll take time. When everything's arranged I'll either ring or come and fetch her. But I'm anxious to keep your name out of it as far as the PIDE's concerned, so until I feel sure they've called off the hunt I won't get in touch. Right?'

'OK.' Davies turned to the girl. 'Pete seems to know what he's doing. So you stay where you belong, sheila.' He grinned wolfishly. 'In bed.'

'Yes, darling. You're right about Peter; he uses his head—butts them with it, I've seen him. But Peter,' she looked at him anxiously, 'what exactly am I going to say? You promised to help me.'

Craig looked at Davies, who nodded sagely. 'You want to talk secrets? OK. Nobody can say I don't know when I'm not wanted.' He stood up on the bed and jumped over Amanda on to the floor. 'I'll have a bath. This is quite an occasion.'

When they were alone Craig said, 'Listen, Amanda. I want you to follow this carefully. We'll tell the truth as far as we can, but all the same there are going to be three versions of it.'

'You old twister,' she said admiringly, 'so the first version is what you told Jack last night?'

'Yes. That's for the PIDE. The whole story except for your previous acquaintance with Rogov. He comes in as a Russian muscling in on Joao's group. We've got him —they must have put him inside last night—and Luiz's body and the transmitter to back it up, and I think I can make Ferreira believe it. There's just one thing, and it may be very important. You remember Joao told you he had something to show you?'

She was on her guard at once. 'Did he?' she said vaguely. 'Oh yes, I'd forgotten. But he didn't.'

'Do you know *why* he didn't?'

She hesitated. 'Peter, this is something to do with his political plans—something we had talked about. But the very first thing I told him was that I wouldn't get involved with his group again, and in the end he knew I meant it. But I'm not going to tell you about it so you mustn't ask me. There are other people involved, still alive and safe, and it's their secret, not mine.'

'That's all I wanted to know. Now, your father and the Ambassador have got to know the real truth about Rogov and your agreeing to spy for him, as well as what actually happened yesterday—all of it. But—I don't like this part of it, but it'll save a lot of unhappiness—I'm going to *imply* that you were working all the time for MI5.'

'But you can't! It's not true. It's not *me*. Look, I don't tell lies to them—my people, I mean—whatever else I do. Not big lies—I mean I don't count saying I've been spending the weekend with a girl-friend when I haven't —but what you're asking for is a whopper. I can't,' she added primly. 'It's a matter of principle.'

'Oh don't be silly. It's a matter of whether you want to make your father thoroughly bewildered and ashamed of you, or not. If he thinks you were acting under orders from the Security Service it makes sense, and what's more neither he nor H.E. can expect to be told details because you won't be at liberty to reveal them.'

'My God, Peter, what a corkscrew mind you've got! You mean under the Official Secrets Act?'

'Yes, of course. You'd have signed the OSA but more than that there is the rule about need-to-know. They won't *need* to know the details of your contacts with MI5. So for Heaven's sake let's give them that straw to grasp at when they're trying to understand your extraordinary conduct. It simplifies the whole thing. Don't you *realize* that if you insist on saying that you were recruited as a spy and *didn't* immediately report the approach to the British authorities, H.E. would have to hold you in the Embassy under guard until Special Branch could fly someone out to take you home. And where would your precious plans be then?'

'But I keep telling you—I never did spy for him.'

'It doesn't make all that difference. You agreed to work for a Soviet intelligence officer. That's quite enough for

Special Branch. They couldn't make a proper case of it but they'd have a lot of fun trying, and all your associations at Oxford and here would come under scrutiny.'

'But if I say this, what happens when I get back to England? Are *you* going to tell MI5 the whole truth? Is that your third version?'

'Yes, of course. They'll have to know, and they'll put you through it when you get back home. But at least, if I tell them you were just playing Rogov along until you felt you had something to report—playing the fool, in other words—they'll treat you only as mentally defective. And serve you right.'

'You're just a policeman after all,' she said resentfully. 'You make all my plans sound so drab and sordid.'

'Oh give me strength! I don't suppose all I'm planning to do to help you—including ruining my leave—will do a blind bit of good. But if I do succeed in getting you off the hook I'm going to make darned sure that you never get involved in the spy game again. Not in England, anyway. The people in Five will see to that, after they've heard what I've got to say. You'll just have to tell your precious co-leaders of the revolt that your speciality will have to be labour relations or anti-pollution. But not espionage, Amanda, oh dear no!'

She looked up at him for a time, thinking. 'What you're doing,' she said, 'is to get my story sorted out by MI5, rather than by your heavy-footed colleagues?'

'Yes, that's what it'll amount to. And they're reasonable people.'

'Oh all right,' she said. 'I'll let you manage my affairs.'

'That,' said Craig, smiling, 'would need a computer.'

'I didn't mean that, you idiot.' She suddenly pulled his face down and kissed him. 'I know that according to your lights you're being very good to me, and I *am* grateful, really. I'll do as you say.' She kissed him again, and whispered in his ear, 'We're a good team, aren't we? And you're a masterful beast, and I love you.'

'You'll scare the pants off me. Stay here until I get in touch.' He was leaving, but turned back. 'Amanda.'

'Yes, darling.'

'Be kind to Jack. He's still in love, you know.'

She lay back on the bed and arranged her hair thoughtfully. 'I'll keep him quiet,' she said. 'You know my methods, Watson.'

The sunlight was brilliant when he came out into the little square. The streets were full of people and as he went down the alley towards the Largo do Chafariz the market was as strident and colourful as before. The Alfama was familiar to him now, and the warmth and vitality of the people stirred his blood. He would have given a lot to stay there, strolling and exploring, through the archways and alleys, and always finding new glimpses of that little medieval society. But the first flight of steps he had to take jolted his arm, and his mind came back reluctantly to his job. He knew he had to have all his wits about him to make a success of it.

The first sign of trouble came when his taxi dropped him at the Chancery entrance. He had expected to see an *agente* on duty, but the man outside the gate was accompanied by an officer in a double-breasted blue serge uniform. There was a big silver star on it, and as he approached Craig could read the words on the blue enamel centre— 'Policia Internacional'. The *agente* was behind him, and out of the corner of his eye Craig could see a black car moving slowly forward.

'Mr Craig, isn't it?' said the officer in excellent English. 'Yes.'

'Would you please accompany me? Sub-Director Ferreira would like to have a word with you.'

'By all means, a little later. I have an appointment with His Excellency the Ambassador.'

'He is at the Ministry at the moment, the Ministry of Foreign Affairs, and isn't expected back for some time. Your appointment must have been postponed. But you could no doubt see him after you have had your talk with the Senhor Sub-Director.'

'I'm sorry. I must see his Excellency first.'

'I'm afraid that will be impossible. I have orders to take you to Headquarters.' The polite tone had hardened, and the policeman had taken out his automatic and was looking down at it speculatively.

'I must protest,' said Craig, 'but to save you inconvenience I'll come with you. Did you have orders to arrest me if I didn't?'

'Yes, sir.' He signalled to the driver of the black car.

The car took a switchback route from the bottom of the Rua Sao Domingos a Lapa, running east, parallel with the river, until they came out suddenly in the middle of the town, where the Rua Alecrim crosses the end of the Rua Garrett, the Chiado. From the busy shopping street the car turned down the Rua Antonio Maria Cardoso, a drab, almost deserted street with a row of old buildings on its left-hand side. There were two faded yellow palaces joined by a terrace garden with an open garage below, in which Craig could see rows of gleaming black Citroëns. There was a line of brown-painted doors, all closed, in the left-hand palace; in the other there was an entrance under a flag and the PIDE escutcheon. It was not an inviting place. The door was opened and he was led in.

Ferreira was dressed in a lounge suit. He was sitting at his desk when Craig was shown in, and he did not rise to his feet. He pointed to a chair. There was no sign of friendliness in his face, or in what he had to say.

'You have a good deal to answer, Craig. You deliberately disregarded my advice, which I could scarcely have put more strongly, you got involved in at least one murder, it appears; you helped the guilty party to escape and finally—and I admit I find this hard to believe—you held up one of my agents at the point of a gun.'

'You're right not to believe that last accusation, Vicente. It's quite untrue. You don't imagine I'd have delivered myself to you like this if I had been guilty of such a thing? And look at this—' he nodded towards the sling—'my right arm had a bullet through it and my hand was in my pocket.'

'And your left hand? What did you do with that?'

'That's something I'm very sorry about, Vicente; but I acted in good faith. Now you tell me it was one of your men I can only apologize most sincerely. I suppose he thought I had a gun in my pocket, poor chap. It all becomes clear.'

'What is clear,' said Ferreira coldly, 'is that you've missed your vocation. You ought to be on the stage. But what you really mean is, that's your story.'

'That's my story. And if it ever came out, instead of remaining just between you and me—I mean if the foreign press heard about it—my account of what happened would be accepted without question. Just imagine,' he added, smiling at Ferreira. 'Who would believe that an armed PIDE *agente* wasn't able to control an unarmed foreigner with only one bare hand to defend himself with?'

'And who would confirm that you were wounded at the time and that you hadn't got a gun?' He laughed cynically. 'Miss Harcourt, I suppose.'

'Yes. Miss Harcourt. May I tell you her story now? It will help to establish her credibility as a witness.'

'That would strain even your powers of invention, but yes, if you wish. I'll revert to the other matter later.'

'First let me say this. Although I've had a lot to say to her in the past twelve hours or so I respected your confidence and I did not disclose to her any part of the detailed information you gave me about her part in the activities of the Gonçalves Costa group. I give you my word as a friend. All I said, and this was necessary to convince her of the danger she had run in agreeing to see young Costa again, was that I had no doubt the PIDE had regarded him with suspicion for his political activities.'

'I see,' said Ferreira noncommittally.

'Costa was pressing her to marry him and insisted on a meeting. She had broken off her friendship with him several months ago, as you told me, because—' he paused to give emphasis to the words which followed—'she had come to realize that her association with the group could lead to serious trouble.' (Strictly speaking, he thought with some satisfaction, it was perfectly true, in those terms.) 'But she did, very foolishly, agree to meet Costa because she hoped to convince him that she hadn't the slightest intention of marrying him. He took her, against her will, to the Quinta dos Cisnes and kept her there.'

'Overnight?' remarked Ferreira mockingly. 'The poor girl!'

Craig ignored the interruption. Now for it! 'Early yesterday morning the Russian turned up.'

'What Russian?' asked Ferreira, his eyes wary.

'The man the police found tied up by Costa's car. Your people did find him?'

'Yes. They found a British subject with some nonsense scrawled on his passport. He was hurt and is in hospital under guard. He hasn't talked yet. But he will.'

'He's a Soviet intelligence officer. The GRU.'

'*Cristo Rey*! That was what was on the passport, but—'

'Yes, I wrote it. I know him and his background. He is the son of Marshal Rogov—the late Marshal Rogov. He is based in England.'

Ferreira stared at him. 'Then what is he doing here?'

'Obviously something in connection with Costa's group. I thought you would have known all about him. Didn't your inside man tell you—'

'No. We had no idea who he was.' He hesitated. 'Are you sure of this, Peter?'

'No question at all.'

'Just a moment, I'll double the guard on him.' He spoke into the telephone. 'Now. Tell me more about him.'

Craig appeared to consider. Then he said. 'Frankly I don't know much myself—it's not my job. But I think I could get you more about him and his activities in England—promoting student unrest and so on—but it would have to be on a completely unofficial basis. You understand, my superiors would have me on the carpet at once if it got out. But just for your background information I might

get you quite a useful dossier. Only you mustn't act on it
—you mustn't use the information in court. Is that under-
stood?'

'Yes. But I hope this isn't another story, Craig.'

'Good God no!' said Craig disgustedly. 'Another man was
killed last night on the same road—you'll see the connection
in a moment—but did you know this?'

'Of course. But he'd been run over. It was a simple
accident, apparently, although there were other contusions
which—'

'I'll be very frank with you, Vicente. That man—I only
know him as Luiz—tried to knock me off. The girl grabbed his hair and I got his gun and hit him with it. But
what killed him was that Rogov ran the car over his neck.'

'Hm. And who is he?'

'I imagine a man supplied by the Soviet Illegal Residency
here, in Lisbon, to help Rogov to get rid of the body. He's
a Portuguese, so you can identify him and check his
background.'

'For God's sake start at the beginning. How did Costa
die?'

'Rogov shot him. They had quarrelled—don't ask me
why—but the girl saw the shooting.' He overrode Ferreira's impatient interruption. 'And later I saw him kill
in cold blood an old woman who looked after the house,
because she had found Costa's body and was going to call
the police. There was nobody else in the house. After the
shooting he locked the girl in one of the towers and that's
where I found her, while Rogov had gone off to get help
to dispose of Costa's body. Before I could take her away
Rogov returned with the Portuguese, Luiz. We tried to keep
them out, but I had no gun and they smashed in the gate
and captured us.'

'Tell me the rest in detail, please. And in order.'

Craig did so. From that point he had nothing to hide.

Ferreira kept his eyes on the other's face until he had
finished. Then he thought for a moment. 'But what I can't
understand—if this extraordinary story is true—is why
Rogov took such elaborate trouble to make it appear that

the house had been attacked—and the old woman killed
—by thieves. And what did it matter *where* Costa was
killed? Rogov and this Luiz could have disappeared. You
said Luiz was wearing a mask and Rogov isn't known here.
He could have gone back to England, once he'd done what
he came to do. And for Heaven's sake, what motive did he
have for killing Costa? The whole thing doesn't make sense.'

'I can't understand it either, unless—'

'And why,' continued Ferreira, 'didn't he kill off you and
the girl at the same time? You were the other witnesses.'

'It was easier to take us on our own legs to where he
could have liquidated us, I suppose. He had some plan
in his mind. Perhaps he'd have held us somewhere until
the enquiry into Costa's death had cooled down.'

Ferreira considered. Then he said, 'You were going to
say something just now, when I asked you why he killed
Costa and took so much trouble to remove him from the
quinta. You said "unless—" and then I interrupted you.
What were you going to say?'

Craig kept him waiting while he rose from his chair and
took a few steps around the room. The whole story fell down
on Ferreira's objections; this was where he had to produce
a solution which really would hold water, and he had prepared it during that painful night on Jack Davies's couch.
And it was the right moment; he could feel Ferreira's
hostility softening.

'There *is* an explanation,' he said, returning to his chair,
'but only you can say if it fits. It was something you said
yesterday which gave me the idea. When you were telling
me about Costa's agit-prop exercise. You said you didn't
know—it was the one thing your informant couldn't tell
you—where the propaganda was to be printed. Is that
right? He still can't find out?'

'That is right,' said Ferreira, with suddenly quickened
interest.

'The *quinta*'s quite extensive. There are a dozen places
where machinery and stores of paper could be hidden. I
wonder *why* Costa was using that great estate-car, unless

he had something heavy to cart around. And I wonder whether Rogov knew or suspected that it was all there—the press or duplicating machine or whatever it was, and the paper, and perhaps the addresses of the distributors and the material for printing.' Ferreira rose slowly to his feet and stood staring down at him.

Craig felt in his pocket. 'When I found Costa's body it was lying in a barn next to the garage, and there was a lot of packing material lying on the floor. Amongst it I found this.' He held out a label, stained with blood—he had pushed it into his right-hand pocket and it had remained there in spite of Amanda's cleansing of the outside of the jacket—but with the address still just legible. Costa's name and Lisbon address were typed under a legend in heavy black print : 'Duploportuguesa SA, Oporto'.

Ferreira looked at it thoughtfully without speaking.

'What does the firm make?' prompted Craig.

'Duplicating machines, including quite big ones for turning out thousands of copies.'

'Yes, I thought it might be that,' said Craig, 'and it occurred to me that Rogov must have seen it too. Or rather he could have seen it, because it was he who carried Costa's body into that barn. So there you are. I've nothing to go on, Vicente,' he added modestly, 'but isn't it possible that Rogov was planning to move in and take over the whole operation, and perhaps give it a Communist slant?'

The Sub-Director slapped his hand down on the desk, hard. 'If that's true, he'll tell us. And in the meantime we'll take that house apart. If we find what we're looking for I shall be in your debt, Peter.'

'You'll have to interrogate him in either Russian or English. He had to speak English to Luiz. And incidentally —there's one thing you *will* find there—the silver. And also the roof-rack, which was badly damaged by the crash. I forgot to tell you that they threw it all into the lake from the windows of the *sala de visitas*. I heard him talking to Luiz about it.'

Ferreira's eyes brightened. 'Well, that's something. We've

got the Ministry breathing down our necks already. But Rogov—are you sure it's the Marshal's son?'

'Yes. There was no mistaking him if you remembered the photographs of his father. As I said, I can't tell you how we know that he *is* Marshal Rogov's son, but you may be able to bluff an admittance from him.' He paused. 'You've got a case for a wonderful row with the Russians, if you want it.'

'Yes,' said Ferreira slowly, 'if we do.' He added, with a sly smile, 'You and the girl would have to give evidence, of course.'

'Make statements, for your own use, possibly, if the Ambassador agrees. But not evidence in court. I wasn't a witness to Costa's murder, which would be the main charge, I presume. As for Miss Harcourt, if I make a full report to the Foreign and Commonwealth Office, as of course I shall, you won't have the ghost of a chance of getting her diplomatic immunity waived. Whatever foolishness she may have been guilty of in the past—and of course I take your word for that; she's said nothing to me—she did nothing wrong this time.'

'That is asking too much of my credulity!'

'But it's true. She really is the most remarkable young woman, and brave—my God, the girl's got guts!'

Ferreira looked at him with an expression of knowing cynicism. 'So she's got you under her spell now, has she?'

'I always have an affection for people who save my life, especially when they do it twice in an evening. But I can tell you one thing, Vicente. *You* won't have any more trouble from her. She's learnt a lesson she won't forget in a hurry.' And that, he thought, was the biggest lie of the lot.

Ferreira considered. 'That's what I want to make sure of. If I let her go, would she come here voluntarily and make a statement to me personally?'

'I think so, but I'd have to ask the Ambassador. And what do you mean—let her go? You haven't got her, have you?'

'You don't have to rub it in, Peter, the fact that a

senior British police officer is hiding her away from my men. You do know where she is?'

'Yes.'

'All right. You can take her to the Embassy, but she won't be allowed to leave the country until I'm satisfied with her story. And you can tell His Excellency that, with my compliments.'

Craig stood up, feeling slightly unsteady with relief. 'You're taking a very civilized line over this, Vicente. Don't think I'm not grateful.'

'We're a civilized people.'

'May I ask you this? Would you be quite glad to see the whole affair hushed up?'

'No I would not. *I* want murderers and enemies of the State tried and convicted. But in the case of Rogov the Cabinet might not be so enthusiastic. As you said, it would mean a first-class row with the Russians, and I'm not sure this is a good moment. But it's not my decision.'

'It just occurred to me. You might swop him.' He used the English word.

'What does "swop" mean?'

'Exchange him. I read in the papers a few weeks ago about that young Portuguese of good family who was convicted of spying in Russia for the CIA. Mondim de Basto, wasn't it? It seemed a bit hard, because he only did it for the kicks, and he's quite well-connected here, isn't he?'

Ferreira laughed shortly. 'That is one of your British understatements. That young man is the reason why I said this might not be a good moment for a quarrel with the Russians.'

'Well, then. What have you got to lose? You could negotiate with them in secret—I'm sure you've got some channel which has been used before—and if they don't want to exchange your de Basto for their Rogov you can still keep the whole thing quiet if you wish, or you can bring Rogov to trial with fanfares, *pour encourager les autres.*'

'We can't state in a court of law that this man is the Marshal's son unless you can give us proof.'

'I know, and it may be difficult to give you anything you could use. But I owe it to you to help get this man tried and even if my Security Service can't give you the proof you want they ought to be able to give you a lot of background information for use in the trial. I'll break my journey and fly back to London today; I shall have to report to my Security colleagues about Rogov, anyway. I'll write to you through your Embassy. Obviously, if you can get Rogov to admit it—but I don't think he will. He's been well-trained, to judge by the way he acted yesterday.'

'You've had a pretty bad time yourself, Peter. I'm sorry about your arm, although it didn't seem to stop you much.'

'Oh yes, that *agente* of yours—he's a good man, Vicente. He was really scared but he went for his gun all the same. And of course, he could have said nothing—just that he'd lost us.'

'That wouldn't have helped him much,' said Ferreira grimly. 'No, he'll be reprimanded, that's all. Except, of course, that he'll be sent on the unarmed combat course again, to refresh his memory. The instructor believes young men should learn his art the hard way.' He smiled. 'I don't think that boy will forget again.'

Craig rose. 'I'd like to pick the girl up now, if you can assure me that she won't be stopped from going home.'

'I said I'd let her go, and that's what I meant. You can have the car that brought you here. Where is she?'

Craig smiled. 'Near the Largo do Chafariz. He could drop me there.'

'Hiding her in the Alfama, were you? All right. We won't follow you this time. You haven't got a regular safe-house there, have you? You and your Embassy. I'd believe anything after hearing this story.'

'No we haven't. She was staying with a friend—a very worthy and respectable citizen who has never given you any trouble and never will.'

Ferreira roared with laughter. 'What a fanciful description of Mr Davies, the artist. Although I must say he seems to be learning manners. He rang Mrs Harcourt yesterday to apologize about something.'

'He's harmless, Vicente. Don't badger him.' He paused. 'You still insist that the girl goes back to England?'

'Oh yes, Peter, don't try to wriggle out of that promise. And remember, I *don't* necessarily believe a word of what you've told me. I shall still await proof before I'm convinced.'

'Of course.' The two men exchanged a look of smiling mistrust. 'May I ring the Embassy? They still know nothing about what's happened.' Ferreira nodded, and he picked up the receiver.

CHAPTER NINETEEN

Clean Up

THE BLACK CAR was waiting, but without the police officer, only the driver. Craig told him where he wanted to go, and the car shot off downhill, round the corner and again down parallel to the Rua Alecrim and out into the Rua Vitor Cordon and so into the Praca do Comercio. Then through the Rua da Alfandega to the Terreiro do Trigo and the Chafariz do Dentro. The driver helped Craig out, saluted, and a moment later the black car roared off round the square and away back towards the centre.

Amanda opened the door. She had a broom in her hand and her head was bound up in a cloth. Her long bare legs were partially hidden by a paint-smeared apron tied round the shirt she had worn in bed. Her cheeks were flushed and there was a fighting look in her grey eyes. She threw her arms round Craig's neck.

'At least *you're* clean,' she said. 'That oaf goes on sitting in the middle of all the filth grinning like a cat with a bowl of cream, and trying to make sketches of me. I can't get him to do *anything*. He just wallows in his mire.'

Craig felt deflated. It wasn't right. The girl ought to have been waiting for him all on edge, and desperately preparing herself for the ordeal she, too, would have to endure later that morning.

'He's an artist, isn't he?' he muttered and followed her into the studio, which looked as if a cleansing wind had swept through it. The bed on the divan had been made, the table cleared, canvases arranged in neat rows against the walls and clean crockery set out on a shelf. In the middle of the floor Davies sat at his easel, working intently with a piece of charcoal on a folio-sized block of paper. The charcoal broke, and he dropped it on the floor and snatched up another. The girl swooped on it with a cry of rage and scolded him, but he paid not the slightest attention until she picked up some sketches he had thrown on to the table. 'Leave those alone,' he said mildly. 'They'll be worth millions one day.'

Craig frowned at the girl as she snorted and went back to her sweeping. This was yet another facet of the girl's extraordinary personality, but at the moment he could do without it. 'Drop it, Amanda,' he said shortly, 'and get yourself ready. We've got to go.'

'Can't I just——?'

'No you can't. It's all fixed, but we haven't got much time.'

'Good-oh, Pete,' said Davies warmly, but without looking up. 'You're a swell operator.'

'Of course he is. That's his job,' said Amanda calmly. 'All right, Peter, I'll only be a minute.' She swept a large pile of dust and debris into a pan and went towards the passage.

'What d'you think of it, sport?' asked Davies.

Craig looked at the sketch on the easel. It was good. There was fury in the lines of the girl's figure as she swept the broom forward. A heavy strand of hair had come loose from the head-cloth and hung towards the floor and her face was half-turned to show the imperious lines of nose and lips. The charcoal strokes thinned and swelled with complete assurance and economy. 'I'll buy it,' said Craig, 'if you'll let me.'

'Not this one, cobber, it's for me. But I'll make you

another and send it to you, if you like.' He stopped sketching and looked up. 'As a thank-you. She told me a lot about you, and if she isn't grateful, I am. My word, yes.' He paused. 'But she is, of course. It's only that—well, cleaning out Augean stables is her main object in life, one way and the other. So she forgot her manners just now.'

'I know,' said Craig. 'She's an odd girl. But thanks, I'd love to have a copy of this. I'll write to you when it's all over.'

Amanda came back, hair brushed, face done, wearing again Joao's shirt and slacks, with the cardigan thrown over her shoulders. She went up to Davies and kissed him fondly, and he clung to her for a moment. 'I'll write, and you're to come to London soon, darling.' Then she took Craig's arm.

'No, lovey,' said Davies, 'it's not my world, and you know it. I don't want to turn over another card. I stick on what I've got.' He watched from the open door as they went down the steps and into the cobbled street.

'I think we'll go uphill to the Portas do Sol,' said Craig. 'It's nearer for us anyway. I've told your people I'm bringing you home.'

As they walked up through the alleys between the high walls he told her about his interview with Ferreira—all except the label and the theory he had evolved for the PIDE to investigate.

'Do you want me to go and see him?' she asked, with a touch of apprehension.

'I made a half-promise that you might, but I'm sure H.E. won't agree. A statement, which I'll draft, should be enough, signed by you in the Ambassador's presence and counter-signed by him.'

'Oh Lord, Sir Roland! I'll have to sweeten him; he'll be furious with me.' She turned to Craig. 'You've been awfully good to me, Peter. I'm devastated that you've got to break your journey and fly to London. But no—it'll be fun. We'll be on the same plane I expect.'

'Oh no we shan't. You follow in a day or two, if H.E.

agrees. I've got to arrange for your reception in England.
But with any luck I'll be able to catch up with *Claudia* in
Barcelona.'

'And then?'

'Friends in Naples and then two weeks in Positano, I
hope.'

She glanced at him sideways. 'Why don't I join you
there?'

'No, ducky.'

'It might even be a *good* idea if I went away for a bit.'

'No, Amanda. You'll stay in London while MI5 try to
straighten out your story and warn you to be a good girl
in future. And I wish them luck.'

CHAPTER TWENTY

His Excellency in Action

As THE TAXI drove into the Rua Sacramento Craig said,
'You've got to tell your mother the whole story as we
planned, all except the real facts about the Security
Service. But you'll have to work out another story for your
friends. Don't *see* any of them, but have something ready
for when they ring.'

'Oh, that's easy. I drove out into the country after the
party to get some fresh air. They won't know I didn't have
my car with me. And I had an accident which shook me up
a lot, but didn't do any serious damage. Only severe con-
cussion. And a kindly peasant took me into his humble
dwelling and nursed me until I recovered my wits last night.
Then Daddy picked me up and I'm still in bed, under the
doctor.'

'Good God! You couldn't make that stick?'

'Why not? Everybody knows me as a truthful girl.'

Speechless, Craig helped her out of the taxi. There were

no visible watchers around. He waited until the maid opened the door of the flat, sent his apologies to her mother for not coming in, and left her. He told the driver to go on to the Embassy.

The messenger at the hall desk was telephoning Dickens. He turned to Craig. 'Would you wait here, sir? Head of Chancery's just coming down.'

Simon Dickens came bounding down the stairs. 'Thank God!' he said. 'H.E.'s getting restive, to put it mildly. What's the matter with your arm?'

Craig told him and added: 'Get Harcourt and let's have a talk before—'

'No dice. H.E. left strict instructions that you were to be brought to his room at once. Incidentally, he's just been given a rocket by the MFA.' They were climbing the stairs. 'And where's Amanda?'

'At home. Look, Dickens, we must get Harcourt in on this.'

'Yes, that's OK. Wait a moment.' He ran into his office, calling instructions to his secretary. When he came back he said, 'Rory's coming and I've sent a message to the Embassy doctor, asking him to come round and stand by. Is your arm in a bad way?'

'No, it's all right. We must wait for Harcourt.'

When the Brigadier came along the passage Craig said to him, 'She's all right and at your flat. But it's been a pretty exhausting experience. She ought to go to bed.'

'Cynthia's just rung me. That's her idea, too. Thanks— it's all I can say now, but I'm very much in your debt. We'd better go in now.'

The Ambassador was behind his desk, glowering at them. 'Good morning, Craig. Morning, Rory. Sit down, all of you. What's the matter with your arm?'

'He's had a bullet through it, sir,' said Dickens.

'Good God!' said the Ambassador disgustedly. 'Was that really necessary?'

'I didn't think so, sir,' said Craig drily.

'No, I suppose not. Has it been dressed properly?'

'Craig says he's had first aid only, sir, so I've asked Dr Leinster to drop in.'

'Good. Well, in the meantime, Craig, perhaps you'd be good enough to tell us what the hell you've been up to.'

'Some of what I have to say is Top Secret, sir.'

'What d'you mean, we're all—' He stopped. 'Oh you mean *really* Top Secret?'

'Yes, indeed,' said Craig impressively. He had to get the initiative in his own hands. 'In the highest degree.'

'Well, this room's all right. It was "swept" only a few weeks ago.' A thought struck His Excellency. 'But no, we'll show you that we know what you people expect. Simon, unplug my telephone and tell Miss Graham to take all calls for the next half-hour. Rory, would you close the curtains, please. We don't want any long-range lip-readers or tele-microphones to hear Craig's secrets. And turn on that damned wireless.' There was a blare of *fado* music from the radio. 'Oh Christ, not that! Speech, for Heaven's sake. Now we'll all sit in the middle of the room. Rory, can you help, please? There, does that satisfy you?' he asked Craig truculently. 'All your damned security circulars implemented, I think, what?'

'Admirably, sir, if we talk quietly.'

'Then talk, please.'

For the second time that morning Craig told his story, but this time it was the truth—or almost the truth. They listened in silence only broken at the beginning by snorts of disgust or disbelief—it was hard to tell which—from His Excellency. But then he became quiet, watching Craig's face thoughtfully. When it was over he spoke.

'You were able to convince Ferreira that young Rogov —I met his father once—had nothing to do with Amanda and was here in order to make a sort of take-over bid for Costa's movement, presumably on instructions from the Kremlin?'

'I think I should say that I left him to come to that conclusion, sir. I didn't propound that argument except as a suggestion.'

'But you made it plain that you thought that must be what Rogov had in mind. It was a very insidious suggestion to make, without authority.'

'As I explained, I tried to consult you first, sir, but was prevented by the PIDE. But I think you would have agreed that I had to suggest some explanation for Rogov's actions and—well, sir, it's almost impossible to disprove.'

'Yes. Yes, that's what struck me. There was only one point, Craig, in your report, where you seemed a bit vague —the girl's link with the Security Service. Who was it who persuaded her to do this highly dangerous double-agent job?'

'I'm afraid I can't help you there, sir.' He drew a deep breath. 'She's got a strong sense of security, and obviously she couldn't tell me that kind of thing. She was very reluctant to tell me what she did. But of course she had no choice, unless I was to treat her simply as a Soviet spy.'

The Ambassador's expression was unfathomable. 'All right. We must accept the situation you have presented us with. Now we turn ourselves into a ways and means committee. Simon, you'd better take Craig's passport and arrange for him to get the berth booked for Amanda on the afternoon plane. And please draft me a little note to the Minister of Foreign Affairs, conciliatory of course, but making it clear that I take exception to the way he spoke to me about Amanda this morning. Craig, you'll want to go back to the boat to get clothes for London, but please be as quick as you can. I want you to start composing the statements for you and the girl to sign. I shall want to see them in draft. There is no question of allowing her to go to PIDE headquarters. Rory, keep her at home unless there's an over-riding reason for her to leave the house; if so she must be accompanied. The other nuts and bolts I leave to you, Simon. That's all, gentlemen.'

Harcourt turned to Craig. 'We are hoping you will lunch with us. Please do.'

'Thanks,' said Craig, turning to the door, 'I'd like nothing better.'

'Just a moment,' said the Ambassador in a silky voice. 'May I have a word with you, Craig, before you go?'

The door closed behind the other men. His Excellency waved Craig to a chair and sat down beside him. The radio was still chattering Portuguese and the Ambassador made no move to turn it off.

'Now, Craig, let's have the truth, and no more bloody lies.'

Craig stood up. 'I think you should withdraw that word, Sir Roland,' he said, the Scottish r's suddenly perceptible in his cold, precise voice.

'Nonsense. Sit down. I said, sit down. Oh, all right, I take it back.'

'Thank you, sir.' He looked at the Ambassador warily.

'Not lies, then, but as neat a bit of *suppressio veri* and *suggestio falsi* as I've heard in years. You never actually said so, but you left Harcourt and Dickens in no doubt that dear Amanda had been a true-blue patriot all along—never a move but under Security Service guidance. Now answer me, is that true?'

Craig hedged. 'There was no need—at least, that's what she thought—to contact MI5 until she was asked to do something against HMG's interests. And she never in fact *did* anything.'

'I realize that, she was being kept on ice. But you know as well as I do that *agreeing* to work for a foreign power is almost as bad. *Did* she have any contact at all with MI5?'

'No, sir.'

'I knew it! The girl's a maverick. She wouldn't ask anybody's permission; she'd do it for the kicks. Just as she did when organizing that band of young hotheads. If she'd been on MI5's books, do you imagine they could have allowed her to do *that*—in my parish? I'd have their guts for garters if they did.'

'It wasn't just for the kicks,' began Craig, 'it was—'

'It doesn't matter what crazy reason she had. But *that* is why you have to go to London today—not to get information to appease your friend Ferreira, but to square the security people?'

'That *is* one reason, sir. But I must try to get some information for Ferreira.'

'I thought so,' crowed the Ambassador. 'You didn't fool me, of course, but my God you fooled the other two. I could see poor Rory's chest expanding with pride. You ought to join the Service, Craig. That honest Scottish air of integrity is a perfect cover for refined diplomatic skull-duggery. These long-haired new entrants are no bloody good at it.' He paused. 'And surely you don't want to end up as a copper?'

Craig ignored the question. A wave of hopelessness had come over him. 'What are you going to do, sir?'

'*Do*? Why, nothing, of course. No one is going to know what you've just told me—except Dickens. Certainly not Harcourt.' He looked at Craig questioningly. 'But I'd be interested to know how you're going to square the Security Service. They're a stuffy lot.'

'I think I can do that; I know one of the senior officers quite well.' He hesitated. 'I'm very glad you're taking this line, sir. It would be an awful blow for the Harcourts if they knew how incredibly irresponsible she'd been. The feelings in that family, between the girl and her parents, are much closer than they appear.'

The Ambassador exploded in a roar of laughter. 'Good God, man, I'm not keeping my mouth shut to save Harcourt's feelings. He's on loan to the Diplomatic Service. He shouldn't *have* any feelings.'

'Then why——?' began Craig, puzzled as ever by this unpredictable little man.

'Oh, surely you must see,' said His Excellency impatiently. 'He'd resign. Letting the side down, honour of the Regiment—all that rot. Can't have the former CO sporting a Soviet spy for a daughter. He'd throw in his gold-braided hat on the spot.' He paused and went on more soberly, 'And I'm not going to have that. I want him here; he's a bloody good attaché. You should see the

Portuguese brass eating out of his hand. They love him.'

'I see,' said Craig, coldly.

The Ambassador looked at him. 'I don't suppose you do,' he said slowly. 'You've lived the sheltered life of a Colonial civil servant; diplomacy in a foreign country is a different matter. Unless you've got a good team it's impossible to put across the extraordinary things the Office tells you to do these days. And that reminds me—young Dickens.'

'He seems very bright to me.'

'He is bright, but he's still a lot to learn. When you were talking he looked almost as starry-eyed as Rory, even when you so delicately touched on the subject of MI5. I had hoped—' his voice took on a plaintive tone— 'I'd hoped to see him glance at me, questioningly, when you did that. Damn it, he ought to have known that the Office wouldn't have allowed MI5 to employ the daughter of one of my staff without telling me—for my ears only, of course—what they were up to. So he should have been curious to see my reaction. But no, he sat drinking in every word you uttered. I will choose some occasion when we've got plenty of time,' he continued, rubbing his hands, 'and take young Dickens step by step through that story of yours and point out the error of his ways. It'll be an excellent lesson for him.'

Craig looked at him with distaste. He was thinking of Ferreira and his proposal to enlighten his wretched plain-clothes agent 'the hard way'.

The Ambassador rose and held out his pudgy little hand. 'But that's another matter. No one can say you haven't done your job, and with resourcefulness and indeed diplomacy. Er—Craig—' He stopped.

'Yes, sir?' To his amazement he saw that the man was somehow embarrassed. He seemed to have difficulty in getting a word out.

'Thanks!' said His Excellency, loudly. Once the word was out he smiled angelically, like a well-burped baby. 'Thanks very much, my dear fellow. You've been a great help. Er—what about lunch?'

'You're very kind, sir, but Harcourt—'

'Of course,' interrupted the Ambassador with evident relief. 'Well, then, some other time.' He patted Craig's shoulder and took him half-way to the door. Then he trotted back to his desk and rang for his Personal Assistant.

CHAPTER TWENTY-ONE

Rogov

As CRAIG listened to Dickens's congratulations on the successful completion of his task he felt awkward. 'It's very nice of you, Simon, but it's been touch and go the whole way, and I owe a great deal to the girl. Hadn't I better see the doctor now, and then go straight to the ship?'

'Yes, of course. You can have the Chancery car. What did you think of H.E.? He's a sharp old fox, isn't he?'

'You can say that again. But not my favourite Ambassador.'

'No, but it's worth it for the odd time when he's talking to you and it's as if—I don't know, it's as if steel shutters opened suddenly and behind his eyes you catch a white-hot glimpse of sheer intelligence blazing away inside. There's a lot to learn from the old boy, even if he is such a bastard most of the time.'

Craig thought of warning him to expect another lesson in the near future, but somehow the Ambassador's dominating authority reached out to him, and he was silent.

The telephone rang and Dickens answered it, and then looked curiously at Craig. 'It's the PIDE, Sub-Director Ferreira.'

'All right. I'll take it here, if I may.'

Ferreira's voice said: 'I thought I'd better get in touch with you at once, Peter. Rogov's dead. So don't bother to get that information for me. You can catch your boat after all.'

Craig glanced at Dickens. 'I'm afraid that's no good, Vicente, but thanks all the same. What happened?'

'Nothing for us to be proud of, but they were very clever. Rogov's friends, the people who were in the furniture van, I suppose. Incidentally, it's been found. They must have tried to turn it on that narrow road and ran it into the ditch. They'd stolen it an hour earlier from a firm in Setubal. No fingerprints, of course.'

'But Rogov?'

'He was under double guard at the military hospital at Outao, near where he was found. He should have been alone, but they had to put him in a ward with three other suspects. He was sitting in a chair, brooding; he'd still refused to say a word and we couldn't interrogate him properly in the hospital, anyway.'

'But what happened?'

'There are hopper windows giving on to the road, and two youngsters were playing outside with a rubber ball. Nobody paid any attention to them, and afterwards, of course, they had disappeared.' Ferreira's voice was tired and very bitter. 'The ball came in through the window and one of the sick prisoners picked it up and started to toss it around—they were all bored, I suppose—and it came to Rogov. He picked it up idly and looked at it, and saw what the police found afterwards—the number 623 printed on it in indelible ink. I imagine it was his symbol, or part of it. Expendable, like him. The others were calling for him to throw it, but he sat staring at it for a moment, and they said his face was white. Then he stood up, and held it in his hands and twisted, and the ball split in two. He pressed the two halves quickly to his face and breathed in.'

'Good God, what was it?'

'Potassium cyanide. They must have had the pellet in a soluble capsule and dropped it into the acid just before they screwed the two halves together. The liquid splashed all over his face, but he didn't scream.'

'He died at once?'

'Oh yes. And so much for our GRU officer.'

Craig felt an immense wave of relief. 'I'm very sorry, Vicente. That's really tough.'

'It is. All we've got now is the dead body of the man you called Luiz, and the little van and transmitter, and we've started to work on that. There was a crystal control of the wavelength, but of course that'll have been changed already.' His voice became more cheerful. 'Thank God you were right about the duplicator and the propaganda material. We found the lot and, *Cristo Rey*! what stuff it is! But that's one little plot that won't come off. I'm grateful to you for that. Now what about Miss Harcourt? I hoped you were going to introduce me!'

'I'm sorry, but His Excellency won't allow it; she's making a full statement about what happened. I'll see that it's in order.'

'Well, I'll have to be content with that, for the record. We've got a list of the distributors, and that's the main thing. But she'll go to England and not come back?'

'Yes. You have His Excellency's assurance. But she's very shaken and won't be able to leave her bed for a day or two. Is that all right with you?'

'I suppose so. But if she does go out she'll be followed —I don't want any contact with her former friends in that group. It's a pity. I'd like to have shown that young lady that she wasn't as clever as she thought she was, but never mind. You can tell her now. We've got them all listed.'

'Thanks for all your help, Vicente. Goodbye.'

'Bon voyage, Peter. I enjoyed seeing you—but don't come back too often.'

'I gather Rogov's dead,' said Dickens.

'They smuggled poison to him in the prison hospital and he died immediately.'

'Then why are you looking so happy?'

'I don't know, quite. But partly because he was very clever indeed, and I didn't trust even the PIDE to hold him for long, once his friends got to work. He must have been hoping against hope that they'd have got him out of the hospital, but when they decided they couldn't they also decided that they weren't going to risk his interrogation by the PIDE. So he was shown the only way out. And he took it like a soldier.' He stopped. 'Don't tell Amanda about this.'

'Why? Surely she wasn't—she wasn't *fond* of him, was she?'

'Good Lord no,' said Craig firmly. 'But he was a highly intelligent man and she had a sort of respect for him.'

'She'll have to be told.'

'I'll tell her, if I see her at lunch. If not I'll write to her.'

'All right, if you want it that way. It's your news. Shall I tell H.E.?'

'Yes, please.'

'Good Lord, Peter, you'll be able to catch your boat—'

'No. I've still got to go to London. H.E. knows why, and if you don't mind I'd rather he told you.'

At four o'clock Dickens accompanied Craig to the airport, and left him while he took his passport over to the counter. Craig was looking at the paper-backs on the bookstand when he heard a voice.

'Hullo, Peter,' said Amanda.

He turned, startled. She was standing beside him, looking like an outdoor girl in a glossy magazine, her face glowing with health, and dressed to kill. 'You're not alone, for God's sake?'

'No, darling. Daddy's over there, talking to Simon. Now, you beast. Why did you run off without saying goodbye?'

'You were asleep when we were having lunch.'

'You could have woken me up. Didn't you want to see me again?'

'Well, yes, and I'm glad to see you now. We've got a few minutes. I want to talk to you seriously.'

'I expect I know it all, but go ahead.'

He took her by the arm and led her into a corner. He was thinking how he could shock her out of her supreme self-confidence and make some sort of lasting effect.

'First, I'm sorry, but I've got to tell you two things which you'll find very unpleasant. Rogov's dead. He committed suicide.'

'Oh *no*! Oh, Peter, how awful! *Poor* Milo!'

'Poor Milo—yes, I guessed you'd say that. But he died bravely. They sent poison to him in hospital.'

'But what a ghastly thing—'

'I know. But there it is.'

'You just pass it off as if it were nothing,' she said bitterly.

'I haven't got time. Now the second thing—and you won't like this either. Do you know what the PIDE call that thick file they've got on the Gonçalves Costa group?'

'It can't be a thick file. They were bluffing you.'

'It's called the MA file. It stands for "*Manda Amanda*".'

She gave a gasp. 'Oh God, how awful! Then they must have known—' She turned on him fiercely. 'And *you* knew, you beast. That's what puzzled me, and I was going to get it out of you but then all the action started. Why didn't you tell me?'

'Because it wasn't my secret. It doesn't matter now, because the PIDE know everything about your plot, the committee, the names of the distributors and the propaganda texts—everything.'

'But it's dreadful! They were my friends, and they'll all be tortured.'

'I don't think so. Ferreira's got what he wanted, and the plot is a damp squib. He's not a vindictive man. They'll all be interviewed and frightened, but I'm pretty sure he won't bring them to trial.'

She said in a dangerously low voice: 'Did you help him to find out?'

'Yes, I did. All the stuff was at the *quinta*, of course. That was what Joao wanted to show you.'

'I don't want to speak to you again.' She started to walk away but Craig seized her arm and held her back.

'I don't care if you don't, but you're going to listen to me. It's for your own sake, Amanda.'

'All right,' she said in a stony voice.

'I was a bit brutal then, I know, but I did it on purpose, to show you that you may be clever but you can't take on an espionage service single-handed. They are clever, too, and what's more important they have all the facilities, the skills and the pressure potentials which you don't have. I have a lot of respect for your brains but I assure you most solemnly that you'd never have succeeded in double-crossing Rogov for long. You were on your own, but he had a whole organization behind him in England—far superior to anything the GRU could have here. In the long run you would have *failed*. Are you listening?' All he could see was a mass of fair hair.

'Go on,' said the cold voice, 'if you must.'

'The same applies to MI5. For God's sake don't try to be clever with them. It would really be best to tell them everything—including your real, lunatic reasons for cultivating Rogov, but if you won't, at least let them think you had a patriotic purpose in mind. I'm going to say that I suppose that was your motivation, but do tell the whole truth if you can.'

'I see.'

'And then, when they let you go—you're in for weeks of questioning, I'm afraid, but they'll be very civilized about it—then you must forget the whole thing. They'll see you're not molested. Now listen very carefully. The safest thing you can do—to avoid giving the Russians any chance to blackmail you—is to avoid going into *any* career which could possibly bring you into touch with classified material. Then, you see, no one can either use you for espionage or accuse you of being used. But best of all, get married.' He stopped with a sigh of relief. He had done his duty.

She was silent for a moment, still with her face turned away from him. Puzzled, he saw her counting on her fingers. Then she faced him. 'I rather think you're right, Peter,' she said gravely. 'That *is* the only thing I can do. I'm pregnant.'

Craig's jaw dropped. 'Oh Amanda, not that! Good Lord, it couldn't have been—'

'I don't know, darling,' she said with a break in her voice, 'but it hardly matters now, does it?' With a swing of the heavy, honey-coloured hair she walked away. She had had the last word.

Craig saw Dickens and Harcourt coming towards him and the first announcement of the plane's departure came over the loudspeakers.

CHAPTER TWENTY-TWO

MI5

RICHARD COURTNEY was a distinguished, scholarly-looking man, very tall, with wavy grey hair rather attractively streaked with white. He stood at the big window of his room in North Audley Street, looking thoughtfully at the Georgian façades of the houses opposite. He had asked no questions while Craig was telling his story, but then he had gone through it, dissecting it logically into its component parts. Now he was silent for a while, and Craig waited.

The MI5 officer came back to his desk and picked up one of two cards which had just been brought in. 'Yes, I thought so, we have traces of Janek. We took a good hard look at the Czech refugees because they were such an obvious medium for infiltration. But Janek—look at the card, any amount of collateral about his record as a resistance man both in Brno and Prague, and at Oxford he behaved admirably. Quite admirably. Looked up to by the undergraduates, a moderating influence on the action committees, never put a foot wrong.' He chuckled drily. 'Not surprising. He's a first-class squash player. Remarkable. If only we'd known then who he was.'

'Then it was news to you that he was the Marshal's son?'

'My dear Peter, I nearly jumped out of my chair.'

'You didn't move a muscle.'

'No? I suppose it's the old po-face *de métier*. But I assure you it was most exciting news.'

'But why?'

'A defector told us some time last year that the Marshal's son was over here, posing as a Czech refugee. But he didn't know his alias. The trouble was that the only picture we had of Rogov's only son was in a *Pravda* article and rather smudgy. And taken when he was seven years old, and there were at least a dozen of the Czechs who had similar features. You've relieved a lot of busy minds in this building.' He flicked the card neatly into his out-tray, and picked up the other. 'Amanda Harcourt, born 17th March 1945, reading modern languages at Somerville (this is a couple of years old, this bit), mixed up with a notorious bunch of Trotskyists for a time, photograph of Trotsky in her study, then anarchists, protest marches, went to Paris to help at the Sorbonne, attended anarchist course, held privately, on making petrol bombs—all routine stuff, nothing of real interest to us, and she appears to have dropped it all, as you said, to work for her Schools. Got a First, too—that's a good girl! She certainly sounds like a person of character but really, what a silly thing to do, waiting to hand the whole thing over to us, tied up in ribbon. Are you sure that's what she intended to do?' he ended, looking sharply at Craig.

'Of course not. I can only repeat what she told me. She said she was going to get in touch with you, that's all.'

'Yes. Yes, of course. But—we've known each other for a long time, Peter, and I get the impression that you are —shall we say a little partisan?'

'It's up to you, chum. You've got the job of sorting her out.'

'Yes. And of course she does seem to have hauled you out of a scrap or two, so you're under a bit of an obligation to her, aren't you? I mean, it doesn't sound like you, trailing a slip of a girl around with you, in case you get into a jam.'

'Oh stop ribbing me, Dick. It's no use. I see the girl quite objectively. But there is one thing. When I gave her a final lecture at the airport she up and told me she was pregnant. So perhaps I *am* a bit sorry that she's got to be put through the mill by your smooth inquisitors.'

Courtney looked upset. 'Good Lord, is that so? I see
your point.' Then his voice changed. 'But is it true?' he
rapped out sharply.

'Look, Dick; I'm not a bloody midwife. Go ahead and
examine her yourself if you want to. But I can't think why
she should have invented a thing like that.'

'Nor can I, but—well, a thought careless of her, wasn't
it? A girl as cold and calculating as you make out.'

'I didn't say she was cold,' protested Craig angrily.
'She's got a very incisive mind, I agree, but a magnetic
warmth, too, that affects—' He stopped. Courtney was per-
mitting himself a quietly triumphant smile.

'Peter,' he said gently, 'I think it's time I took you off to
lunch.'

A fortnight later Peter Craig was lying on the beach at
Positano, reading the letters he had just fetched from
the post office. The sea was blue and calm and the sun
pleasantly hot. His arm had healed nicely, and it was
nearly time to take another bathe. The last letter was
addressed in a bold round hand. There were several pages,
but it was the last few paragraphs which made him sit
up with a jerk.

'Now I must tell you about the interview. Isn't he a *doll*
—Dick, the one who seems to know you so well? It was
rather heavy-going at first, because he was so analytical
and gently *suspicious*, but in the end we got on very well
and he believes in me now. (Which is more than can be
said for some *pompous beasts* I know.) And of course
what made all the difference, as I hoped it would, was
your telling him that I was expecting a little stranger. (Of
course, I knew you *would* tell him, and you'd both wag your
heads over the frailty of women.) He couldn't be *too* tough,
knowing that.

'I admit he was a bit obsessive about it, to start with,
but I soon convinced him, especially after I broke down
once and he was so kind and paternal. And then, to close
that chapter, I didn't turn up for a week and had a
notional miscarriage.

'Because of course, there never was a little stranger, not even a very little one. And I'm glad—I didn't like deceiving Dick. So now I'm seeing quite a lot of him, because I've shown such an interest in his work and he says his Service offers a fascinating career to girls who show the right aptitudes. I mean as *officers*—you have the police at your beck and call (I like that bit!) to do all the heavy work. So perhaps I do have an aptitude, what do you think?

'Anyway, my friends are very interested, because I may be able to play my role after all—perhaps in a different way but the *goal* is the same. (You never let me explain it to you properly.)

'In that hateful lecture you gave me at the airport you told me the best thing I could do was to get married. But you see, you were wrong, and that's one bit of free advice that's going to be shelved. For a while, anyway. After all, a girl must choose the father of her children *very carefully*. When are you coming back to England?

Amanda.'